DANGEROUS ROCK

A Dangerous Noise Novel

CRYSTAL KASWELL

DANGEROUS ROCK

First edition. March 30, 2017.

Written by Crystal Kaswell.
Cover by Okay Creations

Also by Crystal Kaswell

Sinful Serenade

Sing Your Heart Out - Miles

Strum Your Heart Out - Drew

Rock Your Heart Out - Tom

Play Your Heart Out - Pete

Sinful Ever After – series sequel

Just a Taste - Miles's POV

Dangerous Noise

Dangerous Kiss - Ethan

Dangerous Crush – Kit

Dangerous Rock – Joel

Dangerous Fling – Mal

Dangerous Encore - series sequel

Inked Hearts

Tempting - Brendon

Hooking Up - Walker

Pretend You're Mine - Ryan

Hating You, Loving You - Dean

Breaking the Rules - Hunter

Losing It - Wes

Accidental Husband - Griffin

The Baby Bargain - Chase

Inked Love

The Best Friend Bargain - Forest

The First Taste - Holden

The Roomie Rulebook - Oliver

Dirty Rich

Dirty Deal - Blake

Dirty Boss - Nick

Dirty Husband - Shep

Dirty Desires - Ian

Dirty Wedding - Ty

Dirty Secret - Cam

Pierce Family

Broken Beast - Adam

Playboy Prince - Liam

Ruthless Rival - Simon - coming soon

Standalones

Broken - Trent & Delilah

Come Undone Trilogy

Come Undone

Come Apart

Come To Me

Sign up for the Crystal Kaswell mailing list

Chapter One

JOEL

Damn, this beer is watered down. And it still tastes like shit.

I fight my grimace.

The bartender is staring at me like I'm the second coming of Jesus.

He's going on about how much he loves Dangerous Noise.

How he's a drummer too.

The second sip isn't as bad. The third is almost tolerable.

Fuck it.

I down half the glass then offer the guy my best plastered on smile.

The bartender grins. "You do live up to your reputation."

Right. I'm Joel Young, life of the party, the guy who drinks and fucks until he passes out.

The guy who always makes a joke.

Always laughs shit off.

I keep my voice that floaty tone. "I aim to please."

He motions to a blond woman in a tight dress. She's eying me with desire, but I can't tell if it's *oooh, celebrity trophy* or *I want the anonymous hottie in my bed right away*.

He grabs another glass and fills it from the tap. "This one is on me."

"That's all right." I tilt my head back to finish my beer. It's only a notch better than sewer water, but, hey, I'm Joel Young, life of the party.

I don't turn down free beer.

I chug the second glass and leave the guy two twenties.

Two beers and I'm barely feeling a buzz. But then a buzz isn't what I want tonight.

There are only three places where the world makes sense. My drum kit is hundreds of miles away. I'm sore from this morning's workout.

That means I need a beautiful woman in my bed.

Her legs spread.

Her eyes filled with desire.

Her lips parting as my name rolls off her tongue.

That makes sense.

This is a Las Vegas club. It's not packed a week before Christmas, but it's busy enough. The music is pounding. The dance floor is throbbing. And the women are here for the same reason I am.

I cut through the crowd.

The blond woman follows.

Her fingers curl around my forearm then hold tight.

Her red nails dig into my skin as she presses her tits against my back. "I hate to ask, but are you really Joel Young?"

That answers that question.

I turn back to her with a smile. "No, I'm his sexier twin brother."

She giggles. "Joel Young doesn't have a twin brother."

"He can't admit anyone in the world is more beautiful than he is."

This time, she lets out a guffaw of a fake laugh. Those long, red nails rake over my skin. She arches her back to thrust her chest towards me.

It's the kind of gesture that usually calls my attention.

But there's a hollowness to it.

She doesn't want *me*. She wants Joel Young, celebrity playboy. Usually, I'm okay stepping into that role. But right now…

My head refuses to get in gear. My thoughts are drifting back to that look on Mom's face. She needed me to make a joke. She needed me to laugh that shit off, so she could laugh it off too.

But I couldn't.

For the first time in my entire fucking life, I couldn't laugh it off.

God dammit, I'm not in Vegas because I want to think.

"Nice to meet you, honey." I smile and pull away from the blonde.

She pouts, no doubt lamenting the loss of her *I fucked a celebrity* story, but I'm not about to stick around to kiss it better.

I get all the way to the other side of the dance floor before I see her.

Fuck, does she not belong here. Her black dress hugs her lush curves. It's sexy as hell, but it looks more business than pleasure. It looks like something she'd wear to meet with her boss.

If she didn't look so young and awkward, she'd look like a boss. She has that stiffness about her.

She shifts her weight between her long legs. Her milk chocolate hair is pulled into a tight bun. Thick, black glasses frame her brown eyes.

All I can think about is sliding those frames off her face.

Watching her hair spill over her cheeks and shoulders.

Pulling her panties to her knees, diving under that dress, and licking her until she's coming on my face.

She chews on her lip as she leans against the wall.

I'm not about to watch her have a bad time. Not when I'm here.

I couldn't fix my parents' marriage. I couldn't fix my mom's miserable mood.

But I can fix this woman's night.

I move close enough to introduce myself. "I'm Joel."

She looks up at me curiously. It's not *where do I know him from?* It's something else.

"You aren't starting with a line?" she asks.

"If that's what you want." I lean against the wall, copying her posture. I cock a brow. I don't do pick up lines, but I've got a fierce urge to wipe the frown off her face. I can make an exception.

She looks at me, waiting. "Well…"

I give her a long, slow once over. Her brown eyes are dotted with flecks of honey. Her red lips are full and thick. That black dress is tight around her curvy body. And those tits. Nice, big, real tits…

Fuck, I'm getting distracted.

I stare into her pretty brown eyes as I raise a brow. "Baby, are your legs tired…"

She stares at me as if to say *really*?

No. Not really. I hold a straight face. "Because those shoes look uncomfortable."

Her nose scrunches as she laughs. It's a quick thing, but it dissolves all the tension in her expression.

Damn, I love the sound of her laugh in my ears. It's not like with the blonde.

It's real.

No pretenses.

No bullshit.

Just her responding to me.

She offers her hand. "I'm Bella."

I shake. Her hand is clammy. She's nervous.

I can help with that.

I lean a little closer. "You want a drink, Bella?"

"Yes, please. Gin and tonic."

I press my palm against the small of her back to lead her to the bar. She looks at me funny for a moment, then her attention goes back to her feet.

She's really fucking nervous.

There's something endearing about that. I usually sleep with women as *experienced* as I am. This girl, Bella… she's not the one-night stand type.

Which means I get to introduce her to the thrill.

Fuck, I bet I can introduce her to a lot of stuff.

I order our drinks, a gin and tonic for her and a scotch, neat for me. The bartender is quick and he doesn't bring up anything else about the band.

Bella traces the outline of her glass. She gives me a long once-over then her eyes meet mine. "I saw you dancing with that blonde. She was ready to drag you to the bathroom."

"I'm holding out for someone who wants to drag me to the roof."

"It's freezing out."

"That must be why it's taken all night."

Again, she laughs. "Do people really have sex in bathrooms?"

"You're hot, Bella, but I'm not gonna make an exception for you."

She laughs. "Do you have any wiggle room? Maybe a utility closet?"

"Maybe." Absolutely. "Do you always negotiate?"

She sticks out her tongue. "Please don't say what you're about to say."

I cock a brow.

"You know: *Bella, you should be a lawyer*."

"I wasn't about to talk about your career."

"Good. I don't want to know about yours either. No offense. I just—"

"I'm deeply offended. But, thankfully, I'm secretly a criminal assassin, so it's convenient you don't want to know."

She laughs. "You have a hiding in plain sight strategy?"

I nod.

Her eyes go to my bare arms, the left then the right. "I don't think you're an assassin."

"You don't think I could kill someone?"

"I'm sure you *could*. But *could* and *do* are different things. I don't see it."

"I thought you didn't want to talk jobs."

Her smile lights up her brown eyes. Already, her shoulders are softening. Already, she's happier than when we met.

Her eyes meet mine. "I've never met an assassin before."

"That you know about."

She laughs. "True." She tilts her head back to finish the last of her gin and tonic.

My head fills with ideas about her bouncing on my lap, throwing her head back like that as she comes again and again.

Screaming my name again and again.

The tension in my shoulders eases.

It's been a long time since I've wanted someone this much. Already, everything is coming into focus. The music is clearer. My scotch is richer. The air is sweeter.

I finish my drink, drop it on the counter, then order another round. The bartender is quick enough I forgive him for the shit beer.

I grab our drinks, slide my arm around Bella, and lead her to a cozy booth in the corner.

I'm not in the mood to fuck in a bathroom.

But I want to see what her eyes look like filled with pleasure as soon as possible.

She takes a long sip and sets her drink down. Her hands go to the bottom of her skirt. "You're really good at this."

"I have a lot of experience."

She looks up at me. "I… um, actually, it's been a while. A long while."

"Yeah?" I bite my tongue. Fuck. Maybe I'm a pervert, but I love being a woman's first *anything*. Even first in a while.

"I guess… the last time I kissed a strange man, it was because we played truth or dare."

"Truth or dare?"

"I was fourteen. It was normal." She pulls her dress down. "No cheating and saying *I dare you to tell me*."

"Is that cheating?"

"Well, technically…" She smiles, but there's a sadness to it. "No. I'm done with technicalities. I'm done talking for a while. How about a dare?"

I could dare her to do any number of things. With the way she's licking her lips, I'm sure she'd say yes.

But she's still nervous.

I'm not going to touch her until I'm sure she'll be feeling nothing but pleasure.

There are enough fucked up relationships in the world.

This one is simple. I spend the night making her laugh, making her smile, making her come.

In the morning, we part ways.

Nobody gets hurt.

Nobody lies.

Nobody gets married, stays together for thirty-five years, then gets divorced.

Fuck. I'm not thinking about my parents anymore tonight.

Tonight, I'm a man showing a beautiful woman a good time.

Period.

I shrug off the last bit of tension in my shoulders and bring my eyes back to Bella. "I dare you to take off your panties."

Chapter Two

BELLA

My hands go to the hem of my dress. I'm actually pulling it up.

I'm actually reaching for my bikini panties.

Actually pushing them to my knees.

Letting them fall to my ankles.

I reach down to scoop them from my feet.

My hands are shaking so badly, I can barely pull the stretchy straps over my heels.

My heart is thudding against my chest.

My palms are clammy.

I'm in over my head. Way over my head.

But I want to have fun tonight.

No, I *need* to have fun tonight.

I can't be Bella Chase, failing law student, woman completely off track tonight. Or I'll…

No.

I'm not even thinking about that.

I press my panties between my palms. My gaze goes to Joel's eyes. They're green with a little grey. Or grey with a little green. Either way, they're gorgeous and they're filled with this mixture of delight and mischief.

I scoot close enough to press my panties into his palm. "Are we already going to... ahem." I motion to the club exit.

He laughs.

"What?" I pull my hands into my lap. "I... I've never had a one-night stand before."

"I can tell." He takes my panties and slides them into the front pocket of his jeans.

My glance is quick and focused. I can't tell if he's hard.

Okay. That's good. I don't normally think about whether or not guys are hard five minutes after meeting them.

I can do this.

I can be the woman who has fun tonight.

I have to.

My fingers curl around my drink. I take another long sip. It's not enough. My thoughts are still smacking together.

I finish my glass.

Joel's eyes meet mine. "We can take this slow."

"Not that slow."

His smile spreads to his ears. "Shit, we're in Vegas. There's no way to tell the time without checking my cell." He glances around the room. Sure enough, the walls are free of both clocks and windows. "Let's say it's ten."

I nod. "That sounds about right."

"That gives us twelve hours."

"You don't seem like the type who gets up early."

He laughs. "I don't?"

I nod.

I try to suck the last drop of gin from my glass, but the

drink is all melting ice. I pop an ice cube in my mouth and suck hard.

Joel's eyes go to my mouth. His jaw falls ever so slightly.

His pupils dilate.

He really does want me.

The smoking hot bad boy wants me.

I close my eyes and pinch myself.

He's still here. Still staring.

He shakes his head, bringing his attention back to our conversation. He makes a show of flexing his arms in a strongman gesture. "You saying I don't have the physique of someone who hits the gym every morning?"

"I figured assassins worked mostly at night."

"You'd be surprised."

My drink is still ice, and I still need more. I pop another ice cube into my mouth and suck hard. "Maybe it's the tattoos. I don't see you showing up anywhere anytime before noon."

His laugh lights up his eyes. He scoots close enough for the outside of his leg to brush against the outside of mine. "Tattooed guys don't get anywhere on time?"

"No." Damn, my heart is beating even faster. And I'm down to two ice cubes. I pop both into my mouth.

"I'm enjoying the show." His tongue slides over his lips. "But I'm happy to buy you another drink."

"Plus, I'm out of ice cubes."

"True." His fingers curl around his glass. He brings it to his lips and takes a long sip of the amber liquid.

Scotch.

That's the kind of thing my dad drinks. It doesn't seem to fit Joel. But then Joel and I only met ten minutes ago. Maybe he's a scotch kingpin. Maybe his entire life is devoted to scotch.

He hails a cocktail waitress and orders us another round. Once she leaves, he scoots closer.

The back of his hand brushes against my shoulder.

"It's not that I think tattooed bad boys are irresponsible." I'm out of ice cubes. I have no way to occupy my nervous energy. Even though my thoughts are floaty, my hands are nervous. I press my palms against my quads. It helps. "It's more that you seem effortless. Like a surfer."

With the shaggy, dark blond hair, the green eyes, and the incredibly toned physique, Joel really does look like a surfer boy.

But is he effortless?

He turned on like a lightbulb around that blond woman. When she left, he dimmed. Not like he was sad. No, it was more like he was shifting back to his normal self instead of putting up a front.

Right now, the way he's looking at me… he's still on. But it's not at 150 watts. It's more like 60. Or 30 even.

Ahem.

This is a one-night stand. Joel's not my future husband. I shouldn't be psychoanalyzing him.

It's a habit, something I do to everyone I meet.

But it's not why I'm here tonight.

I'm here to get *out* of my head.

And into his pants.

God, that's cheesy… but it's true.

I should be staring at his broad shoulders.

Wondering what his arms will feel like wrapped around me.

What his body will feel like against mine.

I cross and uncross my legs. Somehow, I manage to spread my knees a little wider. It's only an inch. Maybe two. But with my panties in his pocket, that's more than enough to feel dirty.

My eyes meet his.

I swallow hard.

"This isn't a race." He looks down at me. His fingers skim my knee then his hand is back at his sides. "We have all night."

I nod.

My fingers tap against my quads.

Fuck, how can I be this nervous three drinks in. Or is it two? Or four? I'm already forgetting.

Mercifully, the cocktail waitress arrives with our drinks. I practically pounce on my gin and tonic. It's crisp, bubbly, strong. I down the whole thing in three sips.

My head swims.

My throat burns.

But the tension in my shoulders is melting.

The nerves in my stomach are settling.

I can do this.

Joel looks at me curiously. "I like you, Bella. You're charming."

"Weird?"

"Different." He matches my speed, downing half his scotch in one swig. "Fuck, scotch is not meant to be drunk this fast."

"You don't seem like a scotch guy."

"Usually, I drink beer. But the beer here is shit." He downs another half, well, a quarter of the original drink, with his next swig. "And if you're drinking hard liquor…"

"You're a gentleman."

He laughs. "You could say that."

The song shifts from some generic wub-wub club music to a remix of *Poker Face* by Lady Gaga. I can't help but shift my chest. My hips.

My dress presses against my ass. My sex. Fuck, this not

wearing panties thing opens me up to a whole lot of sensation.

Alcohol has my inhibitions falling quickly. I let my eyes flutter closed as I shift my hips in time with the music.

The friction of my dress feels good.

Pleasure pools in my belly.

In my thighs.

Joel's fingers brush against my knee again. His glass clinks as he drops it on the table.

He leans in to whisper, "You want to dance."

It's not really a question. I nod anyway.

He takes my hand and pulls me out of the booth. We cut through the crowd until we find a spot in the middle of the fray.

With his hands on my hips, he pulls my body into his. His cheek brushes against mine. His breath warms my ear.

Fuck, that feels good.

I want him. Badly.

But I'm still not sure about this. I rise to my tiptoes so I can whisper in his ear. "I might get cold feet."

He laughs.

"What?"

His eyes light up as they meet mine. "You might get cold feet?"

"About the sex."

His smile spreads to his cheeks.

"It's an implicit agreement, the one-night stand thing."

"I'm not laughing 'cause you're wrong."

"Then why?"

"You're different than the women who usually approach me."

"You approached me."

"Even so." He presses his palm against my lower back. His eyes fix on mine. "I meant the whole *I like you* thing. I want you to have a good time tonight. I'm more than happy to fuck you, but that isn't my main goal."

"It's not?"

He brushes a stray hair from my eyes. "Don't get me wrong. I want to make you come." He drags his fingertips down my neck. Over my shoulder.

I cringe as his fingertips hit my upper arm. I try to shake it off, but he's not buying that.

He pulls his hand back to his side.

"No. Don't. I mean, keep going." I look up at him. "Please."

He stares back at me. His voice is heavy with desire, but it's even too. "I want you screaming my name loud enough to wake everyone on The Strip."

I swallow hard.

"But only if that's what you want."

"What if you do that… then I don't?"

Again, his smile spreads to his cheeks. "*I* want to make you come. It's for me." His hand goes back to my forearm. Then it's the light brush of his fingers.

The soft, affectionate touch sends desire racing through me.

My eyelids flutter closed. There's some response forming in my brain, but it already seems less important than his hands on my skin.

This is why I flew to Vegas.

I press my cheek against his as I bring my mouth to his ear. "Is that really for you?"

"Fuck yes." He presses his palm against my lower back, pressing my body against his.

He's hard.

Not exactly unusual with the way we're dancing, but still… he's over the thought of making me come—

Because my body is pressed against his—

Damn, I'm hot everywhere.

He brings his hand to the back of my head and undoes my bun. My locks fall over my shoulder.

My hair is going to be a mess tomorrow.

But I don't care.

His voice is loud enough someone else could hear, even with the booming remix. "I want to make you come, because I want to see what those gorgeous brown eyes look like filled with pleasure." His lips brush against my ear.

Against my neck.

He's still moving in time with the beat.

He's still holding my body against his.

Fuck, Joel is really good at this. Between his touch and his words and my three drinks, I'm letting go of every one of my inhibitions.

"I want to feel your cunt pulsing around my fingers." He drags his lips over my neck. "I want to hear your groans in my ears."

Fuck, I'm on fire.

"But only if I can feel how badly you want me." He plants a hard kiss on my neck.

Heat spreads out to my fingers and toes. Despite all my goals to shake off *Bella Chase, cautious stick in the mud*, she's there, whispering in my ear that I'm out of my mind.

I look back at Joel. "You barely know me."

"Tell me something about you."

"Anything?"

He nods.

I reach for something that won't make me think about Dad. Or Anne. Or law school. Okay. That works. "Don't laugh. But I love *Harry Potter*."

He smiles. "The books or the movies?"

"Both. But the books first. I love to read." I grind my body against his. The song transitions into the next. I can't quite catch the beat, but Joel manages to guide me through it. "It's the only time I really relax."

"I get that."

"It's your turn. Tell me something about you."

"I do surf." He drags his lips up my neck and over my ear. "But it's been a while."

"You love it?"

He nods. "You can't be someplace else when you surf. You have to be there, in that moment. Same thing as when I…" He drops his voice to a whisper. "You can have shit sex, where you're zoning out. But I don't do that. I don't fuck someone unless I'm sure I can be there, reveling in every second of pleasure that spreads across her face."

My sex clenches.

The man has a mouth.

And I want it. I want to be out of my head and in my body.

I slide my hand into Joel's hair and I rise to my tiptoes to kiss him.

His lips are soft and he tastes good. Like scotch. Sweet, warm, a little salty.

He kisses back hard. His tongue slides into my mouth. His hands slide to my hips.

I get lost in the motions of our mouths.

Our bodies.

Fuck, that buzz is kicking in.

Who am I kidding? I'm well into tipsy. Drunk even.

But I don't care.

I take Joel's wrist and I bring his hand to my inner thigh.

His fingers brush against my skin. They slip under my dress.

Higher.

Closer.

Almost.

My legs are shaking from anticipation.

I'm about to let a near stranger get me off in a crowded club.

I'm out of my mind.

But I don't care.

I kiss him harder.

His fingers brush against my clit. His touch is soft. A tease. He does it again.

Again.

Pleasure floods my pelvis.

My stomach.

My thighs.

I have to clutch at his t-shirt to stay upright.

He drags his lips to my ear. "You're still nervous," he whispers.

I nod. I am still nervous. "Maybe I should have another drink."

He shakes his head. "After you come on my hand."

His voice is matter of fact, like he's talking about the weather.

Somehow, it's making a lot of sense.

I look up at him. "After I come on your hand."

He leans down to kiss me hard.

Then his fingers are slipping inside me. His thumb is circling my clit.

And I feel so good I can barely stand.

It takes every bit of attention I have to keep my body upright.

To keep from screaming loud enough to alert security.

Everything blurs together—the loud remix, the chatter behind us, his touch, his kiss, the movements of our hips—into this mix of music and pleasure.

My entire world is music and pleasure.

And that buzz of intoxication.

I press my body against his as he works me. Pleasure builds to a crescendo, then I'm there, groaning into his mouth as I come on his hand.

Fuck.

That feels so good.

He drags his lips to my ear as he pulls his hand away. "Next time you're screaming my name as you come."

Chapter Three

BELLA

Six hours later…

My eyelids flutter open.

The room is lit only by the neon of Las Vegas Boulevard.

Not a room. A suite.

But I don't give a fuck about anything but the bed.

About anything but my flesh against Joel's.

His body is on top of mine.

His cock is driving into me.

I look up at him, staring into his green eyes. He smiles. Not the smile of a one-night stand, but more.

This intimacy.

This connection.

My heartbeat picks up.

My stomach flutters.

I rake my nails across his back.

My left hand is heavy. Something catches on his skin. Some memory knocks at my consciousness.

Pleasure pushes it away.

Fuck, that's intense.

I'm not sure I can take more.

I rock my hips against his.

And I groan. "Fuck, Joel. Joel. Joel…"

Chapter Four

BELLA

The next morning…

My head pounds.

No. It screams.

It screams *go back to bed.*

My bladder offers a counter. *Time to pee. Now.*

My eyes blink open then immediately close.

It's too bright in here.

Even in December, the desert sun is luminous enough to make the room this blinding shade of white.

I barely manage to push myself up. My hand plants behind me for stability. There. It gets the soft cotton of the sheets.

Again, I try to pry my eyelids apart.

It's still too bright.

I stumble to the bathroom. Thankfully, I know my way around the room. Joel's room.

We certainly *experienced* every inch of this room.

I manage to open my eyes for long enough to find the toilet.

Ah.

Sweet bladder relief.

My head is aching, my mouth is dry, my stomach is doing somersaults. But my bladder is empty.

I wipe, flush, and stumble to the sink. There. The water turns on. Only it's cold. I reach for the other faucet and turn it until the temperature is just right.

The soap is somewhere. There. I pump it into my palm then rub my hands together.

Only…

No.

It's familiar, but I thought… that was a dream.

Wasn't it?

There's no way.

I rub my palms together. I rinse. I try to ignore the protrusion on my left ring finger. It's hard. Cold. Metal and stone. Rock. Ice. Bling.

Whatever it's called, it's huge.

But if I keep my eyes closed…

If I don't look…

Maybe I'm still dreaming.

I rinse my hands and turn the water off.

Deep breath.

I'm going to pinch myself, and I'm going to wake up for real. I bring my right index finger and thumb to my left forearm, above all the scars.

I'm not supposed to do this, but I don't care.

I dig my nails into my skin.

The pain calls my senses. I *am* awake. My eyes burst open. They catch my reflection then work their way down my naked body—everything is in the right place, as far as I can tell without my glasses—to my left hand.

It's there, on my left ring finger, a massive rock.

It's huge.

Two carats. Maybe three.

That's a platinum band.

A Tiffany setting.

A platinum wedding band beneath it.

Memories try to fight their way to the front of my mind, but the headache makes it too hard to focus. Joel and I met at the club. We flirted. We danced. He got me off.

We had more drinks.

We went somewhere…

We got back here…

We fucked.

Everything between the *somewhere* and the *fuck* is fuzzy.

Did we really get married?

There's no way… I… I know I was drunk, but there's not enough gin in the world to get me to do something that ridiculous.

I take another deep breath. It doesn't help. It only adds to the nausea climbing up my throat.

Maybe this is a joke I can't remember.

Maybe I've got everything mixed up.

I brush my teeth with one of the disposable toothbrushes in the hotel toiletries kit then I force myself to step into the main room.

Joel is sitting on the edge of the bed, his shaggy hair hanging in front of his eyes. But that's about all I can see without my glasses. Only. I think he's holding my glasses? Maybe.

"You look cute when you squint." He motions *come here*.

I think. It's hard to say. My uncorrected vision is terrible.

Slowly, I plant one foot in front of the other. I sit next to him.

He slides my glasses onto my face. His fingers skim my temples then they comb through my messy hair.

His grey-green eyes fix on mine.

He looks happy.

Tired, but happy.

I force myself to keep my gaze on his eyes.

I can't look.

Not yet.

My inhale is shallow. My exhale is forced.

Joel's expression is soft.

Happy.

He looks really fucking happy.

He pulls my body into his and presses his palm against the space between my shoulder blades.

He rubs my back with his hand.

His right hand.

His left arm is there, by his chest.

By his defined, tattooed chest.

God, he's yummy. It's hard to believe someone as hot as Joel wanted to sleep with me much less marry me. It's not that I'm ugly. But I'm more… soft. Round. Chubby is the word Anne uses, though she claims it's lovingly.

My gaze shifts to his taut stomach.

To his lap—he's wearing boxers, tragically.

There's his hand, resting on his tanned knee.

And there's a platinum band on his ring finger.

Fuck.

His voice is even. Sweet. "You okay?"

I shake my head.

"Hangover?"

I nod. Barely. I can't think here. He has a ring. And I have a ring. Well, two rings.

This really happened.

How did this happen?

Joel's touch is soft as he peels my body off his and sets me on the bed. He gets up to get something from his suitcase. Advil I guess.

He pushes himself up as he uncaps the bottle. "I'll order you toast and tea."

"Thank you." I press my lips together. That's far too formal of an address for my husband. But then…

God, my head is throbbing.

He brings me the pills and a glass of water. His fingers comb through my hair. He's being sweet and caring.

He's glad I'm his wife.

And I can't remember our wedding. I can't remember most of last night.

I push myself off the bed. That's enough to make me dizzy. It takes me a second to find my balance, but I do get it.

My eyes go back to the ring. To the massive, expensive, beautiful ring.

Then they go to Joel.

I'm married to this beautiful, tattooed man.

And I'm wearing his beautiful, enormous rock.

I… I'm going to throw up.

I find my dress on the floor and pull it on.

Joel is still staring at me, but now his green eyes are filled with concern.

"I… I'm just going to go back to my room. To change." I grab my purse off the side table.

"Bella—"

I grab my pumps and run out the door before he has the chance to finish his sentence.

In my hotel room, I plug my dead phone into its charger. Then I shower and wrap myself in a towel.

My head is still pounding. Of course it is. I drank my weight in gin last night and I skipped out of Joel's room before swallowing those ibuprofen.

I find painkillers in my suitcase and force myself to down three glasses of water. That takes the pounding to a dull ache, but my stomach continues to do somersaults.

When I'm confident I won't throw up, I grab my cell and investigate. Sure enough, my Gallery is flush with photos.

The first few are familiar. There's me and Joel at the club, laughing, kissing, smiling.

Then we're outside the pyramid shaped Luxor. Riding the monorail to the Excalibur. Joel is pointing at a *Thunder from Down Under* ad and copying a stripper pose.

Then it gets blurry. I can remember bits and pieces of our walk to the Bellagio.

I can almost feel the spray of the water fountains.

The mist was freezing against the cold air.

But I was warm from the buzz.

And his arms were around me.

And I felt safe.

Happy.

Like nothing could ever bring me down.

The next set of pictures is us cuddling up on the gondolas at the Venetian. When I close my eyes, I can almost hear the gondola operator belting out an Italian love song.

And I can feel that affection I had for Joel.

I trusted him.

I really liked him.

Enough to marry him.

The next picture is us in front of Tiffany's. We're both smiling. I look tipsy but not out of my head.

And Joel's smile…

God, he has a nice smile. Real. Honest.

I'm swiping to the next photo when my screen flashes with a text from my sister.

Anne: Holy fuck, Bella. How could you get married without telling me! And to THE JOEL YOUNG!!!

My sister knows my groom's last name and I don't.

Wait. Why does Anne know Joel's last name?

My phone flashes with another text.

Anne: You know how much I love Dangerous Noise. I get it. Eloping is fun and romantic. But I wish I could have at least thrown you a bachelorette party. Tell me you have pictures!

Dangerous Noise. That's a band. And it's a familiar band.

But my head is still fuzzy. I can't remember.

I have to Google "Dangerous Noise."

Oh. *That* band.

They're Anne's favorite. She plays their albums all the time.

And now I'm married to their drummer.

I'm married to a rock star.

The evidence is clear. There are thousands of pictures of Joel Young, the Dangerous Noise drummer. There are hundreds of articles. There's a fucking poster on Amazon.

And it's incredibly yummy too—Joel lying back in bed, his jeans unbuttoned, his hand sliding down his torso, his expression *come here and help me with this, baby.*

I'm still trying to figure out what the hell I should text Anne when there's a knock on the door. That must be him.

I'm out of options.

I shoot a simple *goodbye* text, tuck my wet hair behind my ears, and I head to the door. "Yes?"

"Hey." Joel's voice flows through the heavy wood.

My eyes catch my reflection. I'm still in my towel. I'm not wearing makeup. And my hair… it's not good.

I don't let anyone see me like this.

Not even Anne or Dad.

I pull my towel tighter.

I trace the scars on my right wrist, but all I can see is the giant rock on my left ring finger.

"Bella?" Joel taps on the door. "You gonna open up?"

I guess I should.

The man did marry me.

The least I could do is have an honest conversation about it.

"I'm in a towel." I press my palm against the door. It's a flimsy excuse, but I mean it. It's one thing stripping then jumping into bed with someone. It's another standing here, my face as naked as my body.

"Hate to break it to you, Bella, but I saw every inch of your naked body last night."

"*Every* inch?"

"Just about." He taps the door. "If you need a minute to get dressed, I can wait…"

But he's not leaving until I let him in.

Okay.

That's fair.

We're adults.

We can have an honest conversation.

I pull my towel tighter then I open the door for Joel.

"Thanks." He steps inside and runs a hand through his shaggy hair.

He doesn't look worse for wear. His green eyes are bright. His grey t-shirt—it brings out the grey in his eyes—is tight around his strong shoulders.

His jeans are snug around his narrow hips.

And those tattoos covering his arms and chest…

He really is an attractive man.

I clear my throat and take a step backwards. "I guess there's the instant coffee maker." I motion to it. "I only drink tea, but I do hear hotel coffee is terrible."

"No thanks."

"Or maybe you want water?" I stumble backwards until my calves hit the bed. Then I fall back onto the bed. I manage to do it gracefully. Like it was on purpose. "My sister said congratulations."

"You told her?"

I shake my head. "It was on a gossip site, I guess."

His eyes turn down. "I should have told you I was famous."

I press my lips together. I don't really have the upper hand here, what with my wedding related amnesia. "You didn't?"

"You don't remember?"

"Well… Um. Not everything."

Frustration creeps into his grey-green eyes. His lip corners turn down. His shoulders tense.

He's hurt.

He's hurt that I don't remember.

Even worse, I ran off this morning.

It doesn't take a genius to put two and two together.

Joel shakes his head. He takes a step backwards. "We have to talk about this."

"I know."

"But right now…" He runs a hand through his hair. His eyes fill with that same frustration, but he shakes it off.

He shakes it off enough to go back to that guy he was at the club. Before I met him.

The fun guy. The cool guy. The one who never gets upset or frustrated. The one who lights up the room.

Okay, I'm getting ahead of myself here.

I have an overactive imagination. I blame books. But then it serves me well plenty of the time. Especially on lonely nights, in my tiny studio apartment…

Ahem.

"I'm going to get breakfast at the restaurant downstairs." Joel motions to the door. "How about you meet me there after you get dressed?"

"Okay." I pull my towel tighter.

Again, his eyes flare with frustration.

Again, he shakes it off.

He turns towards the door. "I'll see you soon."

"Yeah."

Then he's gone.

I wait until the door slams shut to fall back onto the bed.

My eyes go to my laptop in the corner.

I tap the trackpad and type in the password.

It's still on my transcript.

This is the first time I've thought about school all morning.

Since I met Joel last night.

I actually did manage to spend the night putting thoughts of my future aside.

I couldn't have done that alone.

I couldn't have done that with anyone but him.

Chapter Five

JOEL

I struggle to smile as I autograph a fan's cell phone case.

Bella isn't here yet.

That isn't a good sign.

"Oh my God, your wedding was beautiful," the fan gushes.

Usually, I enjoy talking to fans. Not so much at the moment. I don't want the reminder that my marriage is all over gossip sites.

Some things should be private.

I shake my shoulders. It does nothing to ease the tension in my upper back.

Okay, time for the nuclear option.

I shoot the fan a panty-melting smile. "It was nice to meet you, honey. But I'm waiting for my wife."

Wrong choice. Her eyes light up. She jumps up and down.

"Really?" Her voice squeaks. "She was so pretty. And I love that she's a normal woman. And not one of those thin super-model types."

I try to stay focused on the task at hand, but my head is filling with memories of Bella's curvy body underneath mine.

Her nails digging into my back.

Her expression filled with pleasure.

Her pretty brown eyes lit up with joy.

Does she really not remember?

I wasn't drinking much more than I normally do, but she was matching me. And she doesn't seem like the work hard, party harder type.

More like the work hard, never party type.

I try to do the math. Five drinks at the first club or was it four, then we shared one of those ridiculous Eiffel Towers filled with vodka slushee. Then champagne to toast our wedding.

What's that? Eight drinks? Ten?

Okay, I can admit ten is a lot.

And I can admit I'm fuzzy on some of last night's details.

That I was joking when I pointed at that *Winter Special. Elvis Wedding Package, $200 Off* poster and pitched the idea of getting hitched.

I was shocked she said yes.

But I was one hundred percent game.

I've always enjoyed making people laugh and smile, but it's next level with Bella. And last night, I didn't feel any of the usual bullshit. I didn't have to step into that Joel Young, life of the party role with her.

Maybe that's not most people's idea of a good reason to get married.

I don't care.

Being with her last night felt right.

Fuck, all I want right now is to wipe all that misery off her face.

This feels right.

What else matters?

The fan is still going on about my beautiful wedding. I should pay attention, but I'm a little distracted here.

This is supposed to be the first day of my honeymoon. I'm not in the mood for celebrity shit.

The fan squeals. "OH MY GOD." She nods to the entrance of the restaurant. Bella is standing there in this prim and proper outfit. She looks like a blockbuster movie's idea of a nerd with her hair pulled into a tight bun and her collared shirt popping out of her sweater.

Nerdy and hot as hell.

Our eyes meet.

She offers me a weak smile. It's plastered on.

But then most people aren't super pumped about celebrity shit.

It doesn't mean she's miserable we're married.

Fuck, this doesn't make sense. She was happy last night. Giddy. And not drunk giddy but genuinely happy.

Right now…

The fan bounces to Bella. Then she's hugging Bella. "Your wedding was beautiful. I'm so happy for you!" She squeezes tightly. "And you, you're so pretty too."

Horror spreads over Bella's expression. She looks to me and mouths *is this normal?*

I nod. It is.

Her brow eases, but she's still wearing tension all over her shoulders.

I motion *come here*. "Sit with me."

Bella pulls away from the fan. Her eyes meet mine. She nods, *okay*.

The fan looks to me. "Can I take a picture of you guys? Please."

No fucking way. "Not right now, sweetie, but I promise to post some on Instagram soon."

The fan accepts the answer with a pout. She throws her arms around Bella again then she scampers off into the casino.

Bella stands there, dumbstruck. Once she's caught her senses, she takes the seat across from me.

The toes of her boots tap the toes of my sneakers.

I motion to her mug of tea. "It's shitty Lipton tea, but it's caffeine."

"Thank you." She pours hot water over her tea bag. Her eyes stay on her mug. "Is that normal? The fan."

"I've never been news before," I say.

She nods. "There was a lot about us on gossip sites."

"Nothing with your name."

"Not yet."

That's a fair point. "It will blow over as soon as a Kardashian does something."

"Even I know that name." She drags her fingers over her mug, the same way she dragged her fingers over her glass last night. "What if that's a while?"

"There will be a bigger story soon. Trust me. I've seen this happen with friends."

"Oh." She glances up from her mug. Her eyes meet mine for a second and she nods. "My family is really traditional. I don't think they check celebrity gossip. Except my sister. But if she found it, someone will."

Yeah. For a second, I feel like an asshole for not telling her I was famous. It wasn't on my mind last night.

But I should have warned her.

Even if this will blow over soon.

I'm about to insist on ordering breakfast before we get to talking—nothing like greasy food to fix a hangover—but something catches my gaze.

A guy in his thirties is taking our picture. Then he's not. Security goes to the guy and points to the no cameras sign on the wall.

But it's too late.

Bella is already freaked.

Better ease her mind. "They take rules seriously in casinos."

"And you know because…"

"Long story."

"I doubt that."

"I climbed the stage at one of those magic shows. I'm no longer allowed at any of the Caeser's casinos."

She laughs. "No way."

"Hey, the magician asked for volunteers. I was taking initiative."

This time her laugh is louder, brighter. "Did you really?"

I nod. "You want to see the article they wrote about me?"

"We were at the Venetian and the Paris last night."

"Neither of those are Caeser's casinos."

"You actually avoid them?"

"Well…"

Her nose scrunches as she laughs. Damn, it's such a nice laugh. I'm ready to get lost in it when I see it.

That's not a fan.

That's a paparazzi big camera.

Fuck.

I motion to the guy and offer Bella my hand. "Security will tell him to get lost, but the second we leave the casino—"

"Oh."

"Let's go to my room."

She gives me a long once-over as she stands. She's not

thinking about privacy or press or anything like that.

She's thinking about fucking me again.

Not that I can talk.

I have a lot of ideas about getting her groaning my name all day.

But first things first.

I take her hand. "Okay?"

She nods. "Okay."

I GUESS IT'S TRUE WHAT THEY SAY ABOUT FAME FINDING those who seek it. Nobody cares about a guy who stays home and watches Netflix, even if he's Brad Pitt. Now, a guy who marries a stranger in Vegas…

Bella hangs close as we step into the elevator. She's squeezing my hand tightly enough to cut off circulation.

We make a strange pair—the uptight good girl and the manwhore rock star. I guess the whole thing about opposites attracting is true too.

The elevator doors slide open.

Again, I take her hand. I keep her close. It fucking stings that she doesn't remember, but I still want to soothe her.

I lead her to my hotel room and point to the room service tray of toast and tea. "The water should still be warm."

She presses her lips together. "You ordered room service even after I left?"

"Yeah." I stick close to the coffee maker to fill it with the cheap hotel beans.

Bella takes a seat at the table. She places a bag of English Breakfast in the ceramic mug then fills it with hot water from the little silver kettle. "Thank you."

She stares at her cup as she stirs.

I wait until my coffee is finished brewing then I take a seat next to her. This is shitty coffee, but I need the caffeine.

She nibbles her toast with tiny, ladylike bites. She even keeps her pinkie raised when she takes a sip of her tea.

When she finishes, she wipes her hands on the cloth napkin folded in her lap. Her eyes meet mine. Her gaze is unsteady. "I'm sorry I don't remember much from last night. Everything between my fourth gin and tonic and, well…" She motions to the bed. "Everything else is fuzzy."

"Besides the sex?"

She blushes. "Yes."

"You're only in this for my body?" I tease.

Her laugh breaks up all the tension in her expression. Her shoulders soften. A smile spreads over her cheeks. Those brown eyes of hers look so good filled with any kind of pleasure.

Her blush deepens. "I've never had sex like that before."

Despite everything, pride bursts through my chest. Memories of Bella groaning my name and sinking her nails into my back threaten to consume all my attention.

I force myself to focus on my coffee.

"I think… we should get on the same page. I… I like you, Joel." She presses her lips together. Her eyes meet mine. She stares at me like she's studying me. I must not be hiding my frustration well, because she's looking at me with an apologetic expression. "I'm sorry, Joel. But I don't think I can really stay married to someone I met last night."

She's staring at me, waiting for a response.

I clear my throat. "Let me call my lawyer."

The word makes her cringe.

Huh.

Dealing with lawyers is never fun, but the way she's cringing is a lot more than *I hate paperwork.*

I grab my cell. "Give me a minute."

"Sure." She offers a weak smile then goes back to staring at her tea.

I push up from the table and move into the other room.

This isn't the biggest suite, but it has a killer view of Las Vegas Boulevard. The Strip isn't nearly as ostentatious this time of day. Sunlight drowns out the flashing neon.

I pull out my cell and call my lawyer.

The receptionist picks up. "Lux and Lawrence, this is Riley speaking."

"Hey. It's Joel—"

"Mr. Young, it's so nice to hear from you! I saw your story on TMZ. Oh my God, that tattoo of her name—so sweet."

Shit. I almost forgot about that.

"Mr. Lux would kill me if he knew I was saying this, but tell me you aren't calling about ending your marriage."

I clear my throat. "I won't tell you."

She sighs. "That's a shame. You two looked adorable. And here I thought I could believe in fairy-tales again."

I give her a minute to opine on the tragedy of my marriage ending. It's kind of nice someone else feels like it's a marriage worth saving.

Bella was on board last night. She was the one insisting. But now…

She doesn't want to stay married.

I do.

This isn't one of those times where we can compromise—divorce is either/or. Either we stay married or we get divorced. There's no half and half.

She wanted this last night.

Demanded it.

There must be a way to get her to remember.

To get her to realize she wants this in the sober light of morning.

I need more time.

Not just to convince her.

But to figure out if my instincts are right.

"Mr. Lux is on vacation. I can refer you to someone else. Either you'll petition for annulment—"

"What's that?"

"It's a way of erasing the marriage. Legally, it will never have happened. California doesn't like to grant annulments. You'll have to admit or prove force or lack of sound mind." She clears her throat. "I'm sure you know your limits, Mr. Young, but people do get drunk and get married in Vegas. If either one of you was drunk, you could argue that you weren't of sound mind. You'd have to admit it in open court."

I clear my throat. "No."

"The paperwork is simple. It's the negotiating that gets tricky. I can get Mr. Lux on it as soon as he returns. But if you want to take care of it right away—"

Shit.

That's it.

This buys me the time I need.

"When will he be back?" I ask.

"In about a week. I know that's a while when you're—"

"No. It's fine. I want him." That *is* true. Maybe it's stupid asking my entertainment lawyer to handle my divorce, but I trust the guy.

"Great. I'll send you a confirmation email for the morning after Mr. Lux returns. Ideally, your wife should attend, but we can do it via conference call or we can have her lawyer attend on her behalf."

"I'll let her know. Thanks."

"I'll email you the details." She lets out a soft sigh. "Good luck."

I hang up the phone.

I have a week to make sure this is what I want.

And to change her mind.

I can do that.

In the bedroom, Bella is staring at her cell phone. She looks up at me. "You got a tattoo of my name?"

I nod. "You don't remember?"

She shakes her head. "Did I…?"

"You were too scared."

"Oh." Her brow relaxes, but there's something in her eyes. Almost like she's disappointed.

Might as well show her the evidence. I pull my jeans and boxers over my hip. I took my bandage off last night, when I cleaned up post-sex.

My skin is still red, but there's no doubting the design —*Bella* in thick, black letters—is visible.

Her eyes go wide. "That's huge."

I have to chuckle.

"I mean. You were, ahem, also, when we… and, uh… that's a massive tattoo." She's as red as a tomato. "Does it hurt?"

I shake my head.

She reaches for my skin. "Can I?"

"Yeah."

Her fingertips graze my skin. The softness of her touch sends desire to every inch of my body.

But there's affection in it too.

She does care about me.

Even if she doesn't remember.

She looks up at me. Her lips curl into the world's tiniest smile.

Damn, even with the sting of her forgetting, that smile does things to me.

My fingers curl around her wrist. My voice is more desperate than I want it to be. "If you keep touching me like that, I'm going to throw you on the bed and make you come."

Somehow, she gets even more red. "Oh. Sorry."

"Don't be."

She pulls her hand back to her lap, but her gaze stays on my hip.

I leave my jeans half undone. "My lawyer isn't in the office for a while. It will be a week before we can get an appointment."

"Oh."

"I'm sure he'd get it done faster if I asked, but the guy's on vacation, and it's almost Christmas—"

"I don't want to be another asshole client." She swallows hard. "I can wait."

"The paparazzi stuff will blow over soon. You're welcome to stay in this suite until it does." I study her expression. This is what she wants. I just have to frame it right. "Or I can send you back to New York, first class."

Dread creeps into her expression. "I don't know about that…"

She didn't say much about her life, but I got the sense that she's not really happy with her family. Even if all I know about them is that they live in Manhattan.

She doesn't want to be there.

She doesn't want to be here.

I'm not sure she wants to spend the week with me. But, hey, she does like me. Deep down, a part of her wants this.

"We have a week. Come to Los Angeles with me. We can have fun while we wait."

"Fun or *fun*?"

I keep my voice playful. "That's up to you."

"Will there be paparazzi?"

"My apartment is in Venice Beach. There's no press there. And I know where to go to avoid that shit." I drop my voice to something low and seductive. "Of course, there's plenty to do in my apartment."

She blushes. "I'll think about it."

No, she'll talk herself out of it. She needs a push. And I have just the thing ready. "I have a limo reserved to take us back to L.A. I'm going to leave after lunch." I push myself to my feet and take a step towards the bathroom. "It's up to you Bella."

Desire spreads over her face as she watches me make my way to the bathroom.

I strip, wash, put A+D Ointment on my new ink.

This is a cheap move, but I don't care. I need a yes here.

I wrap a towel around my hips and make my way to the main room.

Bella looks up from her cell. Her jaw drops halfway to the floor. She barely manages to pull it up.

She barely manages to look me in the eyes. "I thought about it."

"And?"

"I must be out of my mind."

Say it, Bella…

She stares into my eyes. "I want to go with you."

Chapter Six

JOEL

A few hours later, I'm standing in front of Bella's hotel room. I knock on her door.

She answers right away.

She's ready with her suitcase zipped, her hair in that same tight bun, her makeup and outfit as perfect as it was this morning.

Her expression is still hesitant.

"Do anything fun?" I ask.

She shakes her head. "Just reading."

"Anything good?"

"You'll laugh."

"Try me."

"*Harry Potter*."

"I made you come ten minutes after you told me you loved *Harry Potter*. Why would I laugh now?"

She blushes. "I guess that's a good point. But I… I really should read some more new stuff instead of rereading."

"Does re-reading it make you happy?"

"It's comforting."

"Then who cares?"

"A lot of people. You have any idea how many editorials there are about adult YA readers needing to grow up?"

"No, but that sounds like a bunch of pretentious shit."

Her lips press together.

"I do get it. You should hear the shit I get from some of my friends about how they make *real* music and not that pop-rock crap that gets radio play. But I want to make music that's popular enough that I can play to big fucking rooms of screaming fans. If I have to tone it down on a few singles, I can do that."

"Is that what you love about music, playing live?"

I nod. "Yeah, there's an energy to it. It's not like anything else in the world."

"What about the collaboration."

"That's more challenging."

"You're too stubborn to compromise?"

I laugh. "Hey, what about this *I'm okay with making our singles more pop* thing?"

"True. But that's still what *you* want."

She's right. It is what I want. Ethan, our guitarist, is a perfectionist who cares about the song being perfect. If it's not perfect, then he doesn't care if it's popular.

Kit has a love/hate relationship with performing, but he's not as big on composing.

Mal… well, this is the only time we agree. "Mal wants it."

"Malcolm Strong. The singer." She blushes. "I looked you up."

"Smart."

"It felt unfair. I know all this stuff about you, about your life, and you don't know that much about me."

"Most of that stuff is bullshit. If anything you're behind."

She raises a brow. "You don't enjoy drinking a lot and having one-night stands?"

"Fair. But." I motion to my left hand. "I think I'm off one-night stands for a while."

"Oh." She bites her lip. "I don't want to crimp your style."

"Bella, look at me."

She does.

"I didn't invite you to my place so I could go out and fuck other women."

"But, what if I don't… what if I don't want to."

Damn, she must have a real asshole of an ex-boyfriend. Or parents with a fucked up relationship. Does she really think guys are like that?

Or just me?

"You don't owe me shit." I take her suitcase with one hand and offer her the other. "I like you. I want to have fun. If that's sex, fucking great. If not, that's fine."

"Okay." Her brow relaxes.

But not enough.

I need to ease that tension.

I take her hand and lead her down the hall. "I'm surprised you get any shit about *Harry Potter*. That's a fucking great series. The way everybody is always riding around on wood."

She laughs. "On brooms?"

"It's all about the power of riding wood."

"Someone should inform J. K. Rowling."

"And the wands? Don't get me started—"

She laughs.

That's better.

I lead her through the casino then to the parking lot.

Thankfully, no one is gawking. No one is here, really.

Even so, Bella's shoulders tense as we cut through the parking lot and climb into the limo.

She lets out a long exhale as the driver closes the limo door.

Now, it's just us in this den of dim lighting and white leather. This is a seriously 80s limo.

Her eyes go to the minibar. "Is there any water in there?"

I check. It's mostly tiny bottles of liquor and cans of soda, but there is water buried at the bottom. I pull out two bottles and hand one to her.

She's still stiff. Frustrated.

I take a seat on the bench perpendicular to hers.

Damn, she really is beautiful. But it's not just her pretty eyes, her soft lips, and her lush tits. There's something about her.

Her eyes go to the window. "You mind if we stop at the next restroom?"

"Sure." I nod to the button for the divider window. "You can order the driver around too." I roll the window down and nod hello to the driver. "Can we get off at the next rest stop?"

"Of course, Mr. Young," he says.

"You're making me feel old," I say.

"I'm sorry, sir, but I don't feel comfortable calling you Joel," he says.

"How about Your Highness?" I offer.

He chuckles. "I'll consider that, Mr. Young."

I roll the divider up and look back to Bella. Again, she's smiling.

"You're ridiculous. You know that?" she asks.

I'm well aware of that.

BELLA PRACTICALLY RUNS OUT OF THE LIMO. I GUESS I'LL assume she has to pee. I drank enough coffee to feel the same.

After I wash up in the bathroom, I find a seat on one of the rest stop's benches. This would be a cute place for a picnic if it wasn't a spot for people to piss on the way home from Vegas.

My phone buzzes with a new text from Kit.

Kit: You're fucking with me. You did not get married.

I take a photo of my left hand and send it to him. I'm well known for fucking with people, especially with Kit. The bassist has been my best friend since we were kids. Hell, the only reason why he plays the bass at all is that I persuaded him to join me in the rhythm section.

If he'd been into soccer or chess or something, there would not be a Dangerous Noise.

We've been through a lot of shit together. I trust him. I trust him more than I trust anyone. Even so, I'm not sure if he's asking this to test me or because he's curious.

Kit: What's her name?

Joel: Bella Chase.

Kit: Sounds like a fake name.

Joel: I know shit about her. She's from New York. She's smart. And uptight. She loves to read. And she's pretty. Long, dark hair. These brown eyes with flecks of honey. Huge tits.

Kit: That's your wife.

Joel: My wife has nice tits.

Kit: I can tell you really respect her.

Joel: Oh, and you never say Piper has nice tits?

Kit: Point taken.

Joel: I'm trying not to steal your thunder here.

"Hi, um, are you... are you really Joel Young?" A voice asks. It's young, male.

I look up. A teenage boy is staring at me with adoration. Between his tattered jeans, his messy hair, and his leather jacket, he's rocking the wannabe punk vibe.

I nod. "That's me."

His eyes go wide. "I'm a drummer too. Well, not like you, but one day... that song *Love or Lie* is legendary. This is so cool."

I can't help but smile. It's one thing when someone likes our music. It's another when someone actually models his life after mine. I never get used to the pride. And the responsibility. "What's your name?"

"E... Er... Eric." He pulls out his cell phone. "Shoot, I don't have any CDs, but do you think you could sign this?"

"Sure, I have a marker in the car."

He looks to the parking lot, scanning every auto there.

"It's the limo," I tease.

"Right. Of course." His smile is doofy.

I like this kid. He didn't even think to look at the limo. Status doesn't matter to him. Money doesn't matter to him.

Music is what matters.

Sure, he's twelve or maybe thirteen. He has plenty of time to get hung up on status. But it's still good to see someone who plays for the love of it.

I push myself to my feet. My eyes catch Bella's. She's making her way back to the limo. Her long hair is still tied up in that tight bun, but she's no longer wearing a sweater over her button up shirt. And fuck do those buttons not get along with her tits. The top three are undone, and the next two are struggling.

I don't care what anybody says about marriage and respect. My wife has fantastic tits. I'll shout it from the fucking mountaintops if I get the chance.

But I shouldn't stare. I need to inspire this kid. He looks up to me. And that's a fucking responsibility. I'm not going to squander it the way my dad does.

I put my arm around his shoulder to lead him to the limo. He lights up like a pinball machine, babbling about his favorite Dangerous Noise songs.

Bella leans against the limo door, watching us closely.

The driver is standing on the other side of the door. I make the *signature* motion. He reaches into the car, grabs a marker, and tosses it to me.

I catch. I don't always catch.

Eric's eyes go wide. "Wow. You're like… like an even cooler Dave Grohl." He hands over his phone.

I sign the back *Eric, Keep playing - Joel Young* and hand the cell to him.

His eyes nearly burst out of his skull. He throws his arms around me and hugs tightly. He doesn't let go until an older woman, his mom I guess, calls his name.

Bella's lips curl into a smile. "You made his day."

"Just being polite."

"Did it bother you?"

I shrug.

"You probably shouldn't travel in a limo if it bothers you. That's like screaming *look at me.*"

I motion to my face. "People look at me no matter what. It's the curse of beauty."

She laughs.

I pull my t-shirt up my stomach to show off my taut abs. "This doesn't help."

"No, stripping in public would not help deflect attention."

This time, I laugh.

"I'm surprised you've had *this* much attention." Her

eyes light up as her smile widens. "Your band isn't really that big."

"It's not?"

She shakes her head. "Really, have you even had a platinum album?"

"I'll have to ask one of my people. I'm too important to remember those details."

"So you wouldn't know if you'd had a number one single?"

"Not a clue."

"Or how many weeks you've spent in the Billboard Top 200?"

"You Google all those music things in the last five minutes?"

She bites her lip. "Maybe."

"You can Google the answer too."

"I'd rather call one of your people." She stretches her arms over her head. It pulls her shirt up her stomach. "How about a number?"

I shake my head. "I'm too important to remember anything besides how to hold my sticks."

She laughs. "Really?"

I tap my front pocket. "I have them all saved."

"And do you know how many weeks you've spent in the Billboard Top 200?"

Not offhand. I don't pay attention to status shit. I mostly look at the crowd every night. "Do you?"

She nods. "But I'm not telling." She pulls the limo door open and climbs in before the driver can insist on helping.

He holds the door open and motions to me. "Mr. Young."

I raise a brow.

"Your highness." His straight face cracks for a second then it's back. "Should I plan on a dinner stop?"

"Let me ask the queen." I slide into the limo.

This time, I take the seat next to Bella. Bad idea. Being this close to her is sending all my blood straight to my cock. It doesn't help that I have a perfect view of her cleavage.

I force myself to look her in the eyes. "You hungry?"

"Yeah." She presses her lips together. "Maybe we could go through a drive-through."

I have to laugh. "And I'm the one trying to draw attention."

Her cheeks flush. "Okay, we can go in. I'm not the one who hired a limo."

"I flew to Vegas from San Francisco."

"You could have rented a car."

"Excuse me from attempting to start my honeymoon right."

The smile falls off her face. Her gaze goes to the floor. "Oh. Well. That's… you ordered this limo last night?"

"Yeah."

"That's very romantic, thanks."

"I ordered it so we could fuck all the way home."

She laughs.

"I'm not romantic."

"You married a stranger in Las Vegas. That's not something a cynic does." Her gaze goes to her engagement ring. She keeps her voice neutral, even as she stares at the ring. "I am hungry. Don't laugh, but I want Chipotle."

"Why would I laugh?"

"Californians are particular about Mexican food."

That is true, but— "I'm from the bay. We don't know shit about Mexican food."

"Okay, then Chipotle it is." She pulls out her phone and does a search. "The closest one is an hour and a half away."

"Can you wait?"

She bites her lip. "Maybe we should go through a drive-through."

"Flashy."

She holds up her left hand. "*This* is flashy." She stares at the ring. "Can you really afford this?"

"First doubting my fame, now this. That's cold, Bella. That's fucking cold."

She raises a brow. "Can you?"

Jewelry is never a smart financial decision, but I'm not going to skimp on my wife's engagement ring. "Yes."

"Sorry, I guess I'm—"

"Nosy."

"A little. It comes with the territory with…" Her eyes go back to her shoes as she trails off. "Let's not talk about that."

I nod.

She reaches down to unzip her boots. "You mind?"

"Depends on how many articles of clothing you're going to remove."

She smiles. "You're trouble."

"You just figuring that out?"

"No." Bella peels off her boots and sits on the bench cross-legged. She turns to me. "You were looking at your phone."

"Warning my friend Kit… he's planning a Christmas proposal. I don't want to steal his thunder."

"Kit." Her eyes light up with recognition. "Oh, Christopher Lockhart. The bassist." Her expression gets sheepish. "I feel like a stalker, knowing all that."

"I don't mind."

She presses her cell phone into the bench seat. "Did you tell anyone besides your friend Christopher? Kit, I guess?"

"No. But they'll find out."

"My dad… he would think you're trouble. A bad boy phase. A quarter-life crisis."

"Who says I'm not trouble?"

She laughs. "You have tattoos, sure. But you… You're a sweet guy. Deep down."

"How do you know?"

"I remember that. I can't remember a lot of what happened last night, but I still feel this connection. It's stupid."

"It's not."

She presses her lips together. "Joel, um… don't take this the wrong way, but why did you sleep with me?"

"You fishing for more compliments about your tits? I'm happy to oblige if you are, but I demand another look at them first."

Her blush deepens. "No, I mean… we were drinking a lot."

"I tried to turn you down."

She shoots me that same incredulous look.

"You got very demanding."

"No way."

"I'll show you."

"Okay."

"But you have to play me."

She raises a brow. "Do I?"

I nod. My hands go to her hips. I keep the grip loose. "Lie back on the bench seat."

"That's what you were doing, lying down?"

I nod.

She turns enough to lean back on her elbows. She giggles as she falls onto her back. "Why do I feel like I'm being seduced?"

"You're playing Joel. Remind me I'm drunk three times before you give me the time of day."

"Did I really—"

"Yes." It was adorable. And hot. Once Bella is lying back on the bench seat, I drag my fingers up her blouse. I play with her bottom button. "Joel, baby, let's go to bed."

"Did I really call you baby?"

I nod. "Now, stop breaking character."

She drops her voice an octave. "Bella, you're drunk."

I shake my head as I straddle her. Fuck, this is not my wisest move. I'm already getting all sorts of ideas about stripping her out of her clothes and fucking her. But I'm staying in character. "I'm not." I undo her bottom button then I trail my fingers over the soft skin of her stomach. Over the waistband of her jeans. "I want you to fuck me, baby. I want you to make me come like you did at the club. I've never come like that before. I mean came. That's the past tense of come, right?"

Her cheeks flush. She clears her throat, trying to stay in character. "You're too drunk. Later."

"If I was drunk, would I really be able to conjugate the verb to come?" I shake my head. "I'm only a little tipsy." I pull my t-shirt over my head then I take her hand and press it against my pec. "It's okay if you don't want to. Just say that."

"I, um, we should wait until tomorrow."

"If you're sure." I drag her hand over my chest and press her palm flat against my breastbone. "But I don't want to wait. I want to fuck you now. I want you to come right here."

"Oh my God." Her eyes go wide. "I did not say that."

"You did."

"Really?"

"You were a bossy little thing." I smile at the memory. "Not that I minded."

"No… I… No." She shakes her head. "I've never made any demands."

"You did last night."

"Was that it?"

"Fuck no." I play with her top button as I shift back into character. "Take that off now, baby. Take everything off. I want to look at every inch of you." I grind my hips against hers. "I want to feel that hard cock in my mouth."

"No. I didn't—" Her eyes meet mine. Her cheeks turn the color of a tomato. "I did, didn't I?"

"I could go on."

"No. This is embarrassing enough."

"Nothing embarrassing about asking for what you want."

Still, her cheeks flush. "I was so shy with Stan, my ex-boyfriend. Once he asked me to talk dirty and I froze. I couldn't do it."

"Apparently, you learned."

"Really?"

I nod.

She gives me a long, slow once-over. "I guess you bring out my bad girl."

Chapter Seven

BELLA

It's evening when we finally get to Joel's place.

His apartment is on the beach. And it's beautiful. The hardwood floors are clean and sleek. The electric blue walls are adorned with framed prints of musicians.

The TV is one of those expensive flatscreens.

The bamboo bookshelf in the corner is overflowing. One shelf is filled with movies, another is filled with CDs, another with vinyl.

I turn back to Joel. "Of course you have vinyl," I tease.

"You calling me a hipster?"

"If the jeans fit."

He tugs at his belt loop. "I can lose the jeans."

Yes.

Please.

My head fills with ideas about him naked.

About us on that couch. Against the wall. Out on that balcony.

I want him.

Badly.

And I want to feel as loose and free as I did last night.

But sex leads to feelings. And the two of us are getting a divorce in a week. After that, I'll go back to my life. I'm not sure what my life is going to look like after my transcript of Cs, but I know it's not going to fit the whole sex, drugs, and rock n' roll thing.

It's not compatible with Joel's life.

At most, we'll be pen pals. Email pals. Something like that.

I can't fall for Joel.

Which means I need to be careful about sleeping with Joel.

Even if he's near impossible to resist.

Ahem. "Where am I staying?"

"Over here." Joel leads me to the bedroom and opens the door for me.

The room is decorated with a mix of cool jewel tones —red, purple, blue, teal. White string lights line the walls.

There are framed posters here too, but they're all for classic video games. Or at least *older* video games. I'm not really a gamer. All my free time goes to reading.

"The bed's yours as long as you want it," he says.

"And you?"

"You're more than welcome to invite me to spend the night with you. Until then, I'll take the couch."

"Aren't we having *fun*?"

He gives me a funny look. "Would it be fun if I pushed you into fucking me just 'cause I only have one bed?"

"No, I mean…"

"I want to fuck you, Bella. I want to make you come until you forget your name. But I want you to be there, in that moment."

"I didn't mean—"

He nods. "I know." He motions to the bed. "But you should know, that I'm not going to fuck you until you ask."

I swallow hard. "Verbally?"

He nods. "I'm not going to fuck you until you beg me to do it." His pupils dilate. His tongue slides over his lips. "Fuck, I'm getting distracted here. What was I talking about?"

"Sex."

He laughs. "You're not helping." He nods to the sound system in the corner. "You can plug in your phone if the record player doesn't do it for you." He sets my suitcase next to the bed then turns to me. "Have you ever listened to vinyl?"

"I'm not really into music. I mostly listen to Top 40." I cringe anticipating his response.

"What's with that look?"

"I feel like an asshole, telling a rock drummer I don't like music."

"Better than bullshitting me. Besides, you told me last night." He smiles. "You apologized for it a dozen times."

"Really?"

He nods. "It wasn't like you. I get it now. When you're sober, you're a lot more—"

"Polite—"

"Fixated on *pleasing* other people."

My cheeks flush. "Are you saying that because I made all those demands last night?"

"No, but thank you for reminding me about that." He winks then motions *come here*. "Not everyone is into music. It's fine. But you should still try listening to an original vinyl."

He takes my hand and leads me back into the living room.

He crouches down to take a look at the bottom shelf, where he keeps his records. "Any band or song you like?"

"I like girl power stuff. Lady Gaga, Rihanna, Gwen Stefani, the Veronicas. That kind of thing."

He turns back to the shelf and picks out an album by the Bee Gees. He goes to the turntable and pulls open the top.

Something in his posture shifts. He's not putting on a flirty facade.

He's not pretending like he's this fun, party animal guy.

His guard is down.

No, it's gone.

He blows on the record then sets it on the turntable. Slowly, he places the needle on the record.

Music fills the room as Joel pushes himself to his feet and moves towards me.

He sets his hands on my hips. "Close your eyes."

"But—"

"You want to see if you like music or not?"

I do. I always feel like I'm missing some important part of life when Anne gushes over how much she loves a song.

"Bella?" Joel runs his fingertips over my sides. "This isn't exactly slow jam material."

I close my eyes and try to take in nothing but the sound of the song.

It's peppy, fast. I shift my hips, trying to catch the beat. It's not like the music I hear on Top 40 stations, the ones with a thumping drum machine. The beat is a little harder to find.

The more I hear of the song, the more I want to move.

I want to dance.

Like last night.

I want to feel the way I did last night. Excited, floaty, free.

Joel slides his arms to my lower back. He pulls my body against his, swaying in time with the beat. "If you want something easier to dance to, I can put on some Spanish music and teach you to Mamba."

"Mamba?"

"Or we could do cha-cha, salsa, merengue. I can teach you to tango too, but it's more complicated."

"You know how to tango?"

"Mom made me take ballroom dance lessons."

I have to laugh at the thought of Joel in some spandex dancer's outfit. Not that I'd mind the sight of him in skintight material.

"Relax." He pulls me closer. "Follow my lead."

"But, can you really dance to 80s pop?"

"Fuck yeah." He presses his palms into my lower back.

I keep my eyes closed as he guides my movements. Damn, his body feels good against mine. It's comforting in this way nothing else is.

I like the song, but it's not what's making an impression.

Joel's arms around me—

His chest against mine—

His breath warm against my ear—

That's better than any song I've ever heard.

The record shifts to the next song. It's another pop number, but it doesn't have the same beat.

"Here." He places his hands back on my hips and guides them to the beat.

I blink my eyes open to stare back at him.

His green eyes fix on mine.

He really has beautiful eyes.

He's close enough to kiss me.

I really want him kissing me.

I want his lips on mine so badly I'm shaking with desire.

But there's this sound. Not the song. Something else.

And a buzz against my thigh.

Joel takes a step backwards. His brow furrows. "Fuck, that's—" He pulls out his cell. "That's my mom. I have to take this."

"Oh. Do you think she saw the gossip?"

He shakes his head. "Probably not. It's… something else."

"Something important."

"Yeah." His posture stiffens. He motions to the balcony. "It might be a while. Make yourself comfortable."

"Yeah, sure."

I watch him go out to the balcony.

He's on a call with his mom.

And he doesn't want me to know what they're discussing.

I hate that he's locking me out. Even if I'm the one insisting on divorce.

But Joel… I mean, we had a lot of fun last night, but he didn't exactly fight me on the divorce thing. He must want that too.

Then, he must realize we only have a week too.

He has every right to protect his heart.

But I still hate it.

Chapter Eight

BELLA

After I organize my clothes, I move into the main room.

Joel is still on the balcony, but he's no longer on his cell. He has his palms pressed against the railing. His body is turned towards the ocean.

God, that's a beautiful view. I cross the room until I'm in front of the balcony's sliding glass door. My hand goes to the metal handle, but I can't bring myself to join him.

There's something in his expression.

He's hurting.

Over that phone call?

My stomach flip-flops. I want to know what it is that's hurting him. And I want to wipe it away. Not the way I normally do—not by contorting myself into whatever shape will please him most.

I want to be the shoulder he can cry on.

The person who listens.

Who understands him.

Who really cares.

I've never felt like that about anyone. I cared about my

college boyfriend, Stan, but I was always "on" with him. I never let my guard down. I never trusted him enough.

And he wasn't the sharing type.

It didn't bother me then.

But Joel hurting all by himself on that balcony…

I hate it.

He catches me staring and shoots me a curious look. "How long have you been standing there, undressing me with your eyes?"

His eyes light up, but not with joy. He's a lightbulb again. He's stepping into a role.

Do I pull him out of it or play along?

I'm not sure.

I move closer. "I have not been undressing you with my eyes."

"If you want me naked, all you have to do is ask."

"Really?"

He cocks a brow. "Only one way to find out."

A huge part of me wants to find out. Despite the low temperature, I'm hot all over.

Yes, please, Joel. Strip for me. Pull my panties to my knees, bend me over the balcony railing, and get me screaming your name.

My cheeks flush. Where did that come from?

Joel's lips curl into a smile. "Bella, if you're going to think about fucking me, you should really fill me in on the details."

I say nothing.

He motions *come here.*

I do. I'm still red. I'm still blushing. I'm still thinking about Joel and me getting naked on the balcony.

I look to the setting sun instead. "It's beautiful here." It really is. The stars are bright against the dark sky. They cast a glow over the deep blue ocean and the soft beige sand.

I can hear the waves.

I can smell the salt.

"I'm starting to see why people spend a fortune to live on the beach," I say.

Joel laughs. "You care a lot about money."

"No."

He nods. "Yes."

"It's more that my status is important to my family. They're not bad people. My dad is a great guy, a talented lawyer, a pillar of the community."

"That's his bio, not what makes him a great father."

"He is. In his way. But… Chases aren't touchy feely." I look out at the ocean. "My mom died when I was twelve. Did I tell you that?"

"No."

"It was a heart attack. It happened fast. My dad hasn't been the same since. And my sister, she went the other way."

"The other way?"

"I'm the good girl—"

"She's the bad girl?"

I nod. "Yeah, boys and parties and drugs. For a while. She married a doctor last year and now she's a picture perfect housewife."

"There's this tone to your voice."

"Is there?"

"You don't approve."

"She wasn't happy before. She's not happy now. At least before she was free."

He turns away from me. "I didn't realize women bought into that *marriage is a prison* shit too."

"It's not that." I bite my lip. I hate the way he's locking me out. Usually, I push my feelings aside to placate people. But I don't want to do that with Joel. "My parents were happy. But Anne… she became this different person. She tried to pretend she's happy, but she's not."

He nods. "I get that."

"I'm not saying we're that. Well, we're not really anything. We only met twenty-four hours ago."

He turns towards me. "Fair."

"You do a lot of flashy stuff for a guy who doesn't like other people caring about status."

"Also fair."

"How much does this place cost?"

Joel laughs.

"Sorry, that was rude. I get a little… I'm nosy. It comes with the territory—" I bite my lip. "We never talked about what we do, huh?"

"You didn't." His eyes meet mine. "Don't apologize for the questions. I like it. Honestly, I don't remember my rent. I have an accountant who takes care of all my shit."

"You don't care?"

He shakes his head. "Not anymore. I have what I need now. But when I first got this place—" His gaze goes to the sky. "I was over the fucking moon. I couldn't believe I could afford a place on the beach on my own. The first night I moved in, I watched the sun set. I know it's cheesy shit, but I felt like a fucking, well… like I really was a rock star. Like I was someone important."

"Yeah?"

He nods. "Now, I only come out here as a seduction move."

"Oh baby, let's drink some wine on the balcony and take in the view?"

He presses his palms against the railing, pushing his body upright. "Something like that."

"Do you really have to try to seduce women?"

He shakes his head. "Sometimes I want a challenge."

"Why?"

"It's more fun."

"That's it?"

"Here, in L.A., it's easy to find women who are into status. I can head to Hollywood any night of the week and pick up a woman at a club. I'll have at least a dozen chicks approach me, because they want to sleep with *the* Joel Young. I'm not that fucking famous, but it's enough."

I stare back at him. "You don't want a challenge."

"I don't?"

"You want a real connection."

His lips press together. "Maybe. I get tired of the bullshit."

"Me too." I move closer. "We didn't bullshit each other last night."

He nods.

"I know we only have a week together. But… let's make a deal. I don't bullshit you and you don't bullshit me."

"What if you renege?"

"Call me on it."

"And you'll call me on it."

I nod.

He offers his hand.

We shake.

The tension in my chest eases. Joel isn't sharing his secrets with me, but I believe that we're going to be honest.

Even if only for this one week.

My eyes meet Joel's. "The balcony is a seduction move?"

"I don't have moves. I do what I feel in the moment."

"But it happens a lot?"

"You could say that."

"This is a strange seduction."

He cocks a brow. "You wouldn't fuck me right now if I asked?"

"Well, yes."

He laughs.

"In my defense, you're incredibly hot."

His laugh lights up his eyes. Not like the light bulb. Not like he's on. That's real joy in his eyes. "You forgot charming."

"And humble."

"Rich."

"You're not *that* rich."

"Fuck, you're cold, Bella. You know that?"

I nod.

"How rich does a guy have to be to impress you?"

"How rich are you?"

"Not rich enough, apparently."

I look to my engagement ring. I'm not sure about that. "I don't care about money either. I know that's easy to say when you have it, but—"

"You still want to feel self-reliant?"

I nod. My lips press together. "So how rich are you?"

"'Cause you don't care?"

"For the record."

"That's bullshit."

True. Again, I move closer. "I'm curious."

"Less bullshit." His lips curl into a smile. "Three million. Maybe four."

"Oh." That is a lot. And that's a lot of maybe. I can't imagine *maybe* having an extra million dollars hanging around.

"It's contract shit. We hit all our maximums on our last tour, so we got an extra payout. New album drops in January, then we're touring to support it in March. We're opening for a huge fucking band, Wicked Beat. We're going to be selling out stadiums for all twenty-five dates."

"So it will be a nice payday."

He nods. "Even as the opening act." His expression shifts to a playful challenge. "Maybe I'll count as rich then."

I have to laugh. "You're hot and rich."

"And talented."

And good in bed.

Joel chuckles. "If you keep looking at me like that, I'll have no choice but to bring out *Dirty Bella*."

"She's not going to come out when I'm sober."

"She's going to come." He chuckles. "Fuck, that was bad. But you know, my dad, when he taught me to play basketball, every time I missed a shot, he'd look me in the eyes and say, 'son, you miss one hundred percent of the shots you don't take.'"

"He sounds wise."

"In some ways." He gives me a long once over, his gaze settling on my chest. "You keep distracting me."

"Don't blame my boobs."

"It's a compliment."

"Still."

He brings his gaze back to my eyes. "What the fuck were we talking about?"

"You're good in bed."

He laughs. "True." His eyes pass over me, slowly. It's like he's deciding if he wants to talk to me or fuck me. "You don't dance."

I nod.

"You don't party."

Again, I nod.

"What the fuck were you doing at a Vegas club?"

"It was a spur of the moment."

"Bullshit."

"No, it was."

He stares into my eyes, examining my expression. "With all due respect, I don't believe, for a second, that you do things unless you have a reason."

"I was upset about something. I wanted to blow off steam." I wanted to blow off steam without cutting. That's the truth. But I can't tell him that. Not now. He'll think I'm a damaged freak. I swallow hard. "Why were you in Vegas?"

"To have a one-night stand."

"You fucked that up."

He laughs. "You too."

"I want to remember more about last night, Joel. After dinner, help fill me in on what you remember. Please?"

"Yeah, but you have to promise not to ask me to *fill you* in that tone of voice unless you're talking about sex."

I laugh. But there's something about his expression.

He's upset.

And he's deflecting with a joke.

I'm supposed to call him on that.

But I can't bring myself to do it.

I clear my throat. "I want to make dinner. I don't have time to cook during the semester."

"You're a student."

"Maybe."

He cocks a brow.

"How about we talk about that tomorrow?"

"Fair."

I push aside the thought of law school. I'm handling one life crisis at a time. "My place is small. Not much room to cook. And my family doesn't like me cooking while I'm home. I make too much of a mess."

He laughs. "*You* make a mess?"

"I can be messy."

"You can be dirty, but messy?" He shakes his head *no way*. "I bet you've got your socks color coded in my dresser."

"Maybe."

He nods. "Definitely."

I admit nothing.

Chapter Nine

BELLA

I'm far from an expert chef—I don't get a lot of time to practice—but I enjoy cooking.

Well, I enjoy cooking for myself. I don't have to worry about pleasing anyone or failing to live up to their expectations.

There's something about the way Joel is looking at me.

He has expectations of me.

But I'm not sure what they are.

I pluck shrimp and mixed veggies from the freezer. The fruit drawer is packed with lemons, limes, and oranges.

I point it out to Joel.

He shrugs. "Sometimes I want to do tequila shots."

"With everyone in Venice Beach?"

"You never know."

I laugh and I pull two limes from the fridge. This won't be the finest meal in the world, but it will be good. Maybe that's enough. "You have rice?"

He motions to the top cupboard.

It's way out of reach. I'm tall for a girl, but Joel has at least four inches on me. "You're joking, right?"

"About?"

I rise to my tiptoes, press my palm into the counter, and jump for it. Still not close. "Joel!"

"I'm enjoying the view."

"Please check the cupboard for rice, Joel."

"Oh. Of course." He smirks as he reaches over my head to open the cupboard.

Ah. Victory! There is a bag of rice. He hands it to me with that same smug smile. I shouldn't like it as much as I do.

But I really, really like it.

He seems genuinely happy.

And without me smoothing everything over.

I want more of that.

"Why don't you make yourself useful and help me." I bite my lip. Did I really say that? I'm not sassy.

Joel must like it. He's smiling.

He drops his voice to something playfully seductive. "How should I make myself useful?"

My head fills with delicious ideas about where I want his hands, his mouth, his cock.

Ahem.

One thing at a time.

First dinner. Then I'll decide if I can handle fucking my husband.

I clear my throat. "Get out a small pot, one with a lid, and a large pan. A wok, if you have that."

He reaches down to one of the bottom drawers to get them.

"A measuring cup."

He finds one in the silverware drawer.

"Oil."

He brushes his hand over my lower back. "I hope you're this bossy later."

My cheeks flush. I hope so too.

I measure out the rice then get to work on the stir fry. Wok. Oil. Shrimp.

The pan sizzles. "That seems wrong."

"It does."

I turn the heat down. That's better. I add the rest of the shrimp and the entire bag of mixed vegetables. "It won't need attention for a while. It's not going to be a masterpiece, but—"

"You can pick up stuff to cook tomorrow."

"Good."

He slides his arms around my waist. "This looks fucking amazing."

"Don't get your hopes up."

His voice gets low. "Why do you do that?"

"What?"

"Put yourself down like that."

"Just being realistic."

He turns me around so we're face to face. "No. It's more than that."

I bite my lip. I can't explain it. And why the fuck should I explain it to Joel when we're going to part ways forever in a week?

I shake my head. "Forget it."

"No."

"What do you mean no?"

He moves closer. His eyes bore into mine. "Last night, you looked miserable. Were you?"

I bite my lip. "Maybe not miserable."

"Bullshit."

Okay, that is bullshit. I nod. "I was."

"After a while, all that shit slid off your back, and you were happy."

That much, I do remember. "Yeah."

"You're going back to that ugly place in your head."

He's right.

I stare back at Joel. He does care that I'm upset.

My happiness matters to him.

But this relationship has an expiration date.

Fuck.

This is confusing.

He moves close enough that I can feel the heat of his body. Then he's rubbing my shoulders and leaning in to whisper.

"What are you thinking?" he asks.

"Right now?"

"Yeah."

"How can you ask me to open myself up to you when we're divorcing in a week?"

His fingers trail down my arms. "Because you want to."

His voice gets shaky. It's not like him.

He's right, but it's not like him.

"I'll tell you." I lean in to his touch. "If you'll remind me of something from last night. In detail."

"You first."

I press my lips together. "It's hard to explain. I've always been the smart one. Anne, my sister, she's the pretty one. The fun one. The popular one. She was the cheerleader. I was on the debate team."

"Did that bother you?"

"I don't mind people complimenting her looks and my intellect. Looks have never been important to me."

"You're fucking beautiful."

"You don't have to say that."

"You really think I say shit just because it's expected of me."

Actually, yes. I pull back enough to look Joel in the

eyes. "You didn't flirt with that fan because it was what she expected?"

"Not exactly."

"But close?"

He stares back at me. "I'm not bullshitting you, Bella. You're gorgeous."

"Thank you."

"And fucking hot. But I can't get into that or I won't have any blood left in my brain."

My cheeks flush. "You really—"

"Yeah, and if you ask again, I'm going to have to prove it."

God, the intensity of his expression. I believe him.

And I'm tempted to ask him to prove it.

But then this conversation is important.

I shouldn't let him derail it with sex. Even if I really, really want to.

"I don't mind that I'm not the pretty one," I say. "But being the smart one is a lot to live up to. Everyone expects me to succeed. They expect me to follow this path they've set for me. If I step off it, if I fail…" I take a deep breath. This is too close to everything that hurts. "I have to be great at everything."

"Is that what you want or what everyone else expects of you?"

"Both."

He drags his fingertips over my forearm. "You don't try shit if you might fail?"

"I don't think about it like that."

"But you don't."

"I guess not."

"You don't do things unless you're sure you'll be great at them."

My stomach twists. "I... maybe..." I take a deep breath and exhale slowly. "I've never thought about it."

"How about this?" His voice gets soft. "This week, I'm going to ask you to try some shit you've never done before. Shit you might not be good at. Agree to really consider everything before you shoot it down."

"Why should I?"

Joel laughs. "Because you like me."

I do. "But what do I get out of it?"

"Experiencing new things isn't enough?"

I shake my head.

"Not sure I have much else to offer."

"You still haven't told me why you were in Vegas. Not in detail."

He takes a half step backwards.

I press my butt against the counter. There's something in his eyes. This hesitation.

It doesn't seem like Joel.

"You haven't told me either," he says.

True. And I don't want to. But I need to admit this. I need to deal with it. I look back into his eyes. "You go first."

He nods. His eyes go to the window for a minute then they're back on mine. "My parents gave me bad news. I didn't want to think about it."

"So you went looking for a fun distraction?"

He nods. "You."

"I found out I failed at something I thought I was good at." I press my lips together. Already, tears are threatening to sting my eyes. Technically, I haven't flunked out of law school. But I killed myself studying last semester and I ended up with Cs. Classes are only getting harder. Unless I magically find more time to study, or magically get better at school, I'm going to fail. Maybe not next semester. But sometime before my three years are up.

Fuck.

So much for threatening.

I blink back a tear.

Joel wraps his arms around me and pulls my body into his.

One hand goes to my back, my shoulders. He undoes my bun, then he's running his fingers through my hair.

His touch is soft.

Sweet.

Comforting.

Right now, I get it. I completely understand why I married him.

Even though I don't remember most of the details.

He runs his fingers through my hair.

I sink into his chest.

I want, so badly, to collapse in his arms.

To be able to trust him with all the ugly thoughts in my head.

With the secrets I don't share with anyone.

But with our looming expiration date…

I don't know what I'm doing later, but right now, I want to be in his arms.

I soak in every ounce of comfort he can give me.

I FEEL NAKED WHEN I UNWRAP MYSELF FROM JOEL'S ARMS. But I still manage to finish putting together dinner.

We take our food to the couch. I sit, cross-legged, pushing my shrimp around my plate. I'm not hungry anymore.

Too much is happening too fast.

My head is spinning.

Joel isn't lacking for appetite. He eats with greedy bites. It's not exactly messy, but it's certainly not dainty either.

He swallows, wipes his mouth with the back of his hand, and looks to me. "This is fucking good."

"Yeah?"

"Great even." He motions to my fork *try it.*

"I'm not hungry anymore."

"Try it anyway."

I did make this meal. I *should* at least taste it. I stab a shrimp and a broccoli floret and use them to scoop rice.

The shrimp is a little overcooked, but the broccoli is perfect and it's bursting with flavors of garlic, lime, ginger, and fish sauce.

I chew, swallow, dab my lip corners with a paper towel (Joel doesn't have cloth napkins).

His eyes meet mine. He raises a brow. *Well?*

"It's good."

"Only good?"

"It's great, considering my limited options."

"It's great."

I shake my head.

He nods.

I take another bite. To test these claims. Then another. Fuck. I guess I am hungry.

Joel chuckles. "It's great."

"It's very good."

"That's the best I'm going to get from you, huh?"

I nod.

"I'll take it." He turns his attention to his plate but he keeps one eye on me.

Even with the rice a little mushy and the shrimp a little stringy, the dish is good.

Very good even.

But that doesn't feel like enough.

Good has never felt like enough to me.

And I have the scars to prove it.

I trace the faint scars on my wrist as I pour over old memories.

Joel was right. I don't do things unless I can be great. Or maybe I make a point of being great at everything I choose to do.

Either way, I never give myself permission to fail.

Hell, I never give myself permission to be *good enough*.

Forget about *okay* or *terrible.*

It means I close myself off to any activity where I won't excel.

It means I stay planted firmly in my comfort zone.

Only... I'm here, in Los Angeles, in Joel's apartment, spending a week with him before our impending divorce.

That's way, way outside my comfort zone.

I want to try new things. To be the kind of person who can try new things.

But not tonight.

Tonight, I need comfort food.

Like greasy shrimp stir-fry.

Joel finishes first. He waits for me to finish then takes our plates to the sink.

He checks the time on his way back to the couch. "There's a lot of night left."

There is. And I'm tempted to insist we spend it in his bed, naked. I need the comfort right now. Even if it means I break into pieces when we part.

He sits next to me, his body turned towards mine. "I have a pitch."

My breath catches in my throat. "Yeah?"

His eyes fill with mischief. "It might keep you up all night."

Yes. Hell yes. I nod.

"You sure you can handle it?"

I'm not.

I nod anyway.

His smile spreads over his cheeks. "We should start watching the *Harry Potter* movies."

I have to laugh. "Tease."

He plays dumb. "What did you think I meant?"

"You know exactly what I thought you meant."

He pulls me into his lap. His lips hover over my ear. "You thought I'd offer to use *my* wand instead of showing you Harry's?"

I nod.

"You're going to have to request that specifically." He drags his lips down my neck. "Unless I hear otherwise, we're going to Hogwarts."

I smile. "Let's do it."

Chapter Ten

JOEL

Bella nearly falls asleep on the couch a dozen times. By the movie's end, she's barely able to make her way to the bathroom to brush her teeth.

She shifts into my room and closes the door as she changes into pajamas.

Then she pulls the door open and climbs into my bed.

That's an invitation.

But I meant what I said. I'm not rushing things with her. I'm not fucking her until she's begging me.

Still.

I am going to say good night.

It's a few steps into my room. I flick off the light and sit next to her.

She looks up at me from behind her thick, black frames. Her expression is this mix of apprehension and affection.

And exhaustion.

She blinks and stares into my eyes. "I… thanks for the movies."

I pull her glasses from her face. My fingers skim her

temples. Her cheeks. I get lost in the soft purr that falls off her lips as I run my fingers through her hair. "Thanks for dinner."

"It was nothing."

"It was a lot."

She leans into my touch. "Well… you're welcome."

For a second, I consider giving into my body's demands. She wants me touching her. I want her coming on my hand again. It's a win/win.

But she's still nervous.

This is all either one of us is getting.

I lean down and brush my lips against hers. She tastes good. And the way she moans into my mouth—

Fuck, I want every inch of her.

But there's something about stopping at a good night kiss.

It's intimate in a way an easy fuck isn't.

I wait until her eyes flutter closed again then I go back to the main room.

My cock is not happy at this course of events. I could easily take the edge off, but I want to wait to come with her.

I entertain myself by channel surfing.

Law and Order.

Perfect.

I get lost in the show for a while. The grey-haired detective is making a wisecrack when my phone rings.

It's Daphne.

I bite my tongue. I shouldn't ignore my sister's calls, but I'm not sure I can put on a happy face about this divorce shit.

I let it go to voicemail.

She calls again.

Fine.

I bring the phone to my ear. "Yes?"

"Nice to talk to you too, Joel."

Okay, I won't snap. "I'm kinda busy. I don't have time to chat."

"I know Mom called you. I saw her talking to you earlier."

I tap my fingers against the back of my cell. I like my parents. I like my whole fucking family. I don't mind being the person everyone calls when they need cheering up. But I can't do it right now. I can't pretend I'm okay with all this. "They made the announcements. They have the divorce party planned for tomorrow. It sounds like everything is on track." This is about as much of this conversation as I can tolerate.

"Mom is… she needs you here. You're her *funny little man*. Nobody else can make her smile."

I know that. It fucking killed me talking with Mom, hearing that *please, Joel, please laugh this off so I can laugh it off too* tone to her voice, and not being able to deliver. It's still killing me. "I'll make her smile another time."

She sighs. "Promise you'll call Mom tomorrow."

"Yeah, but if she asks what I think about this—"

"Change the subject. You're good at that. Like when I ask if you're dating anyone—"

"I got the point."

"And promise you'll call Dad."

"If you promise not to say the word divorce to me again for a while."

"Okay. Thanks, Joel. Love you."

"Love you too." I hang up the phone. I try to turn my attention back to the storied crime procedural, but I can't find humor in any of the wisecracks.

Divorce is my new least favorite word.

But it's the only word in my brain. The entire episode

of *Law and Order*, and the one that comes after, my brain is screaming *Mom and Dad are getting a divorce*.

Marriage is bullshit.

Until death do us part is bullshit.

It's all bullshit.

I lie back on the couch and try to make my mind blank. No amount of closing my eyes or focusing on my breathing helps me wipe the word *divorce* from my thoughts.

Usually, I know what I want and where I stand. I want to be behind my drum kit. Then I want to be inside a beautiful woman. Then I want to crash in my bed, alone.

Right now, Bella is in my bed.

I want to be inside her, but I don't want to be alone after.

I don't want to kiss her goodbye after breakfast.

Fuck. I've dealt with a lot of weird shit since I started touring, but being a married man takes the cake.

In the morning, I try to get back to my usual routine. I get ready. I head to the gym down the street. It's early enough that no one is looking for celebrities.

I spend an hour sweating through my legs routine, but the entire time I'm lacking focus. Between my parents' divorce and Bella in my bed, I'm distracted.

I try to shake it off on the walk home. I've got three missed calls from Mal. And a voicemail.

A guitar riff flows through the speakers. It's *Good Dirty*, the song that has been haunting the singer for the last month.

This riff is different than what we've got so far. Really fucking different.

But it's perfect.

I text Mal.

Joel: That's it.

Mal: I'll be at your apartment in twenty minutes.

Finally, my thoughts settle. The riff plays in my head as I get home and get into the shower.

I turn the water, wrap a towel around my hips, and I slip into my bedroom.

Bella stirs. Her eyes blink open. She reaches for her glasses on the bedside table and slides them on.

"Hey." She gives me a long once-over. Her tongue slides over her lips. Her eyes fill with desire.

With sunlight streaming in through the windows behind her, Bella really does look like an angel.

I can't help myself. "Good morning, angel."

She cocks a brow. "Angel?"

"You disagree?"

She shakes her head. "I've never had a pet name before." Her lips curl into a smile. She likes it.

Fuck, I like it a little too much. Corrupting the sweet, innocent angel… it's incredibly fucking hot.

Her eyes stay glued to me as she pushes herself to a seated position. She gives me another once-over. This time, her gaze lingers on my hips.

I drop my towel.

She pants.

I stare into her pretty brown eyes. "I'm going to make some noise for a while. You mind?"

"Depends on what you're doing."

Fuck, I like the way she thinks. "Music. Mal's coming over. He figured out the perfect riff."

Finally, her eyes meet mine. "The lead singer. The one who agrees about making your songs radio friendly."

I chuckle. "You have a good memory."

"That's nothing."

"You have dirt?"

She nods. "I shouldn't have been looking, but I couldn't sleep last night..." Her voice gets low, breathy. She might as well scream *I was thinking about you, inside me.*

"You gonna fill me in?" I tease.

She barely managed to drag her eyes from my chest. She shakes her head. "My secret."

The doorbell rings. That must be Mal.

I take a step backwards. "It might be a while."

She nods. "You mind if I watch?"

I let my voice get low and seductive. "Angel, you can watch me anytime you want."

Mal has his guitar slung around one shoulder. He has Kit's practice bass slung around the other.

"Kit's going to kill you if you break that," I say.

"I won't."

I motion *come in*.

He does. He goes straight to my practice room and sets the bass in a stand in the corner.

Usually, Mal is as steady as an anchor. Right now, he's hopped up on *I need to get this song right and I'm fucking close* energy.

I run a hand through my wet hair. "I have a guest. We need to keep it down."

Mal nods. He gives me a paternal once-over. He takes in my left hand then he's looking me in the eyes. He cocks a brow. *Explain.*

"My wife is sleeping."

"Your wife?"

I nod like I've had a wife for years. Like my wife isn't planning on divorcing me in a week.

"You're married?"

"It's all over TMZ."

"I don't read gossip."

"You should. Those sites say a lot of shit about you."

He stares into my eyes. I can see why Mal has no trouble picking up women, but I don't need this kind of intimacy. Not with him.

I motion to his guitar. "Let's get to it."

"Hold on." He turns to his phone and taps out a few messages. "You trust me?"

"You know I don't."

His phone buzzes. "Too bad." It buzzes again. "You've already been outvoted." He shows me his screen.

Mal: Joel has a wife. Who votes we have a show ASAP?

Ethan: I'm in.

Kit: Me too.

"You're an asshole," I say.

"You don't want her to see you play?"

He's still an asshole, but it's a good point. If I want Bella sticking around, I need her seeing me at my best. And behind my drum kit is where I'm at my best.

He taps out another message. "Tomorrow work?"

"Sounds like I'm outvoted. Does it matter if tomorrow works for me?"

He chuckles. "I try to accommodate."

"Tomorrow is fine."

He slides his phone into his pocket. "We go on at ten in Hollywood. Soundcheck is seven."

"How the fuck did you do that so fast?"

"Alessandra owes me a favor."

I raise a brow. Mal cleans up, but I can't imagine him sleeping with our tough as nails booking agent slash tour manager. She's an attractive woman, but she's not Mal's type. He prefers them… inexperienced.

He chuckles. "Not that kind of favor." He shoots me a look. "You're really married?"

"Yeah."

He gives me another prying look. "Congratulations."

"Thanks." I clear my throat. I'm not liking the direction this conversation is going. "Shall we?"

His expression is as incredulous as the day is long. Even so, he connects his guitar to the amp in the corner.

He adjusts his guitar and plays the riff.

There's no cell speaker muffling it. No wind. No city sounds.

It's just my ears and the music.

"Play it again," I demand.

He does.

"It's fucking perfect."

"I know." He nods to the drum kit.

The man doesn't have to ask twice. I pick up my sticks, slide behind the drums, and I start playing.

The old drum line doesn't sound right. This new riff is harder, moodier.

I let my hands take over. They tap out a new beat. That one isn't quite right. I try another. Another. Another dozen.

There.

A buzz fills my body. There's nothing like writing a song, getting every element working together.

I nod to Mal. He nods back. We play the entire fucking song. It's the same chord progression for the chorus. The same breakdown. The same outro. But with the new riff, it's perfect.

We play it again and again, adjusting our parts a little every time. I'm dripping with sweat and my shoulders are aching, but nothing is going to stop me from finishing this.

This is where I belong.

I'm so lost in the song, I don't notice Bella come in. She's in jeans and a cardigan. Her hair is pulled into a loose bun. Those hipster librarian glasses are framing her eyes.

Fuck, she looks good all prim and proper and corruptible.

"Sorry, angel. You know I can't keep it down," I tease.

She smiles and tilts her head to one side. It's like she's analyzing my words. She knows I'm stepping into that *Joel Young, life of the party* role.

Mal looks to me and cocks a brow. *Really, angel?*

I shrug.

"Flirt after you introduce me." He turns to Bella. "Malcolm Strong but everyone calls me Mal."

"Bella Chase." She moves forward to shake his hand. "I'm going to sit in the corner and watch. Or maybe just listen." She holds up her e-reader with her left hand. "I have plenty to entertain myself."

"What are you reading?" Mal asks.

Her eyes meet mine. She winks. "Something about the power of phallic imagery."

"Any chance you play the bass?" he asks.

She shakes her head. "I don't even know what the difference between a bass and a guitar is."

Mal motions to me. *Come on.*

Okay. I see his game.

This will be fun.

I push off my drum kit. "You want to learn?"

Her brown eyes fill with apprehension. "No, I don't think so. I'm not very musical."

"This is an easy riff," I say.

"And there's no way you're worse than Joel," Mal teases.

I laugh. "It's too much to keep track of, the four strings. Much easier to hit things with sticks."

Bella smiles. "You should contribute to this phallic imagery series."

I laugh. "I'll tell you a lot about phallic imagery if you try this."

She shakes her head.

I lean in to whisper. "Because you might not be great right away?"

She says nothing.

I pull her closer. "Give me ten minutes."

Her voice is still nervous. "I don't know…"

Mal shoots me a cutting look. "Save the dirty talk for when I leave."

She blushes. After a deep breath, her cheeks lose some of their pinkish hue. She turns to me with a nod. "Okay. I'll give it a shot."

I pick up Kit's practice bass and I help Bella sling it around her shoulders.

She's incredibly awkward with the instrument. Her shoulders are stiff. Her stance is stiffer.

"Here." I stand behind her, my chest against her back. God, she's warm and soft. It makes it difficult to focus.

I want her in a way I've never wanted anyone.

Not just her pleasure or her laughter, but her heart.

Her mind.

Her soul.

Fuck, that's cheesy. I can barely stand thinking it.

I guide her into position, one hand on the neck of the bass guitar, one hand on the body.

I show her how to pluck and how to fret.

Each time the instrument responds to her, she lets out another little groan.

This isn't my expertise, but I know enough to take her through the entire riff.

She squeals when she plays the entire thing on her own. "I haven't played an instrument since elementary school."

"Violin?" I guess.

She laughs. "How did you know?"

"Lucky guess." I drag my lips over her neck until my mouth is hovering over her ear. "You want to play the song with us or you want to go back to reading?"

She cocks her head. "I'll play it once."

Mal nods to her. "Start on the count of three, all right?"

She nods.

He counts down.

She does start on three. She doesn't quite get keeping the beat, but she manages to play the riff.

This time, Mal belts out the lyrics with his usual breathy groaning style.

When we're done, Bella slides the instrument off her shoulders and sets it back in its stand. Her expression is filled with a beautiful mix of delight and exhaustion.

"You want to go to a show tomorrow?" I ask.

She looks into my eyes. "Your band or another band?"

I mime being stabbed in the gut. "That's cold, Bella. You'd go see someone else over us?"

She laughs. "I like collecting information."

"We're playing in Hollywood tomorrow," Mal says. "Last minute thing."

She shoots me a look. *Is he full of shit?*

I nod. He's incredibly full of shit. But— "It will be fun."

"Sure." She motions to the door. "I'll let you guys finish."

"You can stay," I say.

"I know." She catches me staring at her tits and motions *my eyes are up here.* "But I'm getting this strange feeling I'm not good for your productivity."

That's true.

Not that I'm complaining.

She nods goodbye and closes the door behind her.

Mal shoots me an accusatory look. "Album was due a month ago."

"And?"

"We should get in the studio ASAP."

"Sure."

He stares at me.

I stare back at him.

Fuck, I'm losing this staring contest.

I clear my throat. "Is that all?"

"You like her."

"Why do you think I married her?"

His expression gets serious. "I got a call from our law firm last night. Something about wanting to move an appointment."

I clear my throat.

"For a second, I thought you were getting ready to make due on all those threats to leave the band."

I'd rather not share this detail with Mal, but he's not going to drop this. I keep my voice even. "She wants a divorce."

"And you don't?"

I nod. "Being with her feels right."

He chuckles. "That's it?"

"What else is there?"

"True." He thinks for a moment. When he speaks, his

voice is matter of fact. "So you have a week to convince her to stay married to you?"

"Yeah."

"She's a smart girl. You're going to have to do better than *it feels right* to convince her."

That much I know.

I haven't figured out the how.

But I'll get there.

Somehow, I'll get there.

Chapter Eleven

JOEL

After Mal leaves, I join Bella in the kitchen. She's sipping tea and reading. A mostly empty bowl of cereal is next to her.

I refill her bowl and steal her spoon. "Is that Harry?"

She blushes. "This whole wand thing is making me self-conscious about enjoying a YA fantasy series."

"What book are you on?"

"*Prisoner of Azkaban.*" Her lips curl into a smile as she studies my expression. "Nothing to say about that one?"

"That's the one with the werewolf?"

She nods.

"You know werewolves are one big metaphor for male sexuality."

"They are?"

I nod.

"No offense Joel, but you don't strike me as the intellectual type."

I mime being stabbed in the gut. "How could you? I'm very fucking intellectual."

She raises a brow. *Really?*

I laugh. "My sister. She's a shrink. She used to talk about this shit all the time." I take another bite of cereal, chew, swallow. "Werewolves are all about how male sexuality is dangerous and scary. Men get this urge to become animals and they can't stop themselves from transforming into beasts."

"Huh." She takes a sip of her tea. "What about the full moon thing?"

"What about it?"

"The moon is a metaphor for female reproduction, because the lunar cycle is about as long as the menstrual cycle. And people only change to werewolves during the full moon."

I laugh. "I've got nothing."

"It could be that they become beasts when women are ovulating."

"It's all about making babies?"

"Maybe." She takes another long sip of her tea. This time, she lets out a soft moan. "But then 'moon time' usually means a period."

"You saying my metaphor is falling apart?"

"It needs some finessing."

I steal her tea and take a sip. "You have to admit, those werewolf guys are totally into each other."

"Sirius and Remus?"

"Yeah. Total wolf on wolf action."

She laughs and steals her tea back. "Sirius isn't a werewolf. He's an animagus."

"A what?"

"A shapeshifter. He can turn into a dog."

"But they are fucking."

"Maybe."

"Definitely."

"I never thought about it. I'm not really into guy on

guy."

I raise a brow.

"Really. I guess… I'm not really sure what I'm into. Besides the usual."

"More than happy to help you figure that out."

She blushes.

I could push her.

But I like just talking to her. Even about nothing. It's easy. I don't get that with anyone else.

After I finish my cereal, I leave the bowl in the sink. Then I steal her tea again.

"Hey." She pushes me playfully.

I slide out of my seat and hold the cup over my head.

She stands to reach for it. She's not quite there. "You're too tall."

I nod.

She looks up at me. Her expression softens. Again, she rises to her tiptoes. This time, her hands go to my hips.

Her eyes flutter closed.

Her lips brush against mine.

It starts soft.

Then she's kissing me harder.

Deeper.

I drop the cup on the counter and I slide my arms around her waist.

This is our first real kiss since our wedding night.

Fuck, she tastes good.

I hold her body against mine.

She digs her fingers into my skin.

Her tongue slides around mine.

I've kissed a lot. But this is different. I can feel her affection pouring into me. I can feel our connection. And not just in my cock.

She pulls back with a needy sigh. She's still looking up at me, her eyes full of something I can't quite place.

She reaches for her tea and downs the rest of it.

Fuck, I'm actually speechless.

I clear my throat. "You tried something new."

She nods.

"Did you like it?"

"I didn't hate it."

"You fucking liked it."

"Okay." She sets her mug on the counter. "I did like it."

"We have all day. We can try all sorts of shit."

"I'm not sure I want to spend the entire day trying new things. Sounds exhausting."

"All right." I have a better idea. "You've never been to L.A. right?"

She shakes her head.

"You want to see the city, the beach, or the mountains?"

"This does not count as a city."

"Manhattan snob."

She laughs. "True."

"The beach or the mountains?"

"Both."

"I have just the ticket."

I'm not at all surprised that Bella has workout clothes in her bag.

Or that she insists on sunscreen with at least SPF 30.

Or that she's still wearing that *please fuck me* look in her eyes.

I'm a little surprised by her requesting a hat, but only because my Giants cap looks out of place on her head.

After we change, fill water bottles, and check sunscreen twice, we get in my car and we head towards Malibu. The road is clear. That's one perk of the holidays. Nobody at work means nobody heading home.

We zip up Pacific Coast Highway, the ocean on our left, the mountains on our right, the sun shining high above us.

It's a beautiful, blue day, the kind of day I usually take for granted. But with the way Bella is looking at the sun with a smile, I'm acutely aware of how lucky I am to live in paradise.

She motions to the stereo. "You mind?"

I shake my head. "You can hook up your phone if you want to play something."

"Even if I play Lady Gaga?"

"As long as you're okay with me singing along to *Poker Face*."

She laughs. "You're taunting me."

"Me, taunting? Never."

Her laugh is louder this time. It fills the entire car. "You're a tease." Her voice is needy in that *I'm trying not to think about sex* way. "I should pick something." She attaches the aux cable to her cell's headphone jack and she taps the screen a few times. "There."

Music fills the car. It's not Lady Gaga. It's the Beach Boys.

I shoot her a *really* look. "Am I a California stereotype?"

"You're tan. You're blond. You're famous. You surf. You look great in sunglasses. Start calling people *dude* and you're there."

"Dude, that's not cool."

"If you don't like the music, I'll change it."

"Do you like it?"

She looks me in the eyes. Her voice is confident, assertive. "Yes, I do. It makes me feel like I'm on vacation."

I'll take it.

Bella's eyes go wide as she steps out of the car and takes in the view.

I take her hand and lead her to the start of the hiking trail. She presses her palm into mine, sticking close, breathing deep, taking in every sight and sound.

I'm used to the Malibu Canyon mountains. I'm used to the grey-brown patches of dirt, the mix of green and amber grass, the scraggly trees that cast shade.

I'm even used to seeing the ocean whenever I feel like it.

Bella isn't. She takes in all her surroundings, carefully noting every rock or bump or hole in the path.

I let her get a few steps ahead of me so I can check out her ass. Damn, I want my hands on those round hips. I want to watch her flesh slam into my pelvis as I fuck her doggy style.

Fuck. I'm getting distracted. I can't remember the last time I was around someone I wanted and I didn't fuck her right away.

But that's no excuse. This hike isn't about my dirty thoughts. It's about showing Bella a good time.

I take a few swigs of water to cool off. It doesn't help. Not when I have a prime view of Bella's ass.

I go back to leading the way. The sky is blue. The sun is bright. The ocean is sparkling.

But it's still Bella that has my attention. Every time I turn back to check on her, I get lost in the flush spreading over her cheeks and chest.

Fuck, she looks good in that tight outfit.

Sweat dripping off her forehead.

Her chest heaving with every labored breath.

Damn, I'm getting too many ideas. But I like getting her messy. Dirty. She's not the prim and proper woman running away from… from something right now.

She's in her body.

"What was it you said before?" She drops her voice an octave to imitate me. "If you're going to think about fucking me, fill me in on the details?"

I nod. That is what I said before.

She hipchecks me. "Well?"

"I'm going to be explicit about it."

"I can handle it."

She can't. I shouldn't push her.

But the way she's looking at me, all that need in her brown eyes…

I cock a brow. "You sure?"

She nods.

I motion to the alcove on our right. "I was thinking about taking you into the shade, and rubbing you over your leggings until I got you so wet the fabric was soaked." I lean in to whisper. Already, I'm getting hard. But I don't fucking care. I need her needing this as badly as I do. I need her needing *me*. "Getting you so close to coming you were begging for release, then making you wait the entire drive home, and all through our showers until I'd finally pin you to my bed and fuck your gorgeous ass."

"Oh. Uh. I…" She clears her throat. She pulls back enough to look me in the eyes. A flush spreads over her cheeks. Her tongue slides over her lips. Her nails dig into her thighs, over her leggings.

She wants that too.

Needs it.

Her eyes meet mine. "I don't think you can do it. I don't think you can get me to the edge then walk away." She swallows hard. Her chest heaves with her inhale and falls with her exhale. "I don't think you can resist making me come."

That's a challenge.

But I can't take it until she's begging me.

She clears her throat and moves a few steps ahead.

She's thinking about it.

Then so am I.

We fall back into an easy silence. The wind rustles the brush. Her breath is heavy. Mine too. Our footsteps are soft. Easy. We go like that for minutes.

Bella stops under the shade, on top of a dusty rock. She holds her hands over her eyes to shield them from the sun. "If I lived here, I guess I'd have prescription sunglasses."

"You don't?"

"I do. But I didn't think I'd need them in Vegas." She leans against the rock. Her eyes meet mine, but she doesn't say anything.

"It's bright in the desert."

She nods.

"But you weren't planning on seeing much of outside."

Again, she nods.

"You said you flew there to blow off steam."

"Yeah."

"Why?"

She's quiet for a long moment. When she speaks, her voice is soft. "I'm in law school. I finished my first semester a week and a half ago. Then I got my grades." Her gaze goes to her feet. "Mostly Cs. I'd never got a C before and all of a sudden I had three."

"Never?"

"I got two Bs in college and both were... I was not happy."

"The smart sister doesn't get Bs?"

She nods. "Yeah. My entire life, I had this plan. I was going to be a lawyer. Like my parents. And I did it all right—excellent high school transcripts, great grades at Harvard, admission into Columbia Law School, internships at the right places, summer jobs doing research." Her voice drops. "Then... then I got to school and it was too hard. I tried. All I did, all semester, was study and go to the gym."

"Yeah?"

She nods. "But I got Cs."

"Can you graduate with straight Cs?"

"In theory." She stares at the inside of her wrists. The left. Then the right. "But probably not in reality."

I move closer.

Closer.

She looks up at me. Her voice is shaky. Vulnerable. "I failed. I didn't know what to do. Only that I didn't want to think for a while. That I had to be somewhere else... with someone else."

"So you flew to Vegas?"

She nods. "It would have been easier to go to Atlantic City. Or to go to some club downtown. But that was too—"

"Too close to home."

"Yeah." She bites her lip. "I still don't know what to do. What I'm going to do with my entire life. If I can go back to law school. If I want to." She swallows hard. "I've never failed before."

"Everyone fails sometimes."

She shakes her head. "You have?"

Yeah, but I can't seem to recall anything major at the moment.

This close to her, it's hard to recall anything, period.

"Do you want to be a lawyer?" I ask.

She presses her lips together. "That's the plan."

"But is it what you want?"

"I don't know. I've never stopped to think about what I want." Her voice is a whisper. "My entire life, I've had this plan. Without it, I have nothing. I have no idea what I'm going to do."

"Did you plan on marrying a stranger in Vegas?"

"No. But we're... we're going to get a divorce and that will be..." Her eyes turn down. "I don't know, Joel... I don't know what I'm supposed to do here. I like you. A lot. I don't want to like you. Not if this is ending in a week." Her cheeks flush as she looks me in the eyes. "Right now... it hurts thinking about this."

I get that.

"Did you mean what you said?" Even though no one else is here, she leans in to whisper. "About touching me then making me wait."

My cock stirs. That *will* get her out of her head. And I don't exactly mind. "Yeah."

"Will you do it?"

"Only if you beg."

"Will you... Will you touch me? Please."

I want to.

But I'm not sure now is the time.

I run my fingers over her cheek.

She lets out a soft murmur as her eyes flutter closed. Already, the tension in her brow is easing.

This is what she needs.

She looks up at me. "Please, Joel." She slides her hand

under my t-shirt and presses her palm against my stomach. "Please touch me."

I stare back at her. "Don't blame me when you're desperate and wanting the entire drive home."

Her voice gets confident. "I won't."

Fuck, the fierce look in her eyes…

I slide my hand around her neck and pin her to the rock.

She groans as she kisses me.

Her tongue slides into my mouth.

Her body melts against mine.

Her fingers dig into my arms.

Her touch is soft and hard at once.

Need and affection.

She wants me.

And she likes me.

And that really fucking matters to me.

God dammit, she tastes good.

My cock is screaming to be inside her.

Not yet.

I drag my hand up the inside of her thigh and I rub her over her leggings.

Even with all the fabric in the way, she feels good.

Soft.

Eager.

Pliable.

Her nails dig into my skin.

She nips at my lip.

Then she's rocking her hips, pressing her cunt against my hand.

I want this fabric out of the way.

I rub her harder.

Faster.

I push her closer and closer to the edge.

Fuck, the way her groans vibrate down my neck…

She pulls back to pant.

Her eyes meet mine.

Her eyes scream *please*.

I watch pleasure spread over her expression as I rub her. It's fucking beautiful, the way her cheeks flush, the way her eyelids flutter together, the way her thighs clench around my hands.

Right now, I'm the only thing in her universe.

Right now, she wants to come more than she wants anything else.

More than she's ever wanted anything else.

She's almost there.

I rub her a little harder.

I take her a little closer.

"Joel." She tugs at my t-shirt. "Please."

My cock begs me to keep going, to get her naked on the dirty path, writhing under me.

But my cock is going to have to wait.

I kiss her hard and deep. One more brush of my hands, one more push towards the edge, then I pull my hand to my side.

I step back.

Bella bites her lip. She digs her nails into her outer thigh.

Her face is flushed. She's panting.

She stares at me, that *make me come* plea in her eyes.

I stare back.

"You're really going to wait until we get home?"

I nod.

"Then we need to go home right away."

Chapter Twelve

JOEL

The second we get home, I pull Bella into the bathroom.

She's still flushed and wanting, but she's nervous too.

No. Those nerves need to be gone. I need to bring out her dirty side.

"Take off your tank top," I demand.

She pulls it over her head.

"The sports bra too."

She blushes as she unhooks her sports bra and slides it off her shoulders.

Her tits are perfect. I want them in my hands and my mouth, but I haven't tortured her nearly thoroughly enough yet.

"The glasses," I demand.

She leaves them on the sink.

"Now, the leggings."

She slides them to her ankles and kicks them off. She's standing there in only a pair of black panties.

She looks up at me, need filling her brown eyes.

Her eyelids flutter together as I drag my fingertips over her back, her shoulders, her neck. Gently, I pull the elastic band from her hair.

Her chestnut locks fall onto her shoulders.

I lean down to press my lips to hers. I've never been into kissing, but I fucking love the feeling of her mouth on mine.

She tastes good.

Like she's mine.

I really fucking want her to be mine.

She groans as I slide my tongue into her mouth. Her fingers dig into my skin.

She rocks her hips against mine. "Now, Joel. You need to… You need to make me come now."

I pull her close and I plant kisses along her neck. With each, her groan gets louder, needier.

"Take off your panties." I nip at her earlobe.

She looks at me with all the trust in the world.

I'm used to getting off on bossing women around, but it's different with her.

Knowing she trusts me to deliver on my teasing—

Knowing she trusts me, period—

Her hands go to her hips. Slowly, she slides her panties to her knees.

I press my palm into her hip bone to hold her body against mine. I drag my other hand up her torso and over her breasts.

Bella groans as I play with her nipple. She arches her hips to grind her ass against my cock.

Fuck that feels good. My body threatens to take over. I want to pin Bella to the wall and fuck her hard and fast.

But I want to get her panting with desire more.

I play with her nipple until *I* can't take the friction of

her flesh against my cock. There's no fucking way I'm coming before she does.

"Turn on the water," I demand.

She bends over to reach for the faucet.

"Do that again, and I'm going to fuck that gorgeous ass."

Her breath catches in her throat. "You promise?"

"Fuck yes." The confidence in her voice is pushing me too close to the edge. "Get in the shower."

She does. The water streams over her forehead and down her cheeks. She makes a show of turning around and tilting her head back enough to rinse her hair.

I take in the sight of her for a long moment, then I step into the shower with her.

The tub is small. It's tricky to maneuver. I let her rinse off then I squirt shampoo into my hands and run it through her hair.

Her hands go to my sides, but they don't stay there. She explores every inch of my torso. The soft, slick touch sets me on fire.

Fuck, I need those hands on my cock.

After she comes.

I torture her by soaping every inch of her body except her lush tits.

She groans with a mix of agony and ecstasy. Her eyes meet mine. They scream *you're cruel, you evil tease.*

I lean in to whisper. "If you want something, ask for it."

"Touch me," she groans.

"Where, angel?"

She lets out another groan, a *you know where, you insufferable tease* groan.

She brings my hand to her chest.

My cock quivers. I fucking like her direct.

She keeps her eyes fixed on mine as I tease her nipple again and again. Finally, her lids press together.

Her lips go to my shoulder, my neck, my ear. "Touch me." She takes my hand and place it between her legs.

I pin her to the shower wall—I need to be sure she won't slip if her knees buckle. Water pounds against my side and back as I bring my body closer to hers.

Her thighs are slick against my fingers.

Fuck, those lush thighs feel good.

I slow as I get closer.

She shudders.

Closer.

She groans.

Closer.

"Joel," she whines.

I brush my fingers over her clit as softly as I can.

Again.

Again.

She groans. "You're a tease."

"I know." I drag my lips over her neck as I stroke her. I keep my touch light.

"Joel..." She arches her back, pressing her cunt against my hands. "Please."

I suck on her skin. I stroke her harder. Harder.

She rocks her hips again and again. "Fuck." She slides her arm around my neck. Her nails dig into my shoulders. "Joel... Please... Make me come."

My cock quivers.

I've tortured her enough.

I stroke her harder. Harder.

Her nails sink into my skin.

There. That's it.

I watch pleasure spread over Bella's face as I rub her. It's fucking beautiful, the mix of agony and ecstasy in her expression, the way her nipples tighten and her cheeks flush as her eyes fill with need.

Then her eyes are closed again.

And a groan is falling off her lips.

She's almost there.

I stroke her a little harder, a little faster.

Then she's there.

"Joel." She groans my name again and again as she comes.

Damn, my name sounds good on her lips.

She looks so fucking beautiful wrecked with pleasure.

Her face flushes. Her shoulders shake. Her knees knock together.

Then her entire body is shaking and her moans are vibrating over my skin.

She blinks her eyes open. Her expression is fuzzy for a minute, then it's sharp. Confident.

Her eyes bore into mine. Her voice is shaky, but she gets through her words. "I want you to... ahem, again."

"To?"

Her eyes go to her chest. "Are you going to make me say it?"

"Yes."

Her cheeks flush. "I want you to... to come on my chest again." She places her hands on my hips. "Help me out here."

Fuck yes. I help her lower herself onto her knees, onto the non-skid mat on the tub.

This is exactly why I have a non-skid mat.

Fuck, it's not often I pat my past self on the back for smart decisions, but this non-skid mat—

Great fucking decision.

Practical matters flee my brain as Bella wraps her hand around my cock.

She looks up at me. Her brown eyes fill with desire. "Play with my nipples."

Fuck yes. I keep one hand on the back of her head. I cup her breast with the other.

She rubs my tip with her thumb.

She does it harder. Harder.

She tightens her grip and strokes me.

I run my fingers over her nipples. I try to do it softly, to tease her, but then she brushes her lips against my cock—

Fuck.

She takes her time licking every inch of me. It's torture, the sweetest fucking torture. By the time she brings her tongue back to my tip, I'm shaking.

Pleasure floods my body as she takes me into her soft, wet mouth.

Slowly, she takes me deep.

She does it again.

Again.

Fuck.

I need more. Faster. I press my hand against the back of her head.

I push her deeper.

Faster.

She looks up at me, this mix of lust and power in her eyes.

Damn, her soft, wet mouth. I'm already close.

"Harder," I groan.

She goes harder.

I rub her harder.

She moans against my cock.

Her eyes fix on mine. This dirty, needy, demanding look spreads over her expression.

She's proving something. Not sure what it is at the moment, but I fucking like the way she's proving it.

Bella plants one palm on my ass. She uses it to take me deeper.

I keep my hand on her head, guiding her as gently as I can manage.

My hips rock of their own accord.

She doesn't gag.

She groans with pleasure.

She looks up at me as if to say *more*.

Fuck yes.

My last bit of control slips away. My body takes over. My need to come takes over.

I thrust into her mouth as she sucks on me. The friction of her mouth is fucking heaven.

I squeeze her nipple between my thumb and forefinger.

She groans again.

Louder.

Deeper.

Harder.

I tug at her hair to pull out of her soft mouth.

"Fuck, angel." I groan.

My cock pulses as I come all over her gorgeous tits.

Pleasure spreads over my pelvis, my torso, my legs, my arms. I can feel my orgasm in my fingertips.

Every part of me feels good.

Her expression is full of pride.

Her tits are still dripping, dirty.

I've marked her.

She's mine.

Right now, she's mine.

Chapter Thirteen

BELLA

Even though I'm fresh from the shower, I feel dirty. I feel incredibly, deliciously dirty.

I can't believe how much the thought makes me hot all over.

How much I want to do it again.

I really, really can't believe how much I love feeling dirty.

He's already dressed, already back in the main room, and I'm sitting here, on his bed.

I can't move. I can't think. I can't begin to contemplate what I'm going to wear or what we're going to do for the rest of the night.

My stomach growls. Okay, that's something I need to do. I'm starving.

I let my towel fall to my feet as I push myself off the bed. The bedroom door is open. And Joel is on the couch.

I move into his field of vision. It's not like me to tease. With Stan, I was shy. Inhibited. I only had sex with the lights off. I never, ever wore lingerie. I certainly never made a point of showing off my naked body.

"I like your outfit, angel." His voice is playful. His green eyes light up as he gives me a long once-over. His tongue slides over his lips.

He wants me. It's written all over his face. *Joel Young wants me.*

The heat of his gaze makes me blush, but that doesn't stop me from swaying my hips. I lean against the frame, copping a pin-up model pose.

"You keep that up and I'm going to throw you on the bed and fuck you," Joel growls.

I smile coyly.

He pushes himself off the couch and moves towards me. Joel drags his lips over my neck then his mouth is hovering over my ear. "I have something for you to wear."

I muster up all the confidence I can find. "What if I want you throwing me on the bed and fucking me?"

"Then stay naked." He sucks on my earlobe for a moment then he pulls back enough to look me in the eyes. He cocks a brow as if to say *it's up to you.*

"We haven't eaten lunch. Or dinner." On cue, my stomach growls. "I'm starving."

Joel's lips curl into a smile. He moves to the dresser and opens the top drawer. "How about *Joel, you really worked up my appetite.*"

"How about *Bella, angel, you really worked up my appetite?*"

"You like me calling you angel?"

I nod. I like it a lot.

His smile widens. "You like the reminder you're a good girl."

I admit nothing.

He tosses me a pair of boxers and a t-shirt. "You like feeling like a naughty girl."

It's not a question. There's no need to answer. Even so, the flush in my cheeks spreads to my chest as I pull on

Joel's boxers and t-shirt. They fit surprisingly well, given his fit physique and my curvy figure.

He smiles. "I finally get why women are always trying to steal my shit."

"Why?"

"Seeing you in my clothes." He bites his lip as he slides his arms around my waist. "It's fucking hot."

"Yeah?"

"Yeah." He leans in to plant a soft, slow kiss on my lips.

God, he's a good kisser. I feel warm.

Complete.

I really, really like him.

I force myself to pull back. I don't want to think about how much I like Joel. It's confusing. And I'm starving. "Did I really work up your appetite?"

"Yeah." He presses his palm against my lower back and leads me to the kitchen.

I hop onto the counter to take a seat. Joel starts digging through the fridge. He pulls out red peppers, frozen broccoli, frozen shrimp.

"What are you making?" Whatever it is, it looks good.

"Nothing." He grabs a box of pasta from the pantry. Then sun dried tomatoes. Dried garlic, basil, and parsley. His eyes meet mine. "I'm teaching you to make something."

"What if I don't want your help?"

"Then the lesson is going to take a really fucking long time." His stare is a challenge. *We both know you want to learn from me.*

I hop off the counter. "You're teaching me to make some sort of pasta dish."

"I improvise." He nods to the food on the counter. "You have to know what flavor profiles go together. Shrimp is good with red peppers, garlic, basil, red sauce."

"And it's still the only food we have."

He laughs. "Technicalities."

I nod. That all sounds delicious. But it's beyond my understanding of cooking. I can follow recipes to a T, but I don't have a clue how to improvise beyond combining a meat, a starch, and a vegetable with a bottle of sauce.

"You like shrimp?"

"I love shrimp."

"Name three shrimp dishes you like."

"Shrimp scampi, shrimp arrabiata, shrimp fried rice."

"They're all based around pasta or rice. What else do they have in common?"

"Garlic." I rack my brain for other similarities. Shrimp scampi doesn't seem like it has anything in common with shrimp fried rice, but both dishes are cooked with a lot of butter or oil. Both have lemon. Both are a mix of shrimp, veggies, and starch.

I relay all my findings to Joel.

He nods. "Let's put a pasta dish together. What do you want to put in it, besides shrimp?"

"How do *you* put a dish together?"

"I do whatever feels right. I don't really think about shit in that kind of analytical way." He moves behind me and slides his arms around my waist. "We've got a lot of options here. What else do you want in your dish?"

I grab the box of pasta. "Obviously."

He laughs. "Obviously."

"Red peppers." They're a key ingredient in arrabiata and in shrimp fried rice. And they're amazing. "Garlic, of course. Basil. Frozen broccoli. And—" My brow scrunches. "Hmm, one more vegetable. What do you think?"

"It's your creation, angel."

I recall my last delicious pasta dish. We were at one of Dad's favorite restaurants in Little Italy. The conversation was awkward, stilted. Anne was talking about all the shopping she had to do before some party she was throwing for her husband's work. Dad was shooting her this *why has my daughter been reduced to spending her time shopping* look of disappointment. All I could think about was my impending finals.

The overall experience was awful. But the food was great.

"Artichoke hearts," I say.

He finds a can of them in the pantry. "You want me to lead?"

"Yes, please."

Joel smiles as he takes control. He puts a pan on the burner then walks me through sautéing the shrimp and frozen broccoli. He demonstrates the best way to slice a bell pepper.

He never gets condescending. I don't know how to explain it. When my dad instructs me, I always end up feeling like a child. But with Joel it's like we're equals. Like he sees my potential.

We're only cutting vegetables and boiling pasta, but I really feel like we're a team.

And I really like it.

After we put the dish on simmer—apparently, we need to give the flavors time to bleed together—I slide onto the counter.

Joel leans against the opposite counter. His eyes fix on mine. "You still want something from our wedding night?"

It's weird to think of it as our wedding night, but that's an accurate label. I nod. "Please."

"You remember when we went to the Bellagio fountains?"

"A little."

He smiles, but there's a sadness to it. Then he's shaking

that off, and he's all smile. "We got there right as the water show was starting. The song was *My Heart Will Go On*."

"The *Titanic* song?"

He laughs. "And you wanted to do the *Titanic*."

"That's a thing?"

"According to you, yeah." His laugh lights up his eyes. "You grabbed the railing and you screamed 'Joel, come on. I want to be Queen of the world.'"

"I did not."

He nods. "You did. I tried to talk you out of it."

"Really?"

"Yeah, I figured security would get there fast. I don't mind extra arrests on my record, but I could tell you would."

He's right I would. "I appreciate that."

"Don't. I failed. You started climbing over the railing."

I let my eyes flutter closed. I can hear the Celine Dion song. And Joel's laugh. The spray of the water. It was a cold night, but I was warm from the buzz, then Joel's arms were around my waist, and I felt safe.

Happy.

The memory is faint, but I can still feel every bit of happiness.

Of ease.

It was fun.

I did climb over the railing.

He stayed on the other side of it to hold me tightly.

To protect me.

And I really trusted him to protect me.

His voice gets soft. "You remember?"

"Yeah." I stare into his gorgeous green eyes. "Most of it."

"You agreed I could draw you wearing only your necklace?"

I raise a brow. "Did I?"

Joel shakes his head. "No, but I'm happy to do it."

"You draw?"

"I know how to wield a pen."

I have to laugh. "Brooms, wands, and pens. Joel Young, you have an obsession—"

"You forgot drum sticks."

"I did."

"Guitars." He mimes holding a guitar, the body over his crotch, the neck jutting forward. Then he's fretting his air-guitar like he's touching himself.

Ahem. "You're obsessed with phallic imagery."

"You're thinking about me naked."

"The point stands."

"If it was good enough for Kubrick, it's good enough for me."

My lips press together. "Kubrick, really?"

"Really. I'm not a cretin. I know film."

"I wasn't saying—"

"You were."

I shake my head. "No."

He nods. "A little."

"Maybe, a little." I let my knees tap together. "You don't seem like a Kubrick fan."

"You either."

"Because I love *Harry Potter*?"

"Well, yeah." He takes a step closer. "Kubrick movies are cold, unemotional. *Harry Potter* is full of heart and guts."

"I don't like Kubrick movies."

He smiles. "I figured."

"Do you?"

"Not really."

"Too boring?" I suggest.

He laughs. "Because I have a short attention span?"

"If the taste in movies fits…"

He nods. "They're a little dry." His lips curl into a smile. "And you don't like them because they're cold, and you already do enough thinking all fucking day. You want movies to make you feel something."

It's a perfect description of why I watch movies, read, listen to music. Only I've never thought about it in those terms.

I'm always thinking. And it gets exhausting. Being able to turn that off and get lost in a book and feel—

That's why I read.

How does Joel know that?

Until this very moment, I didn't even know that.

"How did you know that?" I ask.

"You think I don't know you 'cause we met two days ago?"

"That's not a reasonable conclusion?"

"It is." His lips press together. "But reasonable conclusions aren't always right. If I saw you at some club, in that tight all business dress, those work heels, the glasses and the bun—I'd think you were some uptight chick who wouldn't beg me to come on her tits."

My cheeks flush.

"But it turns out, you're an uptight woman who fucking loves when I come on her tits." His smile widens.

I try to reach for something, anything to say. I need my senses back or I'm going to get lost in beautiful, filthy mental images. "You're a know it all."

He shakes his head.

I nod.

He takes another step closer. "I bet I can guess another three movies or books you love."

"You're proving my point about being a know-it-all."

He smiles. "Even so." He places his body between my legs. "I should get something if I win."

I force myself to push past my inhibitions. "A blow job in the shower wasn't enough?"

He slides his arms around my waist. "You're fucking adorable when you blush."

I shake my head.

He nods.

"You…" I lean into his touch as he slides his fingertips under his t-shirt. "You didn't answer the question."

"That was fucking amazing."

"Really?"

"Fuck yes." He looks up at me. "Don't tell me I didn't verbalize that."

God, I'm going to die of embarrassment. I take a deep breath and exhale slowly. Joel is still looking up at me with this *you're cute when you're nervous* smile.

I stare back at him. "I've never been particularly confident about my abilities."

"You mean sucking cock or sex in general?"

I trip over my tongue.

He smiles. "You're amazing on all counts, angel." He slides his hand up my back.

"Really?"

He nods. "Fuck yes." He presses his lips against my neck. "You're giving me ideas about how we should spend the rest of the day."

I clear my throat. "Yeah?"

He nods.

I press my lips together.

Then he's smiling.

And laughing.

Oh.

"You're about to say *Harry Potter*, aren't you?" I ask.

"Am I getting predictable?"

I nod.

"Even so, the offer stands."

"I accept."

Joel and I spend the entire day watching *Harry Potter* movies. We only get up to make dinner, or maybe it's a late night snack.

We're in each other's arms the entire time, but when I go to bed, he doesn't invite himself.

He stays on the couch.

And I toss and turn…

Until I give in to all that desire racing through me and stroke myself to orgasm.

That knocks me out.

I sleep like a log, but when I wake up alone, I feel… well, alone. My eyelids flutter closed. I want to go back to bed.

But my phone is ringing.

And it's ringing in the main room.

And it's a familiar song.

The one I set for my dad.

Shit.

I get out of bed and find my cell charging on the floor. Joel stirs from his spot on the couch.

I grab the phone and bring it back to his room.

Call from *Chase Home*. It's the landline.

Fuck.

I bring the phone to my ear. "Hello."

My dad's voice booms through the speakers. "Isabella, who the hell is this Joel Young you've married?"

Chapter Fourteen

BELLA

My stomach drops. Already, my legs are wobbly.

Dad knows.

I'm going to throw up.

Or maybe I'm going to fall down first.

That would be a hell of a rock star wife way to go, falling face-first in a pile of my own vomit.

I press my back into the wall, but it doesn't give me the stability I need.

"Isabella. Are you there?" Dad's voice is snippy, but there's concern in there too.

I have to say something. "Daddy, you know I prefer to go by Bella." I slink to my feet and pull my knees into my chest. I already feel like I'm back to being fourteen, like I just got caught making out in the living room with the high school bad boy. Only I was never cool enough to kiss any bad boys.

"Your sister tells me he's in some rock band," Dad says. "Where in the world did you meet a musician?"

I can't say that I met him in Las Vegas. But I can tell him most of the truth. "At a bar. I was blowing off some steam. We had a great conversation, and one thing led to another."

"How long have you been serious about this man?" His voice fills with concern. "I suppose that doesn't matter. You two are getting an annulment."

He says it like it's a fact, not an order, but it still catches me off-guard.

"We are?" We can't, not legally. Not unless one of us wants to allege the other was not of sound mind. And I'm not about to do that to him.

"Your sister was reading some article about your impending divorce. It was on that awful gossip website. It had a lot to say about your husband."

Joel may be sporting tattoos and a bad reputation, but he's also sweet and funny and supportive. Those aren't things Dad can see, but he can see that Joel is successful.

He could trust my judgment.

He could want me to live my own life.

"Bella, honey?" Dad clears his throat.

I press my lips together. It should be easy to say *of course I'm divorcing Joel*, even if Dad is being judgmental.

I open my mouth but the words don't fall.

Dad continues. "You're young. You want to have fun. I understand that. I felt the same way when I was your age. But this guy is a fling. You don't marry a fling."

"Of course not." Dad's facts are objectively correct, but they feel wrong. Hell, even the fling part is technically correct. Joel and I agreed to a week of fun. That's all. My stomach shouldn't be twisting. My heart shouldn't be heavy. Dad's words shouldn't feel hollow in my ears.

This is a mess.

I take a deep breath and exhale slowly. It doesn't help me find clarity.

"Are you two getting an annulment?" Dad asks.

"I don't know. We probably have to get a divorce."

"Do you have a settlement conference?"

"After Christmas."

"I have a few friends in Los Angeles. I'll send someone to represent you."

"I don't want his money. It's going to be simple and clean. Neither of us is asking for anything."

"I hope you're right, but just in case—"

"I don't need a lawyer."

"Sweetheart, all lawyers and future lawyers think the 'you always need a lawyer' rule applies to everyone but them. I'm sending a lawyer."

Right. I'm still a future lawyer. That's still the family plan. That's still what I want.

Good law school, good job, well-mannered husband, well-maintained penthouse in Manhattan.

That's supposed to be my life.

The plan makes my stomach churn. But the thought of throwing away the plan and walking into a huge question mark—that's just as bad. Worse even.

Dad is right. It's always best to have a lawyer, just in case. And there's no reason for me to believe that our week is going to end in anything but divorce. This makes sense. "Okay. I have to check, but I think our appointment is at eleven."

"It will be okay, sweetie. This will be over soon. You'll get back to your life."

Right.

I'll be home soon.

I'll be able to get back on the *good school, good job, good future* track.

"I'm going to set this up, then I'm going to call you back tomorrow," he says. "I love you, sweetie."

"I love you too." I end the call.

I should feel relieved, but I don't.

I feel empty.

Lonely.

Like I have no idea where home is anymore.

Like I'm never going to fit into the *prodigal good girl* box.

Like I'm never going to be good enough.

After twenty minutes of sinking into the carpet, I force myself to get up, brush my teeth, wash my face, put on a pot of tea.

Joel is still asleep on the couch.

I want to be in his arms. I want his comfort wiping everything else away. Dad's voice is still echoing in my ears. *You're not good enough, Bella. You made another mistake. You failed again. You'll never been good enough.*

I'm on my second cup of tea when Joel stirs. He throws off his blanket, nods good morning, and moves into the bathroom.

I don't want to mold myself into the shape that pleases everyone else anymore.

But what fucking shape pleases me?

What the hell do I want out of my life?

I don't know.

But there's one thing I'm sure I want.

And the second Joel is in the living room with me, I'm going to have it.

Chapter Fifteen

BELLA

Joel steps out of the bathroom and stretches his arms over his head. He's wearing nothing but boxers and damn does his pose give me a nice view of his sculpted torso.

He looks like a magazine cover model.

He *is* a magazine cover model.

And he's looking at me like he wants to devour me.

I try to channel a version of Bella who goes after exactly what she wants, everyone else's wishes be damned.

It doesn't happen.

Joel moves into the kitchen and places his body behind mine. He rests his head on my shoulder as he wraps his arms around me.

He presses his lips to my neck. "You're tense."

"Yeah." Very, very tense.

"Was it that phone call?"

I nod. "How much did you hear?"

"Only the ringing. Your dad?"

"Yeah. He wants to make sure I have a lawyer at our meeting."

"Prudent."

"Yeah." I press my lips together. Tension is already creeping into my shoulders. "Can we not talk about this right now?"

He drags his fingertips over my forearms. I cringe as they drop. He's close.

But I need his comfort right now.

I can't let him know how much I don't want him feeling my scars.

I take a deep breath. With my exhale, I melt into his body.

His voice gets low and flirty. "How about I get your mind off it?"

"How will you manage that?" I try to make my voice just as flirty, but I sound more apprehensive than anything.

He slides his hands to my hips then pulls my ass against his crotch. "That's a surprise."

I very much like the direction this is going. I tease back. "You want to eat now or… after."

He plays coy. "After what, angel?"

"Whatever you're doing to get my mind off things." I press my lips together. If he's playing coy, I'm playing coy. No matter how badly I want the comfort of his body against mine.

"After." He takes my hands, leads me to the couch, and sits me down.

He goes to the TV. I enjoy the view of him crouching over to grab something from the cabinet, but I have no clue what he's doing.

The more I take in the hard lines of his back and shoulders, the less I care.

The TV turns on. The screen flashes with a familiar logo. Joel moves to the couch with two Nintendo-64 controllers.

He hands the purple one to me. "We're playing *Golden Eye.*"

I cock a brow. "We are?"

He takes a seat on the couch then he pats his lap. "Come here so I can show you how to play."

I'm not big on video games, but I like where this is going.

I slide into Joel's lap.

He wraps his arms around my waist and places his hands on top of mine. He walks me through the game's controls, then through a tutorial level, then we're starting the single-player mode.

It's difficult. My lack of hand-eye coordination doesn't help. Computer characters keep finding me. And I'm incredibly bad at aiming well enough to kill them before they kill me.

Joel laughs as he helps me finesse my skills. By my fifth death, I get the hang of aiming.

I actually enjoy the second level. Even if it takes me far too many tries to get through it.

By the third level, I finally get why people sink hours and hours into video games. This is fun.

Joel presses his lips to my neck. "You're kicking ass, angel."

I laugh as I die, again. "I'm not sure about that."

He drags his lips over my skin. "Want to test your concentration?"

He slips one hand under my t-shirt.

His fingers brush my stomach.

He slides his hand up my torso.

"Joel," I breathe.

"Yeah?" His voice gets rough, needy.

The controller slips from my hands and lands on the floor with a thud. I no longer care about the video game.

I no longer care about anything but Joel's hands on my skin.

He cups my breasts, rubbing my nipples with the pads of his thumbs. The friction sends waves of pleasure to my core.

I need this distraction.

But I also need his touch.

I trust him.

I want him.

Fuck, there are too many feelings swirling around my stomach. I want this to be *just sex*.

But I want more than that with Joel.

I press my neck against his mouth.

He growls as he sucks on my skin. His hands stay on my breasts. He toys with my nipples again and again.

I get achy.

Desperate.

"Don't stop," I groan.

He rubs me with soft, slow strokes. His groans vibrate down my neck as he drags his lips over my skin. The softness of the gesture makes me achier.

I need more of him.

I rock my hips to grind against his cock. He's hard. He's hard because I'm in his lap, because his hands are on my breasts, because he wants me.

There's too much fabric in the way of our bodies connecting.

"More," I demand.

He lets out a low grunt of approval as he pulls my t-shirt over my head. Then he's adjusting our positions so I'm straddling him.

One hand cups the back of my head.

The other toys with my nipple.

He pulls me into a deep kiss. It's messy in the best possible way.

It's deep.

Intimate.

Like this *is* more than sex.

When our kiss breaks, he looks up at me, his green eyes wide with desire. "You want to come on my hands or my face first?"

My sex clenches. I want to be as dirty and bold as he is. I muster up all my confidence as I stare back into his eyes. "Your face."

He lets out another one of those low deep groans. Then his lips are on mine. Desire pours between us.

Affection too.

I want more of him than his body. I want all of him.

But this is all I can have.

It has to be enough.

I tell myself it's enough.

I don't believe it.

Then Joel's dragging his lips down my neck and I don't fucking care if it's enough.

I don't care if I'll break when this ends.

I need him inside me.

Now.

He palms my ass, lifting me enough to bring my chest to his mouth. He sucks on my nipple. Then it's flicks of his tongue. Fast. Slow. Hard. Soft.

He scrapes his teeth against me.

"Fuck." I have to tug at his hair. "More."

He does it again. Again. It's hard enough it hurts, but it hurts in the best possible way.

I take his hand and bring it between my legs. Dirty Bella is taking over. I don't even have to try. Hell, I'm not sure that I have a choice in the matter.

Not when I'm with Joel.

"Touch me," I groan.

He pulls my shorts off my hips and he strokes me. The friction of his fingers against my clit sets me on fire. I'm going to come on his hand quickly.

I groan.

I tug at his hair.

I tug at his hair enough to bring his mouth to my other nipple.

Joel slides his fingers over me until he's teasing my cunt.

Holy fuck I just thought cunt.

It feels right.

It feels good.

"Please," I groan.

Slowly, he slides a finger inside me. Then another. Then his thumb is working my clit.

The pressure is so intense my knees wobble. I have to plant my hands on his shoulders for support.

He fucks me with his fingers as he sucks on my nipple.

Pleasure floods my body. Almost.

Almost…

Joel pulls his hand away. "On your back. Now."

I collapse on the couch.

Then he's between my legs, pulling my boxers off my feet.

"Joel," I groan as I reach for his hair. There. I've got it. I tug him towards me.

He plants his hands on my inner thighs and he pries my legs apart.

One falls over the side of the couch. The other presses against its back.

Joel drags his lips up my inner thigh. Then his mouth is on me.

He licks me from top to bottom again and again. Then

he's plunging his tongue inside me, sucking on my lips, ever-so-gently scraping his teeth against my tender flesh.

I tug at his hair as I rock my hips against his mouth. My conscious brain shuts off.

I don't stop to think about what I want.

I just demand it.

"Make me come, baby," I groan.

He licks me up and down again. Again. Again.

Then his mouth is on my clit. He digs his fingers into the flesh of my inner thigh as he licks me.

God that feels good.

I press my thigh back into his hand.

I tug at his hair.

He goes a little harder. A littler faster.

Then he's there, exactly where I need him.

"Don't stop," I groan.

I writhe.

I rock my hips against him.

He licks me with just the right pressure, just the right speed.

There.

My sex pulses as I come. Pleasure spreads out to my fingers and toes. I'm still shaking, still writhing.

I'm screaming loud enough to wake the entire building.

"Fuck, Joel." I hold his head against me. "Don't stop."

He licks me through my orgasm. And through the after-shocks.

I groan with a mix of ecstasy and agony.

He pulls back enough to nip at the flesh of my inner thigh. "Say my name again, angel."

Fuck, the way his voice gets low and needy when he calls me angel…

He makes me feel like it's sexy that I'm a good girl.

"Joel." My voice breaks into a whine. I've come down

enough that I need his mouth on me again. I can't believe how badly I need his mouth on me again. "Make me come again, Joel."

He groans into my skin.

Then he's sucking on my clit. Harder. Harder.

Fuck, that's intense.

Pleasure wells up to a fever pitch. Almost. Almost.

There.

I groan incomprehensible things as I come.

He keeps me pinned to the couch, licking me through my orgasm. My entire body is wrecked with pleasure.

He looks up at me, his green eyes heavy with desire, and suddenly I need more.

I need Joel in a way I've never needed anyone.

I need him so much it's terrifying.

"Fuck me," I groan.

He reaches for something in the bookshelf. A condom. Of course he has condoms in the bookshelf. He has a non-skid mat in his bathtub. I'm sure he has condoms in every nook and cranny of the apartment.

I don't even care that it means he's a manwhore.

It's good that he's safe.

"Fuck me," I groan it again.

He unwraps the condom and rolls it on. Then he's sitting on the couch. He pulls my body on top of his so I'm straddling him.

His hands go to my hips.

He looks me in the eyes as he pulls my body onto his.

His tip strains against me. Inch by inch, he enters me.

I stare back as I take him. It's intense. A good intense. A really fucking great intense.

Our bodies are one.

We move together. With his hands as my guide, I shift until I only have his tip, then I take him as deep as I can. I fuck him with long, deep strokes. I fuck him until I'm dizzy. Until I can't take it anymore.

He pulls my chest against his mouth and sucks on my nipple. Enough pleasure floods my body that I can't take more.

Everything but the motions of our bodies falls away. The room is filled with our breath, with our groans. A neighbor is pounding on the wall to tell us to quiet down, but that only makes me hotter.

His fingers dig into my skin.

His lips close around my nipple.

He looks up at me, his green eyes wrecked with pleasure.

Then he's groaning against my chest. His eyelids press together.

He's close.

"Touch yourself. I want you coming on my cock."

My sex clenches as I groan out something resembling a yes.

I want that too.

I hold onto his shoulders tightly with one hand. With the other, I stroke my clit. Pleasure wells up inside me.

He's almost there too.

I want to come with him.

But I want to come too badly to worry about timing.

A few more brushes of my hand and I'm there.

Our groans run together like beautiful music.

Pleasure spreads out to my fingers and toes.

Then he's there too, his cock pulsing inside me.

"Fuck, Bella." Joel rocks me through his orgasm, his shoulders shaking.

His entire body is shaking.

It's the best thing I've ever seen.

He holds me close for a minute then he separates our bodies and takes care of the condom.

He smiles as he rejoins me on the couch. He pulls me back into his lap.

I melt.

Right now, I know I'm exactly where I'm supposed to be.

Chapter Sixteen

BELLA

We have breakfast and tea (coffee for Joel) on the couch.

We're not talking about anything important.

We're not really talking even.

Quiet isn't what I expect from Joel, but it's comfortable. Easy. Like we're a normal married couple, two people who have been together for years.

There's no tension between us.

There are no pretenses.

Even though I'm keeping my thoughts about the divorce and about Dad's phone call to myself, I don't feel the usual burden of secrets.

It's not like quiet breakfasts with my family. Joel isn't looking at me with expectations. He's not waiting for me to convince him I'm doing well in school.

That I'm doing well, period.

Hell, I'm not thinking about school.

I'm not even thinking about life outside this apartment.

The sun is streaming through the wide windows. Waves are crashing against the beach. The sky is blue and bright.

This place is beautiful.

It's distracting how beautiful it is.

I finish my last bite of scrambled eggs, take my plate to the sink, fix another cup of tea.

Joel looks up at me from the couch. His green eyes are filled with affection.

He *does* like me.

A lot even.

But he seems okay with this ending. At least, he hasn't said otherwise.

Joel pushes himself to his feet. He moves close enough to slide his arms around my waist then he pulls me onto the couch, onto his lap.

My tea sloshes over the sides of my mug. "This is hot."

"Angel, you flatter me."

I nod to my mug.

His lips curl into a smile. Gently, he peels my fingers off my cup, takes it into his hands, and places it on the side table. His voice is low, seductive. "We have until six."

"That's a lot of time."

"I'm more than happy to help you beat *Golden Eye*." He nods to the remote. "But we can watch TV if that's more your speed."

Would it be out of line to demand more sex?

I don't want to start thinking yet.

Right now, I never want to think again.

But there's something about Joel's expression. He wants to cheer me up. But not physically.

Get ahold of yourself, Bella. He fucked you thirty minutes ago.

Games can be fun, but TV is more my speed. I grab the remote. "Thank you. I'm sure it means a lot, giving up control of your magic stick."

He laughs. "I would say that."

"You would." I settle into his lap as I turn the TV on and flip through channels. My body is humming from the feeling of his body against mine, his arms around me.

He feels so good.

Like he's meant to be mine.

I sink into his body. All of my attention is on his breath, his heartbeat.

"Stop." Joel's fingers curl around my wrist. "You flipped past *Law and Order*."

"Yeah?" I force myself to stare at the TV. I channel down until *Law and Order* appears on screen. "I thought I had the controls."

"Don't tell me you don't like *Law and Order*."

"Does it have some connection to *Harry Potter* I don't know about?"

"Bella, you're killing me." He drags his fingers through my hair. "This show is fucking brilliant."

"It's entertaining, but brilliant?"

He laughs. "Brilliant."

"It is interesting, the way it puts so much emphasis on the lawyers. Most of these shows treat the lawyers like stupid suits who don't get it because they care about Miranda warnings."

His voice gets bright. "You do like it."

"I watch a lot of TV at the gym."

"You love it."

"Love is a strong word."

"You want to marry *Law and Order* and have its babies."

"*Law and Order* has done enough reproducing."

"Take that back."

"I won't." My fingers curl around the remote. I *do* enjoy police procedurals and courtroom dramas. But they're close to that place that hurts. "I like shows about defense attorneys better. Or the ones where you see more civil cases. Like *The Good Wife*."

"Fuck, I love that one."

"Yeah?"

He nods. "I watch a lot of TV on tour. Kit loves thrillers. He's easy. Ethan always wants to watch monster movies, but he'll give up the TV. And we play a lot of—" Joel nods to the video game console.

I can picture Joel on some tour bus with his friends. Even if I'm basing my image of a tour bus off a Google Image search. And I'm going by his friends' Wikipedia pages.

"I have a long list of awesome defense attorney shows." His voice gets soft. It's like he knows this is a sore spot.

The word attorney is enough to make my heart heavy. This hurts. But it's not going away anytime soon.

Either I go back to law school, put my nose to the grindstone, and really get my shit together.

Or I give up on the plan of Bella Chase, attorney at law.

Those are my only two options.

Either I succeed or I fail.

And the former isn't looking likely.

I adjust my t-shirt. My boxers. My hands refuse to still. My entire body is antsy. I don't want to sit here and talk about this. I want to run far, far away from it.

I can't fail. Not like this.

Joel pulls me closer. "Bella?"

Shit. He can tell I'm upset. He's going to ask. Then I'm going to have to literally run away or I'm going to have to talk about it.

I need to reply. "There's something about standing in open court and saying *I am this person's advocate. I will use the law and all evidence I can find to get them what they want. I'm their ally, no matter what.*"

"You like to support people?"

"Don't tell me that's surprising."

"No." He brushes my hair behind my ears. His hand slides down my shoulders, over my forearm. "Just, you don't have to be a lawyer to support people."

"I know."

"There are a ton of jobs where you can support people."

"Maybe."

"Definitely."

I pull my hands to my lap. This is pressing on that *Bella, you're a failure* bruise. I need it to stop. "Don't tell me you want to do a naughty nurse roleplay."

"Fuck yeah, but that's not my point." He pulls me off his lap then turns me so we're face to face. "There's a huge world of careers."

I'm sure there are, but I don't want to talk about it.

"You could be an executive assistant."

My nose scrunches in distaste. "An assistant?"

Joel shoots me a cutting look. "Damn. That tone—"

"It's not that."

He raises a brow.

"Okay, maybe I'm a snob. But it's not just me."

"The prodigal daughter is supposed to do better than someone's assistant?" he offers.

"Exactly." My gaze goes to my bare feet. This conversation needs to stop.

But I can't run away from this forever.

I can't hang out in Joel's beautiful apartment forever.

I don't get him comforting me forever.

Eventually, I have to get back to my life.

If that's not law school, then what the hell is it?

I play with my t-shirt. "Have you always wanted to be a drummer?"

"Since I can remember."

I look up at him. "What's it like, knowing exactly what you want?"

"I'm not an introspective guy."

"Try."

He thinks for a moment. When he speaks, his voice is steady. Confident. "You ever feel like you know exactly where you're supposed to be?"

I nod. "When I read." And sometimes, when I've been around him. But that's confusing. I don't get to be around him for long.

"It's like that." He runs his fingertips over my ankle. "You want it so fucking bad. When you have it, fuck. It's like chocolate and bourbon and sex all mixed together."

"At once?"

"No, but it feels that fucking good, the satisfaction." He looks into my eyes. "When you want it but you can't have it—it's like if you were naked on my bed, spreading your legs, shooting me a come hither look—"

"It's like me naked on your bed?"

He laughs. "I'm not finished."

I nod *go on.*

He does. "It's like you naked on my bed, inviting me to fuck you, but then you're too far away. When I reach out to touch you, I get air. I'm close, but I can't get there. It feels good to want it. But it hurts too."

Somehow, I get that. "Desire feels good."

"Yeah."

I lean back into the couch and pull my knees into my chest. I can't bring myself to look Joel in the eyes. I try to pay attention to the TV, but the car commercial isn't particularly entertaining. "I've never felt like that."

"Not everyone is passionate about work."

I shake my head. "I've never felt that kind of passion."

Joel copies my posture. He leans into the couch, but instead of pulling his knees into his chest, he places his palm over the back of my hand. "Never?"

"Never."

"What about *Harry Potter*?"

"That doesn't count."

"Why not?"

"It's a book series."

He looks me in the eyes. "And?"

"I don't know…" I unwrap my legs. My gaze goes back to my thighs.

"Bullshit. You know."

"Let's say I do."

"You do."

No, I don't. And where does he get off telling me how I feel? I shake my head. "It's a hypothetical."

"Admit you do."

But I don't. I think. I've never stopped to ask myself what I want. I've never questioned the grand plan.

I've never really thought about my interests or hobbies.

After all, they're not part of the plan.

They're not nearly as important.

He brushes my hair from my eyes. "I'll spend all afternoon watching those movies with you if you don't admit it."

My laugh breaks up the tension forming in my chest. "That's a terrible threat."

"Yeah?"

"If you really believe I'm passionate about *Harry Potter*. Why wouldn't I lie to get you to watch the movies with me?"

"Because you're honorable."

I want to stay mad at Joel, but his voice is soft, sweet.

And the way he's looking at me with all this affection…

He cares about me.

But how much?

"Who says I'm honorable?" I ask.

"I do. Besides, I want to watch those movies with you all afternoon." He takes my hand and presses it between his palms. "Go ahead. Make it hypothetical."

"Say I'm passionate about *Harry Potter*."

He nods.

"What good does that do me?"

"You get to escape into that world whenever you open a book."

"But that's not a job."

"Could be. You could be an editor. You're a smart girl. You'd be good at a lot of shit."

"Maybe."

"Maybe you're smart?"

"I'm failing out of law school."

"Cs aren't failing."

"You don't get it—"

"I get that you think anything less than perfect is failing."

I shake my head. "There's no way I'll pass next semester. Not with how hard I worked to get Cs."

"Do you even like law school?"

"I don't know. We can't all be rock stars."

He shrinks back for a second. Then he blinks and his expression is back to confident. "You'd hate being a rock star."

"Says who?"

"Me."

I say nothing.

"Deep down, do you want to be a lawyer?"

"I don't know."

"I think you do."

"I think it's none of your business. If this is a fling, then why do you fucking care what I want to do?" I push myself out of Joel's lap and off the couch. "You can't do this, Joel. You can't pry me open if you're going to leave."

He looks up at me. "I want to help you."

"I've never talked about this stuff with anyone. I can't… if we're divorcing in five days… don't convince me I can trust you and rely on you if you're going to leave."

He nods. "Okay."

"Okay?"

"Yeah." His voice gets soft. "I like you, Bella. I want to help you."

"You're bossy."

"I know."

"I…" I'm fucking lost here. I like him too. And the way he's looking at me… it's like he's promising he's going to stick around.

Like he's screaming *I don't want a divorce.*

But he isn't saying that.

He isn't saying anything.

My deep breath does nothing to calm me.

His expression does nothing to illuminate his feelings.

My stomach churns. It's not just *Bella, you're a failure.* It's also *what the hell does Joel want?*

I need a break from this.

I take the remote. "I'm going to watch more *Harry Potter.*"

He nods and pulls me back into his lap.

It still feels like I'm exactly where I belong.

Chapter Seventeen

BELLA

My thoughts refuse to settle.

Joel wants me.

He likes me.

He cares about my future.

But we're divorcing in less than a week.

That doesn't make any fucking sense.

I try to push my thoughts aside through *Harry Potter*, but they stick. Even as we dress and take his flashy sports car to the venue in Hollywood.

We're right by the walk of fame. The sidewalk with stars' handprints is familiar. The white Hollywood sign is bright against the dark hills.

But here, on the street, our surroundings aren't glitz and glamour. It's dirty, and gritty, almost like a real city.

We park at an underground garage and walk three blocks to the venue.

It's a brisk night. I feel incredibly uncool in my flats, jeans, collared shirt, v-neck sweater combination, but I'm grateful for the layers.

Joel slides his arm around my waist. He holds me close as he leads me to the venue.

It's confusing how good his touch feels. The sexual part I understand.

But there's more to it.

This feels like the touch of a husband.

Or at least a guy I could see as my husband, one day.

I push the thought aside as we walk into the dark venue. It's all black with a rock and roll vibe.

The bouncer nods hello. "Hey, Joel." His eyes linger on my chest. "Who's your friend?"

Joel pulls me closer. "My wife."

The guy continues staring at my boobs.

Joel glares.

The bouncer offers an apologetic shrug. He motions to the door behind him. "Head in. Everyone is ready for you."

We do. But Joel isn't walking with his usual bouncy steps. He's clearly irritated. Is he jealous?

I study his expression. There's something protective about his stance, but there's this frustration in his eyes.

It's not jealousy.

It's more that he doesn't like people thinking he treats women like interchangeable sex toys.

Maybe.

I'm not sure.

I should ask.

That's the key to marriage, communication. But when I open my mouth, words refuse to fall.

I don't want to talk about this.

I don't want to talk right now.

I want to run away from everything and everyone and find some magic clarity.

That's not going to happen. I might as well enjoy another few days as a rock and roll wife.

Sound check at a cool, nearly empty club is a good start.

This place looks big enough to fit a few hundred. Right now, it's about a dozen.

Roadies are setting up gear on stage. Bartenders and servers are mulling around by the bar. There are hanger-ons there too.

A tall guy with dark hair nods and moves towards us. Oh, that's Ethan Strong. The guitarist. I remind myself of the gossip—he was mowing through lingerie models until he got back together with his ex-girlfriend. There aren't many pictures of them together, but the ones I saw stood out. She's a strawberry blond with a noticeable and incredibly hot goth style.

She's not here. At least, not somewhere I can see her.

Ethan extends his hand. "I'm Ethan Strong. You must be Bella."

I shake his hand. "Bella Chase, yeah." Or did I take Joel's last name? I don't remember seeing any paperwork.

Joel nods. "You kept your name."

My cheeks flush. How did he know exactly what I was thinking?

Ethan is mostly hiding his *what the hell* expression, but he isn't quite there. I don't think it's anything about me. I think it's more that he can't believe Joel is showing up with a wife.

I clear my throat. "It's nice to meet another friend of Joel's."

He nods. "Yeah, Mal had a lot to say about your jam session. Well, a lot for him. My brother isn't exactly talkative." He turns to me. "He said Joel tried to teach you to play the bass."

"Only for a few minutes," I say.

"You want to learn a guitar riff?" he offers.

"No thank you," I say.

Joel slides his arm around me. "My wife prefers the rhythm section."

Ethan looks to me and cocks a brow. "Is that right?"

"I prefer the audience section," I say.

Ethan laughs. "Nothing wrong with that." He brushes a dark lock from his blue eyes. "Joel treating you well?"

"He is my husband." It's not an answer, but I don't feel compelled to share my personal life with anyone. Even one of Joel's friends.

His expression shifts to something playful. "If he gives you too much shit, call me. I'll talk to him."

"Will you?" I ask.

"I can't promise he'll listen. But you must know how hard his head is by now," Ethan says.

"Not just my head, Strong." Joel winks.

I shake my head. "That was bad. You're off your game."

"Angel, you're brutal." Joel slides his arms around my waist and pulls me into a slow, deep kiss.

Thoughts flee my head at an alarming rate. I don't care why we're here.

I don't care what he expects of me.

I don't care that this is ending soon.

I need his body against mine.

I need him.

Now.

He pulls back with a smile.

My expression is needy. Desperate even.

Ethan motions to Joel then to the stage. "Kit's not going to be here until showtime. You're up."

"Duty calls." Joel takes my hand and leads me to the stage.

We go up the stairs on its right. It's smaller than I expected. Actually, the entire venue is smaller than I expected. Everything Anne has told me about Dangerous Noise shows suggests they usually play to a much bigger crowd.

"This venue is smaller than normal?" I ask.

Joel nods. He takes his seat at the drum kit in the middle of the stage. His eyes meet mine. "Mal orchestrated the whole thing so Kit and Ethan could meet you."

"Is that why I feel like an exhibit at the zoo?"

"That's probably everyone checking your tits."

I motion to my baggy sweater. "In this outfit?"

Joel's smile spreads over his cheeks. "Even in that outfit, I can tell they're fucking nice. Then there's your ass in those tight jeans."

My cheeks flush.

"Of course you're welcome to lose the sweater." He picks up a pair of sticks. "And the button up blouse."

"You're okay with your friends seeing me in my bra?"

His voice drops to something low and seductive. "I don't mind being watched."

Oh.

My head fills with all sorts of beautiful mental images.

My chest heaves.

My sex clenches.

I'm a filthy pervert.

Who knew?

Joel's smile is something truly, beautifully evil. He winks at me.

His expression shifts as he turns his attention to his drum kit. He's focused.

Intense.

At peace.

Serenity spreads over his face as he pounds at his drum kit. This is exactly where Joel belongs. He knows it. Everyone in the venue knows it.

His movements are precise and loose at the same time. God, his arms are moving so fast I can't keep up.

It's incredibly sexy.

But it's more than that.

There's something about seeing him excelling at the thing he's meant to do. It makes me jealous and proud at the same time.

I'm ready to watch him all night when someone bumps into me. An older woman, in her 40s or 50s. She's short with a muscular frame and a sharp black suit.

"Sorry, sweetheart. I thought you were one of Mal's *friends*. I can't keep up with these boys." She offers her hand. "Alessandra Rodriguez. I handle all this shit." She motions to the venue. "Booking, touring, dealing with Mal's constant requests."

"Bella Chase. Nice to meet you." I shake her hand.

She looks to me then to Joel then back to me. "You married the drummer, huh?"

"I did."

"And it's sticking?"

"Oh. Well. I, um…"

"I wish it was none of my business sweetheart, but these fucking artists and their fucking feelings. They make every little thing my business. I need to know if the boy is going to be canceling shows because he's devastated. Musicians are always listening to their hearts instead of their bottom lines, running off to Maui or skipping recording sessions because they have to look for inspiration in some model's cunt." She just stops herself from rolling her eyes. "I'm sure you're used to it."

I nod like I am.

"You have a minute, sweetheart? I could use some help putting out a fire."

I like to help. And I need a distraction from the feeling whirling around my stomach.

I'm jealous of my husband.

I want what he has, this place where I belong.

This passion for what I do.

My voice is weak, but I do manage a nod. "Okay."

Alessandra leads me to a spot backstage. It's not much of a backstage. It's more of a hallway behind a curtain.

She motions to a room at the end of the hall. "Dressing room's down there if you need to do some pre-show *ritual* later. You don't have to pretend or be shy with me. I've seen it all before."

My gaze goes back to Joel. He's still in a trance. He has no idea I'm back here.

This is a nice angle. I can see all the action, but I'm well out of the fray. Joel's friends can't look at me like I have two heads.

I can't get caught up in the jealousy monster threatening to swallow me whole.

Alessandra motions to a printed paper with a list of names, phone numbers, and email addresses. There are some huge names on here. Some of the biggest names in rock.

She taps the first four names. They're highlighted in pink. "These fucking assholes tell me they'll take any gig they can get, then they give me shit about showing up by nine. If they aren't here at nine, they don't go on. End of story." Her voice is tough but all-business. She's not irritated or emotional. She's making a decision.

I'm jealous of her too. I want to feel badass and in

control. Only the thought of calling strangers and demanding they bend to my will has my palms sweaty.

I promised Joel I'd try new things, even things that terrified me.

This certainly qualifies.

"You want to use my phone, sweetheart?" She offers me her cell.

I take it. "Okay. I can do that."

"You're calling on behalf of Alessandra Rodriguez. Don't give them a name. Just tell them not to fuck off."

Okay, maybe she's a little irritated. But I'm glad to help someone who helps Joel.

I do really like helping people.

It makes me feel good.

Useful.

Productive.

I dial the first number and bring the phone to my ear.

A deep voice answers. "Yeah?"

"Is this Kell?"

"Don't you know who I am?"

I don't know who anyone is. I look to Alessandra. She's already onto her next fire, chewing out one of the guys who works at the venue.

A deep breath helps calm my racing heart. I channel my sister. "I know you need to be at Club Lurid at nine o'clock or you won't be going on."

"Who the hell are you?"

"I'm calling on behalf of Alessandra Rodriguez."

"She finally got an assistant?"

"I have other calls to make." My palms are so clammy I nearly drop the phone. I wipe my left palm on my jeans then shift the phone to my left hand. "Will you be here at nine or not?"

"Yeah, I'll get to it."

"Thanks. Goodbye." I hang up the phone before I can say anything embarrassing.

My heart is thudding against my chest. I just told off a rock star.

And he listened.

He believed my threat.

The tension in my chest melts into something lighter. I'm nervous, yeah, but I'm also exhilarated.

I feel like a badass.

Alessandra nods approval. "That was good. What was it— Isabella?"

"I go by Bella."

"Of course." She gives me a long once-over. Her expression fills with confidence. "You okay to make the rest of those calls?"

"I think so."

She nods. "You are. I can tell."

I'm not as sure about that. But I know I want to feel as badass and exhilarated as I did after the first one.

I nod. "I've got it."

Chapter Eighteen

BELLA

I make the rest of the calls without any additional clammy palms. Then Alessandra has another task for me. I should probably object to doing her bidding, but I'm enjoying the break from my thoughts too much to care.

I get caught up helping her until I feel an arm around my waist. Joel pulls my body into his. He drags his lips up my neck, then they're hovering over my ear.

His breath warms my skin. "The venue is filling up. You should grab a spot by the front or head to the VIP area upstairs."

I press my back against his chest, melting into his body. It feels good being this close to Joel. Too good. "Can't I watch from backstage?"

"Eventually. But the first time you see me perform—no fucking way." He takes me to the curtain, to that spot where you can see the stage. "This is not a view of a concert. You don't see the show. You don't feel the energy."

"Where is the view?" I don't see his point, not yet, but I

can admit that this isn't my area of expertise. I haven't been to a concert since high school.

"By the front of the stage, with everyone pushing to try to get closer to the hot singer." He presses his lips to my neck. "Mal has fucking crazy fans."

"And you don't?"

"Watch the show. You'll get it."

"Okay." It's not hard to imagine the singer drawing a crowd. But then it's not hard to imagine women screaming Joel's name and throwing their panties on stage.

My stomach churns.

This is a fling until one of us says otherwise.

After our divorce, we go our separate ways.

That's what I should want.

I shouldn't want Joel around all the time.

I shouldn't care that thousands of women want to get in his pants.

His voice pulls me out of my thoughts. "You've been hogging my wife." He nods to Alessandra.

She smiles. "I like her. I only wish I could find an assistant half as competent. She's smart, no sass, and she doesn't check out the talent."

Joel looks me in the eyes. "Tell me that last part isn't true."

"If you'd like to strip for my viewing pleasure, I'm more than happy to ogle you." My cheeks flush. Where did that come from?

Joel laughs. He pulls his t-shirt up his stomach, showing off inches of taut abs.

Mmm.

Must.

Screw.

Husband.

Now.

Joel shoots Alessandra a knowing look.

She nods back. "Nice to meet you, sweetheart. I'm sure I'll see you soon." She heads down the hall.

Then it's just me and Joel.

And my raging libido.

I'm considering asking him to pin me to the wall and fuck me here, in front of anyone who could walk by.

What the hell is wrong with me?

He brushes a stray hair behind my ear. His grey-green eyes fix on mine. "You keep looking at me like that and I'm going to put you out of your misery."

"My misery?"

"You want to fuck me." He runs his fingertips down my neck. "You're desperate to fuck me."

Yes, but I'm confused too. I can't fuck him again until I know what we're doing here. "I should get a spot for the show."

He looks to the stage then back to me "If you insist."

I could stay here.

I could demand his lips, his hands, his cock…

God dammit, I need to get ahold of myself.

I take a step backwards. "I, um… break a leg." I turn before I can give in to how badly I want the comfort of his body.

Back in high school, I went to a ton of concerts with Anne. I went to a few with my best friend.

I even saw a few indie bands with Stan.

But I've never been alone.

And I've never been to a show like this.

The opening act is playing. I recognize the singer's voice from one of my phone calls. He's good, and he's charismatic, and he's strutting around the stage like he owns the place.

Women in the audience are screaming and singing along with the lyrics and jumping up and down.

And even though I don't know the band, I'm caught up enough in the energy to do the same.

I can actually feel the music. It's vibrating against my chest.

And the crowd is bumping and bopping in time with the beat.

The room is dark except for the stage lights, and they're casting the opening act in a hazy glow.

I get caught up in the music until the singer is announcing it's the final song. Then he's singing, and I'm trying to listen, but I'm not.

I'm thinking about Joel on that stage.

About how women are going to react to him.

About how *I'm* going to react to him.

I'm already going out of my mind with desire.

Can I really handle him in full on rock star mode?

My mind is spinning. I barely notice the guys bow and take their leave. I barely notice the way the crowd quiets, then eases, then starts to grow again. Ten minutes pass. Twenty.

Then the lights are dark.

And the crowd is chanting *Dangerous Noise*.

And I can't think. Period.

My gaze goes to the stage.

It's all dark. I can't see anything. I can't do anything but dig my heels into the ground to hold my position. As uncool as I feel in my jeans and flats, I'm glad for the comfortable clothes. I haven't got a clue how the women in cocktail dresses and heels are managing.

The stage lights turn on.

Joel is the first to walk onto stage. He blows kisses to his fans. His eyes pass over the crowd.

They meet mine.

He winks.

I melt.

Right now, Joel isn't the one-night stand I accidentally married.

He's not the guy I might want to stay married to.

The guy who's incredibly unclear on whether or not he'd like to stay married to me.

He's a fucking rock god.

And he's winking at me.

I didn't think I cared about rock stars.

But the way he commands all the attention on stage…

The way he's blowing a kiss at me as he takes a seat at his drum kit…

All the girls in the audience want him.

But they can't have him.

He's mine.

Only for a while, yeah.

But he is mine.

Joel is fucking amazing.

Mal and Ethan and Kit…

They're amazing too.

Mal sings with this breathy voice. He sounds like he's in pain. Or in the middle of an incredibly vigorous fuck.

And Ethan has this adorable boyish charm.

And Kit is all mysterious and sexy.

But Joel…

Joel is an animal. He's there, lost in the music, exactly where he's supposed to be.

Halfway through the set, he tosses his shirt aside.

He's even sexier without it.

My eyes stay glued to him for the rest of the show. The music, the energy of the crowd, the way my hips are swaying with the beat—I love everything about being up in the front row.

But it can't compare to watching Joel play.

He's a fucking rock god.

And I want him.

I want him so badly I can't breathe.

But I can't have him again. Not until I know where we stand.

Chapter Nineteen

JOEL

The second I get off stage, Kit shoots me a *come here, now* look.

"You want some, you'll have to ask, Lockhart. I'm a married man now," I say.

He shakes his head, not buying my banter for a second. "You were calling her angel before."

"You heard that?"

"Mal told me."

"You and Mal are speaking?"

He nods. "Never seen you call someone you didn't like by a pet name."

"I don't like Mal and I still call him Strong."

"You don't like that he gets his way more often than you do."

"I don't like that he was willing to throw you under the bus just because—"

"I don't blame him."

"He didn't handle it like an adult."

"And you did?"

Fair enough. Our last tour, Mal discovered that some

money went missing. He blamed Kit immediately. Just cause Kit had done a lot of shitty stuff when he was using.

Maybe Mal had his reasons. I don't care. Nobody throws my friends under the bus.

But I can admit that getting wasted after shows didn't do anything to help matters.

Kit hands his bass off to a roadie then motions for me to follow him to the dressing room in the corner.

I do. It's busy with hustle and bustle but no one is paying attention to us. "You have a problem with me calling my wife *angel*? You call Piper *baby* every three and a half seconds."

"No shame in wanting to corrupt the good girl." He waits for a roadie to move out of earshot then he leans in to whisper. "You gonna keep pretending like it's normal you got married in Vegas?"

"When have I ever been normal?"

"Not relevant." Kit runs a hand through his mass of curly black hair. "You gonna offer more details?"

"Not planning on it."

He cocks a brow.

I say nothing.

His voice drops to a whisper. "No bullshit, why did you marry a stranger?"

I stare back at him.

He stares back at me.

Fuck, I always forget how intense Kit is. No wonder women fall all over themselves trying to unlock his heart. He has this stare that makes you feel like he can see into your soul.

Which is more than I need from a guy, even if he's my closest friend.

"Well?" he asks.

He *is* my closest friend. And I'm not exactly happy about how this is ending.

I don't usually tell people about shit that makes me unhappy.

I don't usually let people know anything, save for somebody fucking with one of my friends, makes me unhappy.

"Must be bad if you can't come up with a bullshit answer," Kit says.

"My parents are splitting up."

"Shit, really?"

"Yeah."

"Fuck. Can't believe my parents' marriage outlasted theirs. They're actually… I think they're done with their 'arrangement.'"

I'm happy for him, I am, but I don't need to hear this right now. "They announced it that morning. They wanted to warn me and Daphne that they were going to tell all their friends at their divorce party the next night."

"Divorce party?"

"It's a thing, apparently. And it's over. So fuck that."

"Fuck." Kit chuckles. "Your parents are getting a divorce."

I cringe at the word. "Not getting. It's done. Official."

"So you head to Vegas and get married?"

"It wasn't like that."

"Explain it."

I'm not sure that I can. "I wasn't planning on matrimony. I wanted to find a woman to take back to my hotel room, one who would make me forget every fucking thing in my life."

He nods *I've been there.*

"Fuck, she was wearing this tight dress that was all business. She looked uptight. I wanted to help her let her hair down." My thoughts go back to that night, to the way her smile lit up her brown eyes, to the way she sighed with pleasure as I ran my fingers over her skin. A lot of that night is fuzzy, but I remember enough. "I didn't think we'd end up at a chapel."

Kit chuckles. "Why are you always looking for a challenge?"

"It's boring getting handed everything you want."

He gives me a serious look. He's not buying it. Kit's always been the thoughtful type, but now that he's a year out of rehab he's particularly introspective.

Fuck. That could work. I pretend like I'm not trying to change the subject. "Hey. It's been more than a year you've been sober now, hasn't it."

Kit doesn't take the bait. At all. He shoots me a *try harder next time* look. "You really think that would work?"

"You miss a hundred percent of the shots you don't take."

He chuckles. "Take another."

I rack my brain for the perfect button to push. That's it. I make my expression serene, my voice even. "You ever fuck Piper in the ass?"

His eyes flare with a protective glare. "None of your fucking business."

"Is that a yes?" I ask.

Kit shoots me that *you're ridiculous* look of his. "Why do you care?"

"There's no law that says I need to stop enjoying details because I'm married."

"You fuck your wife in the ass?"

"Not yet. But, soon."

He shakes his head. Then he's laughing so hard his shoulders are shaking. "Of course. The uptight wallflower is a challenge. She's not going to hop on the bed and spread 'em."

"Don't pretend like you haven't fucked a hundred women who only cared that you were famous, who would have literally done anything you asked, who didn't have a fucking clue that you were an actual human being."

He nods, conceding my point. But then he gets this knowing look in his dark eyes. "Awfully fixated on screwing women who aren't your wife."

"It's not like that."

His expression gets sympathetic. "I know."

I shove my hands into my pockets. I'm not sure that I should tell Kit, but I want to tell somebody, and he's the only person I trust. Well, maybe Daphne but I'm not interested in her opinions on the matter.

I drop my voice to a whisper. "You can't tell anyone this."

"When have I ever spilled a secret?"

"Shit's different now."

He nods. "Go ahead."

"I better start at the beginning."

I tell Kit more than I should. I tell him about meeting Bella in the bar and daring her to do shit that got her blushing. And the way she dared back, even though she was nervous.

It was easy to talk to her. At first, I thought it was because I'd never see her again. At first, it was a typical one-night stand. I wanted to show her a good time. I wanted to make her laugh.

Making her smile made me feel good in a way that casual sex never had.

It made me feel whole.

I tell Kit that I knew some part of me was trying to

prove some point about love and marriage. I was trying to prove my dad wrong—when he announced the divorce, he looked me in the eyes as if to say *of course, you get this Joel. You're smart not to settle down. It's a drag, having a wife and two kids.*

Marrying Bella felt right.

Being with her still feels right.

But keeping that from her? That doesn't fucking feel right.

Shit. I don't know what to do here. I want her around. But I don't want to hurt her.

Kit steps in. "You always get people to go along with what you want."

I nod. I'm capable of getting people on board with things.

"You can't stay married to her unless you're sure you're in love with her."

"Why's it have to happen in that order?"

"You think she'd be okay staying married to a guy who isn't in love with her?"

Probably not. "It's only been a few days."

"Okay. Talk to her. Mutually agree to give it a month. But that is not a decision you make for her." His expression gets stern. "She deserves to know you're evaluating her as a potential wife all week."

"It's not like that."

"It's not far from that."

Technically, he's right. But the way he says it makes it sound ugly.

I do fucking like Bella.

And I want her around.

I'm giving myself time to get certain.

What the hell is wrong with that?

"Hey." That's Bella's voice. She smiles as she moves

closer. "I was looking for you." She turns to Kit. "You must be Kit."

"Yeah." He shakes her hand. "It's nice to meet you."

"You too. Joel speaks highly of you," she says.

Kit raises a brow. "Does he."

"Yeah, but you should know that he is trying to teach me to play bass. You might want to do something to secure your place in the band," she says.

Kit chuckles. "I have bad news for you, Bella. Joel is a fucking terrible bassist."

"Oh yeah?" she asks.

"He's not gonna teach you well enough that you could take over." He smiles. "But I can teach you to play drums."

She laughs. "Maybe you could teach me bass and he could teach me drums."

Kit shoots me an *I like her* look.

"I'll teach you to play drums." I slide my arms around her waist and pull her body into mine. She's soft and warm and she smells so fucking good. "I've got all day free tomorrow."

"Maybe." She nestles into my chest. Her eyes flutter closed for a minute then she forces them open. She turns to Kit with a smile. "You mind if I steal my husband back."

"No." He nods goodbye. "It was nice to meet you. I have to get back to my parents."

"And your soon to be fiancée," I say.

He blushes, a rarity for him. Then he flips me off.

More normal.

I return the gesture.

He takes one more step backwards and raises a brow. *Don't hurt this poor girl.*

I shoot him an *I'm not going to do that on purpose.*

We've known each other too long if I can read his face this well.

Bella waits until he's out of earshot to move closer. She plants a slow, deep kiss on my lips.

I've never been shy. I'm not about to start now. My hands go to her hips. I pull her body against mine as I groan into her mouth.

She sighs with pleasure as she pulls back. "You've got me all distracted."

"Yeah?" The warmth of pride spreads over my chest. It's not like this is the first time I've distracted a woman with my body, but seeing the contentment on Bella's face… it does something to me.

She nods. "Oh, I remember." She leans in close enough to whisper. "You're not as 'on' with him. Maybe even not at all. You two are good friends?"

"Since we were kids. He lived next door."

Her expression gets serious. "In his bio, it said he went to rehab."

"Angel, you're going to get in trouble memorizing our Wikipedia pages."

"You said to ask if I wanted to know."

I did, but I don't feel right sharing any of Kit's secrets. Even if they're my secrets too. "We all used to party too much. He didn't know when to stop."

Bella's eyes fix on mine. She's studying me like she's deciding if she believes me. She must settle on not because she shakes her head. "That's not it."

How can she tell? It's not it. It's technically true, but it's only a tiny part of the story.

"It's okay. He's your friend. I won't ask you to betray his trust." Her eyes light up as she smiles. "Did you push him the way you're pushing me about school?"

"You could say that."

"He's lucky to have you as a friend." She slides her arm

around me. "And, well, I'm glad you have someone who… who sees through your bullshit."

"Angel, you keep romancing me like this and I'm going to have to drag you to that utility closest."

"Is that a dare?"

"Yeah."

She smiles like she's thinking about taking it.

Chapter Twenty

BELLA

The next morning, I wake to Joel fixing tea and coffee in the kitchen. He's fresh from the gym, shirtless and dripping with sweat.

And tempting.

Very, very tempting.

His smile spreads to his ears as his gaze meets mine. There are no pretenses on his face. His expression is pure joy.

He's happy to see me.

Because he wants to fuck me again?

Because he's enjoying our one week fling?

Or because he wants me around forever?

Getting married puts a hell of a lot of strain on a relationship. If we'd met and fucked and decided to have fun in Vegas, we wouldn't have to worry so much about these questions.

We'd be able to step back and relax.

In theory.

In practice, I spent my entire relationship with Stan worried about where it was going and which one of us cared about the other more. He was a great guy, but it never felt quite right.

I was never myself.

I was never relaxed.

Usually, I only relax when I'm alone with a good book. That's the only time I can shut out everyone else's expectations.

But with Joel…

He motions to my cup of tea. "You want honey in this?"

Dammit, I'm getting stuck in my head here. If this is it, if we are getting a divorce, then I need to decide what I'm doing here.

Either I'm going to enjoy the hell out of the few days I have with Joel.

Or I'm going to pull back enough to keep my heart from breaking into a million little pieces when we part ways.

Either I put my heart on the line or I lock it up tightly.

"It's a complex decision, honey or no honey." Joel takes a sip of his coffee. "I don't want to overload you, but I have sugar too."

"No honey. Thank you."

He nods and hands over my mug.

The tea is hot enough to scald my tongue and sting my throat, but it has that perfect robust flavor. The familiarity is comforting. Even if it burns.

Joel studies my expression. "I want to try something today."

I take another sip. It's still comforting, but it doesn't bring any clarity. "Yeah?"

He sets his mug down. "I want to teach you to play the drums."

Huh? "You do?"

He nods.

"I was kidding last night."

"I know."

"I liked watching you play. The band is great and you were amazing—"

"Shirtless," he offers.

I laugh. "That was a perk." I take another long sip to buy myself time to think. I'm not musically inclined, but it might be interesting to try something new. "Joel, you know, I'm not going to turn into some loose and free rocker chick."

He laughs. "Thank you for the mental image."

It is a hilarious mental image. But— "Why do I feel like this joke is at my expense."

"Imagine me in a suit and tie, showing up to work at a corporate job."

That is funny.

"Saying *yes, sir* to a boss."

Funnier. "You're lucky music worked out."

He nods. "I'm not fit for anything else." He crosses the distance between us. His fingers slide over my exposed forearms. "Let me teach you to play a song."

"Maybe."

"Give me one hour."

God, his touch is making me hot and warm at once.

"You can teach me something after."

"What can I teach you?"

"You tell me. I hear you learn a lot of shit in college."

"You didn't go?"

"I dropped out after a semester."

I shoot him a *really* look.

He nods.

"I majored in English. Do you really want to learn about analyzing literature?"

"I haven't read a book in a while."

"Hmm." I rack my brain for things I can teach Joel. "We could do it with movies, instead."

"You're passing up the chance to analyze *Harry Potter* with me."

I have to laugh. "God, your thesis would be exclusively focused on phallic imagery. It would be disturbing."

"That's a funny way of pronouncing *genius*."

"Uh-huh."

He takes my mug of tea and sets it on the counter. Then he's sliding his arms around my waist, pulling my body into his.

Already, I'm forgetting my anxieties.

I can't pull back from this thing with Joel.

His touch makes me feel alive in a way nothing else does.

How can I give up even a minute of that?

"I'm a bad student. I can see why you don't want to teach." He brushes my hair behind my ear. "How about you force me to try something new instead?"

"Is there anything Joel Young hasn't tried?"

He shrugs. "There must be."

Hmm. This needs to be something that challenges Joel. He's good at convincing everyone else he's the up for anything life of the party guy.

But I know that's a put on.

Which means, I need to find something that will challenge his desire to seem like the cool, fun, nothing bothers me guy.

Ah.

That's it!

"How about I give you a facial," I say.

His pupils dilate. "You're going to have to explain this—"

"Not that kind of facial."

"That's all I'm thinking."

"It's for your skin."

"Yeah, I hear it's great for your skin."

I laugh. "Like at a spa. We can make homemade masks. We need to pick up some food anyway."

"You do *that* at a spa."

My laugh spreads all the way to my belly. I have to clutch at my stomach so I won't double over.

"If you want to get kinky about blowing me in public, I'm not about to complain."

I shake my head. Okay, I'm getting back in control of this conversation. "You know that isn't the kind of facial I mean."

He tries to keep a straight face, but he doesn't quite get there. He's laughing.

"We'll do an avocado and honey face mask."

"You turning down my offer?"

I nod.

He cocks a brow.

"I'm not opposed to doing that kind of thing in public." My cheeks flush, but I press on. "But I don't want you coming on my face."

His pupils dilate.

"I want you coming on my tits or in my mouth. Or... well. I want you coming inside me. I'm on the pill. And I'm safe. If you're safe—"

"Fuck, don't tease about this."

"I'm not."

"You want to go bareback?"

Yes. Badly. But then I'm supposed to be waiting until I'm sure I'll survive losing him.

Only I'm never going to be sure of that.

And, really, there are no guarantees in life...

Maybe I'm letting go of caution. Maybe I'm thinking with my libido. I don't care.

I need to have Joel again.

I nod. "I do. Not right now. But… sometime."

"Now is good."

"What happened to drums?"

"I'd rather bang you."

I laugh. "That was terrible."

"Not *terrible.*"

"Terrible. Joel Young makes terrible jokes." I push him playfully. "That would sound better if I knew your middle name."

"Joel Oscar Young."

"Your initials spell joy?"

He nods. "My mom is a hippie."

Again, I laugh. "Joel is Joy… wow, that puts you in a whole new perspective."

He's still wearing that slack-jawed expression. "We're talking."

"We are."

"We could be fucking."

"Here?"

"Yeah."

I shake my head.

He nods to the couch. When I fold my arms and raise a brow, he nods to the bed. Then to the balcony. The kitchen counter. The expanse of wall.

"You want to go bareback that badly?"

"Never have."

"Never?"

"Never been in a monogamous relationship."

Monogamous relationship.

How can such a matter of fact description set me on fire?

How can it make my heart flutter and my stomach churn?

I let my head fill with ideas about me and Joel. I wash up, dress, join Joel at the nearest grocery store, drive back to our place. The entire time, I'm in my head, imagining the possibility of this being forever.

We *are* married.

Maybe...

There's a reason for that.

Maybe it's enough of a reason for us to stay that way.

———

AFTER WE PUT OUR GROCERIES AWAY, WE GET SET UP IN Joel's practice room.

This apartment is cozy. It's not Manhattan cozy, but it's not exactly a big expanse of space. With the walls covered in beige soundproofing foam, the room is even smaller.

There's something nice about how DIY this room feels. It's not the fancy studio of a stuck-up millionaire musician. It's this thrown together *I need to play here and I need to play now* thing.

Joel motions to the stool behind his drum kit.

I sit.

He kneels behind me, his chest against my back, his cheek against my neck. His breath is warm on my ear.

It's incredibly difficult to concentrate. Somehow, I manage to listen as he shows me how to hold the drumsticks with a loose grip. How to tap the drum or the cymbal. How to smack the leather hard enough to make a lot of noise but not so hard it snaps.

"It would be very fucking rock and roll of you to burst a drum, but I don't want to be without my kit if I can help it." His hands curl around my wrists. It's a tight grip.

He's looking too close.

He's going to feel those scars.

He's going to know.

He can't know.

I look back to him. His expression is the same. He's an eager teacher. He's either not noticing the scar tissue on my wrists or he doesn't care.

"Angel, I know it's *hard* to think about anything but fucking me when I'm this close—"

Okay. I have to shake this off and joke back.

Only that isn't what I want with Joel. I want to tell him. I want to tell him everything.

His voice softens. "Hey. You okay?"

I want to tell him everything. I do. But not right now.

I make my voice light. "Are you trying to talk me out of thinking about you naked?"

He laughs. "I know you have an active imagination with all the reading you do, but if you want me naked, you only have to ask."

"That's not good teaching. You should make it a reward."

"Are you trying to talk me out of getting naked?"

"No. But…" I press my back into his chest. He's warm. And I can feel his chest rising and falling with each inhale and exhale. "I guess I want to channel my inner rock star."

"Yeah?"

"Yeah." That is true. I want to learn this. If only to prove I can. "I want to try things even when I'll be terrible at them."

"You're sure you'll be terrible?"

"When the odds are good I'll be terrible." Right now, I don't try things if the odds are good I'll be terrible. Or even just okay. But I want to get there. I want to stop closing myself off to every experience that might end in pain or failure. I look to Joel and nod. "Let's go."

IT TAKES NEARLY THREE HOURS FOR JOEL TO TEACH ME THE Billy Idol song *White Wedding*. I'm pretty sure the choice has everything to do with Joel's love of 80s music and nothing to do with our quickie nuptials. Hell, I even manage to put the *what the hell is happening with our marriage* question out of mind while we practice.

Drumming is hard. I'm terrible at keeping a beat. I miss a ton of notes. Every time I take a misstep, that little voice in my head screams *give this up and do something you know you're good at*. But I fight it.

I fight it enough to learn the song… well, I know it okay.

Joel is beaming with pride. "Play it one more time."

"I'm tired." I try to keep my voice even, but it's distinctly whiny. "And hot." I toss my cardigan on the floor.

Joel's gaze goes straight to my chest. "You're more than welcome to do this shirtless."

"That sounds like a reward for you."

"Only while you play. After…" He barely manages to bring his eyes back to mine. "We'll both like what happens after."

"One more time," I say.

He nods.

"Okay." I tap the drumsticks together. I feel silly counting down, but when I manage to turn off the part of my brain that cares what everyone else thinks, I enjoy it. "Three, two, one."

I go.

I play the entire song. And I only mess up a dozen times.

When I'm done, Joel knees in front of me. He pulls me onto the floor with him.

His lips find mine. His kiss is full of affection. Tenderness. It's hungry too, but it's more *I adore you* than *I need to fuck you, immediately.*

God, he tastes good.

And the way he's been smiling at me all afternoon…

Feelings whirl around my stomach.

The possibility of failing at playing drums is nothing compared to the possibility of this ending just as I'm falling in love with him.

I'm not there yet.

But I'm pretty sure I'll get there if this keeps up.

God, he's a good kisser.

His hand slides under my dress. He presses his palm against me, over my panties. Desire pushes concerns from my mind.

It pushes thoughts from my mind, period.

I'm losing interest in everything except Joel's hands on my body.

His lips on my lips.

His cock inside me.

Yes.

We need to do this.

Now.

I'm about to tear his clothes off when there's a knock on the door.

Then the bell rings. It's three rings in a pattern. I can't quite place the pattern but it seems intentional.

Joel pushes himself up with a heavy sigh. "Fuck."

I stare up at him, but his expression doesn't offer me any clarity.

"That can't be…" He looks at me apologetically. "Give me a minute."

I nod and adjust my dress.

His footsteps move through the apartment. Then he's opening the door.

"Sweetheart, you look good," a voice says. It's older. Female. "It's really true."

"Yeah," he says.

"My son really is married."

Chapter Twenty-One

JOEL

Bella pulls her arms over her chest as she steps into the main room. It doesn't do much to hide her cleavage. Her tits are fighting that tight dress.

I have no complaints, but I can read the nervous look on her face. She doesn't want my mom thinking she's trashy.

She doesn't realize that my mom doesn't think anyone is trashy.

"I'm sorry to pop-in, but I couldn't reach Joel on his phone. And, well, I had to come when I heard the news." Mom nods hello. "You can call me Trish."

"Bella."

"Don't let me stop you two from whatever you were doing." Mom smiles.

Bella blushes. "No, that's fine. We were just, ahem—"

"Practicing," I say.

Mom nods. "Yes, I can tell you two were working hard."

"Excuse me." Bella motions to the bathroom. "I'll be a few minutes."

Mom offers her a friendly smile.

Mom offers everyone that friendly smile.

She waits until Bella is in the bathroom to look to me. "She's pretty."

"Yeah."

"Smart?" Mom asks.

I nod.

"She seems polite too."

"She's nervous. Almost like she didn't know she was going to meet my mom for some reason."

"I called a few hours ago."

I'm sure that's true. For the last few hours, I've been thinking of nothing but teaching Bella to play. Okay, maybe I thought about making her come here and there. But I was mostly in music mode.

Mom's voice is teasing. "How did someone like you end up with someone so polite."

"I'm very fucking polite." I slide my hand into my pocket. "I'm a fucking gentleman."

Mom's eyes light up as she laughs. "Do gentlemen marry women who haven't met their mothers?"

"Apparently."

She makes that mhmmm noise. Her posture is still confident, in control. She's wearing her usual loose sweater, jeans, comfort shoes outfit.

She looks the same as always.

Except that she isn't wearing her wedding ring.

I try not to stare at her unadorned left hand, but I can't help it.

"You haven't told me how you two met," Mom says.

"I haven't?" I make my shrug effortless. "You'd think I'd mention that."

"I would." She stares through me. It's not penetrating the way Mal or Kit's stare is. There's something soft about it. Understanding. "You were home for a week and you didn't say a word about a girlfriend."

I clear my throat.

"Joel, I understand that you aren't happy your father and I have divorced. I'm not mad that you wanted to skip our party." Her voice softens. "You can be upset. That's okay. You're allowed to grieve however you want."

I want to not talk about this.

"Your model of love, of marriage, was broken. It's normal for that to hurt."

"Daphne tell you to say that?"

"No. Sweetie, my parents divorced when I was young. And back then… it wasn't nearly as common. I know how much it hurts. But it wasn't your fault. It was us making that decision."

I appreciate that Mom wants to help, but I don't want to discuss this shit. She sees the divorce as sunshine and roses. I see it as darkness and lilies on tombstones.

There's no middle ground here. There's no way we're going to agree.

I need to make a joke. I need to laugh it off. I need to convince her I'm fine with this.

At the very least, I need to change the subject.

But when I rack my brain for something, anything, to say, I come up empty.

I can't laugh this off.

But I can keep my hands occupied. "You want coffee?"

Mom nods. "Sure."

I fill two mugs with what's left in the carafe and hand one to Mom. Both of us drink it black.

My gaze goes to Bella as she slinks out of the bathroom and into the bedroom.

"Kit seems to like her," Mom says.

Good for him. Fucking traitor. Not that I can talk. I would have done exactly the same thing in his shoes.

"Don't blame him sweetheart. He was worried about you."

"Was he?"

"Hearing your parents are getting a divorce then running off to Vegas to get married." Mom takes a long sip then sets her mug on the counter. "It's not hard to draw a line between the two things."

"I like her."

"Do you love her?"

Why is everyone asking me that? I offer Mom my best smile. From the look in her eyes, I'm not sure she's buying it. But it's all I've got. "Being with her feels right."

Mom makes that mhmmm sound again.

"She's a fucking amazing woman. Don't give her shit."

That gets Mom smiling. "I may not be a 'fucking gentleman,' but I am always polite."

I have to laugh.

Right on cue, Bella steps out of the bedroom in that same cute dress, a different adorable cardigan covering her shoulders. Her hair is in a loose bun. Her lips are pink.

Damn, my fingers are itching to pull those glasses off her face. My lips are itching for hers.

This conversation is torture. I need to be someplace where the world makes sense.

And Bella in my bed—that makes a lot of fucking sense.

Mom slides off her stool. She goes to shake Bella's hand. "It's very nice to meet you officially."

"You too," Bella says.

"Forgive me if I seem surprised. It's nothing personal. You're a lovely woman and you seem smart," Mom says.

Bella taps her glasses. "I get that a lot."

Mom laughs. "They are lovely frames. They suit you."

Bella smiles. "Thanks."

Mom's voice lifts to a playful tone. "Joel has never even mentioned a girlfriend before."

Bella blushes. "It happened pretty fast."

"There's nothing wrong with a whirlwind romance." Mom laughs. "I understand the rush. Joel is one of a kind. You don't want to let someone like him slip through your fingers."

"True." Bella moves into the kitchen and takes the seat next to mine. "Tea?"

I motion to the kettle. "The water is warm."

"He's always been such a special young man. And always so good with women. Even when he was in marching band," Mom says.

Bella laughs. "Joel was in marching band?"

Mom nods. "He was a Drum Major." Mom winks at me. "They're basically team captains."

"A chance to boss everyone around." Bella fixes a cup of English Breakfast. "That sounds like Joel."

"You should have seen him running theater crew," Mom says.

"Theater crew?" Bella shoots me a *really* look.

I nod. Really.

"Yes. Oh, he was the president of the A.V. club." Mom sips her coffee. "Has he told you about the time he accidentally broadcast a, um… a private session with a friend instead of the school's weekly news."

Bella presses her back against the counter. She stares into my eyes. "A private session with a friend?"

I have to laugh. "Especially private."

"So, even as the A.V. club geek, you still cleaned up?" Bella teases.

I wave my hand over my face. "Some people know what matters in life."

Bella laughs. "You have your priorities in order."

She stares into my eyes like she's lost in them. There's something going through her head, but I don't have a clue what it is.

"Have you seen the pictures of Joel in his band uniform?" Mom pulls out her cell. "He really was adorable."

Bella takes in the photos on the screen. "He was. And those braces. They suit you, baby." She winks at me.

"You like the pictures?" Mom asks.

Bella nods.

"Good." Mom smiles. "I have plenty more where those came from."

It's a quiet weekday afternoon at that time between lunch and dinner. This place is dead. There's only one other group here, and from the way they're dressed like they're going to church after this, I'm pretty sure they have no idea who I am.

Mom delights in embarrassing me all through whatever this meal is called. She's on wine glass two. Bella's still abstaining. And I'm three beers in, which is two more than I should have given how much I need to pay attention. This is one of the rare times when I need inhibitions.

I can't tell Mom what I think about the divorce.

Not in front of Bella.

I don't mind Mom sharing stories and pictures from my childhood. It's part of the whole meeting the parents thing. Not that I've ever experienced it firsthand.

I'm glad to see Bella smiling.

I'm glad to see Mom laughing. Even if I don't get how she can be this happy days after announcing her divorce.

Mom and Bella finish laughing over a picture of my first drum performance.

Under the table, Bella squeezes my hand. "It's all over little Joel's face. He wants to drum more than he wants anything else in the world."

"He's always been passionate." Mom looks from Bella to me then back to Bella. "You have to forgive me for talking your ear off. I could go on about Joel and Daphne all day. But I do want to hear more about you too, sweetheart. Joel tells me you're from New York."

"Yes, my parents... just my dad now. We live in Manhattan. I have my own place by school. Columbia. It's tiny, but it's mine. I could live at home with Dad. He works so many hours that I would have the place to myself."

Mom makes that mhmm noise. "Yes, I know the type. Joel's father is the same way. Forgive me for asking sweetheart, but it's just your father now?"

She nods. "My mother died when I was twelve. She had a heart attack." Bella presses her lips together. "Dad stepped up to take care of us, but it wasn't the same."

Mom nods.

"Anne, my older sister, she did a lot too. She taught me about clothes and makeup. And boys. She's good at all those practical, life things. I'm much more academic. I can ace a test but I can barely boil water." Bella looks to me. "She would like Joel. Actually, she *does* like Joel. She's a big Dangerous Noise fan."

"And you?" Mom asks.

"They're pretty good. But I'm more into pop," Bella says.

Mom laughs. "I don't know, the music today, it all

sounds like pop. I'm showing my age now, but it's not the same as when I was younger."

Bella laughs. "I know what you mean."

"Be honest, sweetheart, do I sound old when I say that?" Mom asks.

Bella presses her lips together. "A little."

Mom looks to me.

I nod. "A little."

"My son—you can appreciate his honesty. But then, he also thinks I don't realize that he lies to spare my feelings. I sound ancient complaining about the kids' music." Mom smiles at me then looks to Bella. "I was worried when he dropped out of school to play music. It's a hard road. He's done well."

Bella smiles. "He's a machine. And the way he knows exactly what he wants… it's admirable." She gets a dreamy look in her eyes. "Mom would have liked Joel. She would have been taken aback by all the tattoos, but he's so charming—"

"He is," Mom says. "I'm not sure where he gets it."

Bella laughs. "You two have the same green eyes."

"Thank you." Mom smiles. "What do you do in New York, sweetheart?"

"Oh." Bella chews on her lower lip. "I'm a student at Columbia Law School."

"A lawyer." Mom looks to me and raises her eyebrows *nicely done*. "Do you know what kind of law you'd like to practice?"

"Well…" Bella stares at her roasted potatoes. "I… Um…"

Her expression is the picture of misery.

Mom's voice gets softer. "What was that, sweetheart?"

"Well… I…" Bella pinches her pointer finger. Then the

middle. The ring. Pinkie. Then she's doing the same to her other hand. "That's... it could be a long way off. Maybe."

I shouldn't step in here.

I know that.

But I have to do something about the pained expression on her face.

"Bella's thinking about leaving law school," I say.

"Joel." Bella's eyes meet mine. She glares *what the hell?*

"You don't want to go back," I say.

"Maybe." She stabs a potato.

"Not maybe. You hate law school," I say.

"No. I just..." Bella stares at the silverware like it has the answers to every question in the history of the world. "Let's talk about this later."

"So you can make another excuse?" I ask.

"Not right now." Bella's voice breaks. Her eyes stay on the table.

"Are you going to run away from this forever?" I ask.

She looks to me. "Does what I do forever really matter to you?"

Mom's brow furrows as she attempts to work that out. I'm not about to explain. Or concede Bella's point.

Mom clears her throat. "You're young. You have time."

Bella stares at me. *Let it go.*

I stare back. *No fucking way.*

Bella sets her silverware down. She pulls her napkin from her lap and tosses it on the table. "Excuse me. I'm going to... actually, I don't feel well. I think I'm going home."

"Bella—"

Mom clears her throat. "Great idea, sweetie. We'll get some coffee and see you later."

"Yes. Good. I'll, um. It's been really nice talking to

you." She offers Mom a pained smile. Her eyes catch mine. They scream *how could you.*

But she says nothing.

She walks away, calmly, like nothing has ever bothered her.

Mom leans in to whisper. "Sweetheart, what was that?"

"You saw her expression when she brought up law school." My eyes stay on my plate. "I'm not going to stand back and let her ruin her life."

"It's her life to ruin."

"She's my wife."

Mom's expression gets serious. "You and Daphne are everything to me. But you've only been married a few days. You don't get to claim she's your wife like it's been thirty years."

"And you know what about marriage?"

She doesn't shrink back. "I gave your father everything I had. He didn't give back."

I bite my tongue.

"You know that's true, Joel. He's not a bad man. I still love him. I always will. But he isn't the kind of partner I want anymore. I want my own life." She looks to the bathroom. "And your wife, she wants her own life too. Not one curated by Joel Young."

"I'm not—"

"You are."

Maybe. But— "She needs a push."

"From you?"

"From somebody."

"Have you tried looking at things from her perspective?"

"I'm not going to let her throw her happiness away."

"Have you?"

Not exactly.

But Mom already knows that. It's written all over her face.

Fine. I take a deep breath and I try to put myself in Bella's shoes.

I just married a hot stranger and found out he's famous. I'm worried my dad is about to disown me for that.

Then I have my law school grades to worry about.

The law school grades part isn't clicking. But if it was an album that bombed…

If the band was breaking up, or I was giving up on music, and I had to face everyone I know and tell them I'd failed at my life's work.

Even if I fucking hated music, I'd be terrified. What the hell else would I do?

How would I deal with the constant pity?

Mom's voice is soft. "I wanted our marriage to work. Your father wanted it to work. But it was always his way or the highway. And I couldn't live like that anymore." She pats my hand. "Deep down, you know that. Deep down, you know that we weren't happy."

Maybe.

"I can tell you two are new, but you seem good together." She looks me in the eyes. "If you want to help her, listen to her."

"Yeah."

"We can meet for breakfast tomorrow." Mom motions to the lobby. "Go, fix things with your wife."

Chapter Twenty-Two

JOEL

I practically run to the apartment. It's only half a mile, but it feels like an eternity. By the time I arrive, my heart is thudding. My breath is in my throat. My sweat-soaked t-shirt is sticking to my chest.

Bella is sitting in front of the door, cross-legged, her eyes on her phone.

"It's the same." She motions to the cell screen. "I still have Cs." She blinks and a tear rolls down her cheek. "I'm still a failure."

I take a seat next to her. "Don't say shit like that."

She pulls her arms over her chest. "Avoiding the words doesn't change the facts."

"Cs are passing grades."

"Technically. But they aren't good enough. I'm not cut out for law school and nothing is going to change that." She wipes a tear with the back of her hand. "I've failed at what's supposed to be my life's work. My future." She takes an unsteady breath. Her eyes go to her hands, then to the inside of her wrists. "What the hell do I do now?"

I resist my urge to argue. I don't know shit about law school, but it's plausible that Cs really are a failure.

I have to trust Bella here.

I have to take her at her word.

I lean in to whisper. "Do you want to go back to school?"

"You're actually asking?"

"Yeah."

She looks up at me with those pretty brown eyes. "You don't want to lecture me about how I'll be miserable?"

"I got the point across."

Her eyes go to the floor. "Did your mom give you shit?"

"Yeah."

"Good." She presses her lips together. "She seems nice, your mom."

"She's the nicest person anyone's ever met." I move closer. "And I don't mean that as an insult the way people normally do."

"I know." She looks up at me for a second. "I'm nice. People say that about me. They mean passive and boring."

"Or maybe they're struggling for something to say to your face because they're talking about your tits behind your back."

She lets out a sound that's half laugh, half sob. "That must be it." With her next breath, her eyes go back to the floor. She blinks back another tear. "Right now, you're the only person who knows."

"Do you want to change that?"

"I have to tell my dad soon. And other people, they'll ask why I left law school. I'm not sure which is worse, the truth or a lie that I dropped out to follow my husband around on tour."

"You mean, you don't want to be my pet?"

She shakes her head. "You... you wouldn't want that, would you?"

"No. But I wouldn't mind it. If you wanted that, if you never wanted to work again, I'd take care of you."

"You mean if we... if we stay married."

"Hypothetically, yeah."

She looks up at me. "It's hard caring about someone. They can really hurt you." Her brown eyes fill with frustration. "Joel, that stuff you said... how could you ambush me like that?"

"I shouldn't have said that shit in front of my mom." I slide my arm around her shoulders. "I shouldn't have said that shit, period."

She nods.

"I'm sorry. I get out of my head when I see you doing shit that will make you miserable."

"How did you know it would make me miserable?"

"You get this expression when you bring it up. It's like... what are those things called, in *Harry Potter*, that eat your happiness?"

"Dementors."

"Like that."

"Law school is like a soul-sucking dementor?"

I nod.

She looks at me like I'm crazy. But also like I'm right.

Deep down, she knows she doesn't want to go back to law school.

She must.

Damn, all I want to do is wipe her pain away. I'm not good at this relationship thing. But I want to try. For her.

I lean down and offer her my hand. "This will be more comfortable inside."

"I'm not sure I'm ready to go inside yet."

That's fair. I take her hands and pull her to her feet. "I

do know you, Bella. Maybe not every inch of you, not yet, but I want to."

She keeps her gaze on the floor. Her voice is still filled with uncertainty. "You don't mean..." Her eyes go to her ring. "We're getting a divorce in less than a week."

"We could change our minds."

She stares at me like I'm crazy.

"Hypothetically."

"We barely know each other."

"We did it out of order, got married then got to know each other. So what?"

She stares into my eyes. "You really want to stay married?"

I run my fingers through her hair. "We have a few more days to get to one hundred percent certain."

She laughs and rests her head against my chest. "I like you, Joel. But there's a lot of room between *I like you* and *we should stay married*." She bites her lip. "I don't know what I'll want later. But right now..." She looks up at me. Then her eyes flutter closed and her lips press into mine. She kisses me hard and deep.

I kiss her back.

Fuck, we need to be inside.

And I need to be inside her.

When our kiss breaks, I unlock the door and whisk her into the apartment.

I pin her to the door.

She looks up at me with all that trust.

All that affection.

I pull her glasses off her face and set them on the bookshelf.

Her hands go to my hair. She brings my mouth to hers. She's soft and she tastes good and there's all this affection flowing between us.

She sighs as our kiss breaks. "We fight a lot."

"Because we call each other on our bullshit."

She nods.

"No one else does that to me."

"Me either." Her fingers dig into my skin. "I think… even though it's only been a few days… I think you know me better than anyone does."

"Yeah?"

"I don't let my guard down with anyone." She slides her hand under my t-shirt and presses her palm against my stomach. "You either?"

I nod.

"Joel, I know you can't promise how you'll feel tomorrow. Or the next day. Or the day we're supposed to divorce." Her eyes bore into mine. "But, your mom… she had a tan line on her left ring finger."

"You noticed that?"

"I notice everything." She stares back at me expectantly.

Fuck. I should tell her about this. Even if she'll get the wrong idea. "My parents just got divorced."

"When did you find out?"

"That morning."

"Oh." She presses her back against the door. "I thought the timing would be, but that's fast—"

I undo her bun and run my fingers through her hair. "It's not like that."

"At all?"

"Maybe somewhere in my subconscious I'm proving a point about marriage being forever, but that's not what's in my head. Bella, I really fucking like you." I cup the back of her head. There's too much space between us right now. I need to erase it. "What do you want, right now?"

"I want to believe you."

"Then?"

"I don't know." She runs her fingers through my hair. "In the last week, my life has gone completely off track." She stares back into my eyes. "I want to feel the way you do when you play drums. I want to know I'm where I belong in the world."

I nod.

Her eyelids flutter closed.

She rises onto her tiptoes.

And she kisses me like the fucking ship is going down.

It's fast.

Messy.

Perfect.

She pulls my t-shirt over my head.

Her hands rake over my bare torso. She looks up into my eyes. "Make me believe you. Please."

I nod and I kiss her back.

She presses her palm against my hard-on, over my jeans. "Nothing in the way of us connecting."

Fuck. That last bit of blood flees my brain.

I let go of conscious thought.

I do away with my jeans and boxers.

She steps out of her panties and pulls her dress to her waist.

Fuck, we're going bareback. There's nothing in the way of our flesh connecting.

I drag my hand up her thighs and stroke her clit until she's groaning against my mouth.

She's wet. Even so, I slip a finger inside her to warm her up. Then two. Three.

She bucks her hips against my hand.

Her nails dig into my skin.

She blinks her eyes open and pulls back from our kiss. "Joel, please. I need you inside me."

My breath gets heavy. "Say that again."

"I need you." She tugs at my hair. "I need you inside me."

I bring my hands to her hips.

Slowly, I bring her body towards mine.

My tip strains against her.

Fuck.

One inch at a time, I slide inside her.

Damn, she feels good.

And there's nothing in the way.

That's my flesh against hers.

The trust of this—

The intimacy—

Feelings fill my gut. Too many. I'm not good at this kind of thing.

I really fucking care about her.

I want the fucking world for her.

I can't stand the thought of this ending.

She groans into my mouth as I pump her with long, deep strokes. Her hands tug at my hair.

My fingers dig into her skin.

We stay locked together, groans bleeding together, tongues dancing together.

Her legs are wrapped around my waist.

My arms are wrapped around her chest.

Our bodies are moving together.

Then she's moving faster, nipping at my lips as she groans harder and deeper.

I pull back enough to watch pleasure spread over her face. Her eyelids press together. Her teeth sink into her lip.

Her nails rake across my back.

"Fuck, Joel." She groans it again and again. Then she's blinking her eyes open, staring at me like she's staring into my soul.

It's not like when Kit or Mal looks at me like this.

With her, I really fucking like it.

I want her seeing every inch of me.

The ugly shit too.

Her hand goes to the back of my head. She pulls me into another slow, deep kiss.

Fuck, the way she's rocking her hips, groaning into my mouth like she needs my pleasure—

A few more thrusts and I'm there. I groan into her mouth.

I dig my fingers into her skin.

I pin her to that fucking wall as I fill her.

Once I've spilled every drop, I set her down.

She looks up at me, her brown eyes filled with affection. Then her hands are in my hair and she's pulling me into another deep kiss.

And it's like when I play.

I *know* this is where I belong.

Chapter Twenty-Three

BELLA

It's night now. The light streaming through the windows is a dark blue, marked only by glittering silver stars.

With the quiet murmur of the waves pounding the sand, Joel's bedroom feels like *our* beach view, our safe haven, our universe.

Joel slides his arms around my waist and pulls me closer.

I nestle into his body. He's warm and hard and the skin on skin contact is filling me with a pleasant buzz.

He's offering forever.

The potential of forever.

If I don't do something to throw up guardrails, I'm going to fall for him.

I'm not there yet. But I'm close.

If he doesn't catch me…

I don't know what I'll do if he doesn't catch me.

His lips brush against my neck. My body fills with that same buzz. It's a beautiful mix of need, desire, affection, trust.

My eyelids flutter closed.

For a moment, I let my thoughts float away. I let everything but the sensations in my body float away.

His lips are soft against my neck.

His chest is hard against my back.

His strong arms are around me. And I feel so fucking safe.

One hand is on my forearm. He drags his fingertips over my skin, that absent minded lovers' gesture.

His touch gets closer.

Closer.

Almost…

My teeth sink into my lip. My stomach tenses. I haven't told him this. Aside from my college therapist, I haven't told anyone this.

Ever.

He murmurs something incomprehensible against my neck.

"You falling asleep?" I whisper.

"I could. But no." He strokes me with that same gentle touch. "You're getting tense again."

I can tell him now.

But what if that changes his opinion of me?

What if I transform from *the woman I might want to spend my life with* to *the damaged freak I need out of my bed, ASAP*?

I try to make my voice light. "Is that a surprise?"

He murmurs a no. "It does mean I'll have to make you come again."

I close my eyes and try to push my thoughts away. He's touched me plenty. Even my wrists. He hasn't noticed yet.

Maybe he won't.

Maybe this can stay a secret forever.

"Hey." He runs his fingers through my hair. Over my ear. "You're going off some place."

I nod.

"Take me with you."

"I... I don't know if I can."

"Yeah?"

"Yeah." I take a deep breath and exhale slowly. Still, my chest is tense. My stomach is twisting. "I don't want you to think differently of me."

"You kill someone?"

"Nothing like that."

"You secretly love Justin Beiber?"

My laugh breaks up the tension in my chest. "No."

"I'd forgive you for bad taste."

"I appreciate that."

He nods. Again, he runs his fingers through my hair. The joking tone drops from his voice. "This is a big deal?"

I nod. "I wasn't exaggerating to get in your pants earlier. I think you do know me better than anyone." I press my lips together. "But the way you look at me... it's like you really think I'm this good girl who could never do bad. You really think I am an angel."

His touch is soft. Sweet.

I want to tell him.

I want him to know and not think of me differently.

But there's no way to guarantee that.

My breath catches in my throat.

This is a risk.

I've spent my life avoiding risks.

This time, I'm not running away from potential hurt.

Here goes nothing.

"Joel, I..." I take his hand and bring it to the inside of my wrist. "I used to cut... though... I guess 'used to' is a little strong."

"You still do?"

"A few times over the semester."

He runs his fingertips over my skin in a back and forth pattern. Then his finger catches a scar. He traces its line.

"Only when it was really bad. The pressure from the tests… I didn't know how else to handle it."

He keeps tracing scars.

He doesn't say anything.

Fuck.

What does that mean?

My eyelids flutter closed. My body goes numb. I can't feel anything but the crushing weight of expectations. This is changing how he looks at me.

"Bella." His voice is still soft. Still sweet. "When was the last time?"

"Finals."

"Where?"

"Here." I take his hand and bring it to my upper arm. That's an easy spot to hide. I've gotten smarter as I've gotten older.

"That was what, two weeks ago?"

"About that."

"Bella… Fuck." He turns me around. His hand goes to my chin. He tilts my head so we're eye to eye. "Thank you."

"Thank you?" A tear stings my eye. I can't make sense of any of the feelings whirling around my stomach. Why is he thanking me?

Why isn't he reacting… why…

"For telling me. I know that shit is hard." His hand curls around my wrist. Gently he brings my arm to his mouth and places a soft kiss on the inside of my wrist.

My chest is still heavy. But this… this seems good.

Is this really okay?

Is he really accepting this?

I barely manage to exhale. "You're... you're not horrified?"

"No."

"Nothing?"

"If you're still doing this, then I'm not gonna fucking rest until you're getting help."

"But... you don't think there's something wrong with me?"

"Of course there is. Angel, you hurt yourself because you bottle up everything you feel instead of asking for help. But that doesn't make you a bad person."

"You do that too."

"I know." He takes my other arm, brings it to his mouth, plants kisses on my wrist. "I can't talk shit about coping mechanisms. I've drank, fucked, or laughed my way out of everything that bothered me for a long time." He sets my arm down. His eyes find mine. "I get it."

I blink back a tear. "You do?"

He rests his palm on my cheek and brushes a tear with his thumb. "Not exactly, but enough."

"Joel, I..." Fuck. There's another tear. Another. I can't stop them. He's not running away. He's not calling me a freak.

He's accepting this broken, ugly part of me.

The tension in my body is releasing.

The relief is overwhelming.

This time, I don't blink back my tears. I let them fall. I've hidden this for so long. And now he knows... and he's not running away.

He presses his palm between my shoulder blades. "You don't have to justify it. But you can explain." His eyes find mine. "I want to know every part of you, Bella."

"Even the ugly parts?"

"Especially the ugly parts." He leans down to press his lips to mine.

Relief pours out of me. He's here. He's not running.

He's kissing me.

Holding me.

Is this really possible?

When our kiss breaks, I'm shaking.

I look into his gorgeous green eyes. They're filled with understanding.

This time, my exhale isn't quite so heavy. "It started after my mom died. My family, we're not feelings people. I didn't know how to process it. I was mixed up all the time. One day, I bombed some test and I felt like shit. And I didn't know how to deal with that. I don't even remember how I thought of it. Maybe it was a friend or a TV show. The first time I tried, I was so scared I passed out before the razor hit my skin."

He pulls me closer.

"I tried again. That time, it worked. And that pain was concrete. Real. I felt like I deserved it. I felt better, punishing myself. It became a habit. A way to hurt physically instead of mentally. A way to punish myself for failing." My voice drops to a whisper. "The only person I've ever told was my college therapist."

"Yeah?"

I nod. "Stan, my ex… he saw the scars once. He looked at me with this horrified expression. I could tell he knew. And he could tell I knew that he knew. But neither one of us said anything. We never mentioned it. It wasn't that he was a bad person. Just not really… he thought I was this girl who had it all together. I was stepping into that role with him. I never let him see the cracks."

"I get that."

I press my forehead to his. "Tell me you're not getting ready to run away."

"It's going to take a lot more than this to get me to run off."

"You promise?"

He nods. "Cross my heart and hope to die."

Chapter Twenty-Four

BELLA

The next day, we get up early to meet Joel's mom for breakfast.

She's all smiles and stories about Joel. She doesn't mention our fight, or that I ran off, or that we're clearly moving faster than we should here.

She carefully avoids the subject of work as she asks about my life and my interests. I tell her everything I can about my dad, the strong but gruff lawyer who lets us know he loves us in a stoic, I'll take care of you but don't expect any hugs kind of way.

I tell her about my sister Anne, the party girl turned life of the party wife, who loves shopping and clothes *and* Medieval European history. Anne is as smart as I am, smarter even, but she's never had an interest in academics.

I tell her about my tiny apartment by Columbia, about how I've painted the walls a pastel pink, and adorned them with rose decals. I tell her about how I've always loved roses, especially the thorns. How my mother used to garden. I took over her garden when she died, but I was helpless.

I tell her about my undying love of reading. Not just *Harry Potter* and assorted YA books, but anything and everything I can get my hands on. I read plenty of contemporary stories, but fantasy is what really grabs me. There's something about escaping into another world. It takes me away from my life. It convinces me anything is possible.

Thankfully, Trish reads as much as I do. It was her main hobby while she was a stay at home mom—which was pretty much until Joel went to college. She doesn't say it aloud, but it's clear that the trouble in her marriage started when she went back to work.

When she realized she wanted her own life.

Mostly, we talk about books. And about Joel. All through coffee, shopping, lunch, more coffee, we talk about books and we talk about Joel. I don't feel like a failed law student around Trish. I don't even feel like I'm only here because I'm Joel's wife.

I feel like a human being who loves tea, reading, and long cardio sessions.

Maybe I don't know what the hell I want out of life right now, but I'm starting to figure out what I don't want.

We spend the entire day with her. By the time we get home, Joel and I are exhausted. He's still shaking his head over all the ways his mom mocked him.

"I can't believe how much you enjoyed this picture of me as a child," he says.

"You looked cute with braces."

"I'm going to get you back when I meet your dad."

I laugh even though the thought of Dad meeting Joel is terrifying. "Dad doesn't share pictures. He's not sentimental."

"No?"

"No." I collapse on the couch and grab the remote.

"He'll probably have one of his investigator's get background on you then grill you about every horrible thing you've ever done."

"Law firms really have investigators?"

"Yeah, and his investigator is even tougher than Calinda," I reference the tough as nails investor on *The Good Wife*. "Not as pretty though. He's more the type who could beat you up."

"You saying I couldn't take him?"

I laugh. "Shouldn't you protect your hands."

"Drumming is more in the wrists. You should know that."

I nod.

"I'll take it you're concerned about my hands for your sake."

I admit nothing.

Relaxation spreads through my chest as I sink into the couch. I'm ready to have a quiet night with Joel. This is the perfect Christmas Eve, the two of us on the couch.

Maybe we'll make some cookies too.

The kind we can decorate with frosting and sprinkles.

But Joel's phone is ringing.

It goes to voicemail.

It rings again.

"I don't mind if you get that," I say.

He nods. There's something in his eyes, some apprehension.

Still, he pulls his cell from his pocket and glances at the screen.

His voice is bright as he answers the phone. "You shouldn't booty call me anymore, Strong. You know I'm married now." He laughs into the phone. "You do realize it's Christmas Eve?"

Joel looks to me and motions *come here.*

I do.

He slides his arm around my waist and brings his mouth to my ear. "Mal's organized an emergency recording session."

"Has he?"

Joel nods. "You want to come?"

I like watching them work. There's something about seeing people who know they're exactly where they belong. It's thrilling.

He turns to the phone. "You're lucky my wife gets off on watching me play." He ends the call and tosses his cell aside. His eyes meet mine. "We have an hour till we have to leave."

"Do we?"

He nods to the bedroom.

Well, I'm only human.

An hour later, I follow Joel into the non-descript building downtown. It's dark and the streets are dead. Nobody is at work today. Nobody but perfectionists like the guys in Dangerous Noise.

There's no one at the front desk of the lobby, but that doesn't stop him.

He leads me through the door on the right, down the hall, to the suite.

It's like something out of a TV show. Mal and Ethan are already here, in the other room. That must be the sound booth. It's encased in glass and the other three walls are some padded beige material.

Ethan is strumming his guitar. He has no idea we're here.

Neither does Mal. Both of them are lost in the song.

There's a guy here with his hands on the controls. He nods hello to us, but he keeps his attention on his task.

I wait until Mal is finished with the song to whisper in Joel's ear. "Does this really need to happen today?"

"Fuck no." He pulls me closer. "But you know artists."

"I don't, actually."

"They're temperamental."

"You included?"

He shrugs, feigning innocence.

"Bullshit."

"Maybe," he says.

The door opens behind us, and a deep voice flows into the room. "Joel, bullshitting, that's hard to believe."

That's Kit. His dark eyes really are intense.

He offers me his hand. "Nice to see you again, Bella."

"You too. Thanks." My shoulders relax. He isn't looking at me like I hail from outer space.

Kit motions to Joel. "Did this really need to happen today?"

"Wasn't my idea," Joel says.

"You've never had trouble getting your way before," Kit says.

"I've been preoccupied," Joel motions to me.

"You buy that Joel ever gives up on what he wants?" Kit teases.

I shake my head. I don't buy that.

"She's smart. I like her." Kit greets the operator, then he's pressing the button to communicate with the soundproof room. "You have one hour, starting now."

Joel looks to me and raises his brows. *You think we can do it?*

I'm not sure. I better tease him. "Anything is possible."

He smiles. "I like you brutal, angel." He winks as he makes his way into the sound booth.

I sit next to the sound operator and I watch the guys attempt to record the song.

The sound guy is friendly and he likes having someone who wants to listen to him for once. He explains every step of the process to me. Each of the guys needs to record his track separately. In theory, if they get the first take perfect, the recording can take half an hour.

In reality, an hour is not anywhere near enough time.

They make a valiant effort, but they spend half their time debating changing this note or that riff or this line of the chorus. No one is shy about making suggestions or shooting down ideas. It's real collaboration. Real team work.

At the end of the hour, Kit does leave, but the other three guys stay. And they go at it for another hour.

Another.

Ethan leaves.

Another hour.

We take a coffee break.

Another hour.

I'm exhausted just watching them, but Mal and Joel are ready to go all fucking night. Never mind that it's Christmas Eve. Hell, by now it might be Christmas.

As far as I can tell, the sound guy would rather be here than anywhere else.

He doesn't say anything about his personal life. I fill in the blanks. He could be a recent widower. Or perpetually single. Or someone with no interest in love or dating.

Or maybe he's freshly divorced and his heart is about to break and he has to fill every moment with work.

I lose my ability to take even breaths.

In a week, that may be me.
Not even a week.
Our settlement conference is three days away.
In three days, I might be a divorcée.
I might not get Joel anymore.

Chapter Twenty-Five

JOEL

I nearly tumble out of the booth. I think I'm seeing stars. My arms are aching. My head is aching. My entire body is stiff and strained. And I never fucking want to see Mal again.

Really, the only thing I want is Bella in my bed right away.

But she's not here.

I say my goodbyes to Mal and to our sound guy, and I look for her. She's not in the hall or in any of the other suites.

But she is in the lobby.

With Alessandra.

What the hell is our tour manager doing here?

Alessandra's gaze catches mine. She waves hello and motions for me to join their conversation.

Bella turns to me, holding up a coffee cup. "I was bribed."

"Is it working?" I ask.

Bella shakes her head. "Not yet. Maybe if this was loose leaf."

Alessandra laughs. "Your wife tells me the song is going well, yes?"

I nod.

"Good. The label is annoyed, but that isn't my problem. Hearing about it… that is a problem." She shoots me a knowing look. "I know it's Malcolm who's the diva, sweetheart, but he's pretty enough to pull it off."

"And I'm not?" I tease her back.

"You don't have the pipes." She winks at me. "Joel, will you hate me if I offer your wife a job?"

"Depends on the job," I say.

Bella's eyes flair with something I can't quite place.

"I could use someone like you. I've needed a good assistant for ages. And you have a knack for it. And I can trust you not to sleep with the talent, present company excluded," Alessandra says.

Bella shakes her head. "That's very generous, but—"

"Think about it." Alessandra leans in to hug Bella goodbye. Then she does the same to me. "Merry Christmas. I'll see you two at the New Year's show."

I wait until she's out the door to slide my arms around Bella.

"You must be tired after all that." She rests her head against my chest. "I was tired just watching you."

"Yeah?"

She nods. "You guys work well together."

"We spent half the time fighting."

"Because you're all passionate and headstrong."

"We do have to compromise."

"You got there, didn't you?"

More or less. I undo her bun and run my fingers through her hair.

She leans into my touch.

She purrs.

Usually, after we record, I go out and get wasted.

But right now, I don't want that kind of shit.

I want Bella.

I want to talk to her.

To hold her.

Yeah, I want to fuck her, but I want to just be with her more than I want to be inside her.

Her voice is a whisper. It's barely there, like she's already drifting off someplace. "I'm not very rock n' roll."

"That's what we need. Someone with her shit together. Someone who insists on wearing sunscreen and baseball caps hiking."

"That's common sense."

I laugh. "You don't know musicians."

"Maybe."

"You should give it a shot."

Her posture stiffens. She shrugs off my arms.

She takes a long step backwards. "I don't know. That's all, still…" She looks up at me. "It's late. I don't want to have this conversation when I'm tired and grumpy."

"You're grumpy?"

"A little." Her expression softens. "It's Christmas Eve. I don't want to get in another fight."

I don't want to fight either. But this isn't a conversation we can put off forever.

I'm about to object when she yawns. Her jaw drops. Her arms stretch over her head.

She blushes. "I am tired."

I can tell.

This time, I'll go easy on her.

I slide my arms around her waist and pull her body into mine. Again, she purrs, and I'm incredibly fucking tempted to stay here like this all night.

Her chest against mine.

Her heart beating with mine.

Fuck, holding her satisfies me in a way nothing else does. I should be high off recording our song, but she's grabbing all my attention.

I brush her hair behind her ear. "What do you normally do on Christmas Eve?"

She looks up at me, her expression coy. "That's a secret."

"Yeah?"

She nods. She tries to hold a straight face, but it only lasts a few seconds. She breaks. Laughs. Blushes.

Her fingers skim my chin.

She rests her head on my chest. "I stay up late to watch *The Nightmare Before Christmas*."

"Secret emo girl." I laugh.

She taps her frames. "I have the glasses for it." Her lips curl into a smile. "But I think emo is before my time."

"You calling me old, angel?"

She nods as she digs her fingers into my t-shirt. Her voice is low, this mix of exhaustion and desire. "What do you normally do on Christmas Eve?"

"Usually, I'm at home." I always thought my family had picture perfect Christmases, but looking back… I missed all the signs. I fed myself a lot of bullshit.

Things have been fucked for a while.

She traces the neckline of my t-shirt. "We haven't talked about your parents, about the divorce. Not really."

"We will. But not now."

She nods. "Maybe… well, watching that movie was *my* tradition. Maybe we should make our own tradition."

"You trust me?" It's late. This might be a bad move. But it feels right.

She nods.

"Good. I have just the idea."

The bouncer nods to me with recognition. He lets us into the club, and points us to the VIP area, without checking our IDs.

Bella's eyes go wide. "I don't belong here."

"You don't want to dance with me?"

"I mean—"

"If you want to dance, and you're here, you belong here."

She nods. "This is a strange Christmas Eve celebration."

"You don't like it?"

She looks around. "I don't know. I was ready to collapse at the studio. But with the music and the lights." She looks to me. "The only time I've ever had fun at a club was our wedding night."

"That's why I'm here."

Her eyes light up. "Yeah?"

I nod. "And I'm thinking about a repeat of what made that night especially fun."

Her pupils dilate. "Oh."

"You game?"

She nods. "Very."

I slide my arm around her waist and pull her closer. This is a nice club. It's not a busy night, but the room is still pounding with house music. If anything, the less than packed dance floor makes this more difficult.

But I don't mind.

"You want a gin and tonic?" I lead Bella towards the bar.

She presses her lips together. "Just one."

Just enough to lower her inhibitions so she's not nervous about fucking me in public. It's in her eyes, in the way she's pressing her palms into her quads and biting her lip.

She looks so fucking good in that dress, all prim and proper.

She does seem like she has everything together.

I'm the only person who gets to know how dirty she is.

I'm the only person who knows how deeply she hurts.

Fuck, the responsibility of that fills me with pride. But it *is* a responsibility.

She's letting me in.

I have to do the same to her.

I want to do the same to her.

But we still have that divorce date looming. It's only three days away now.

I lean against the bar, hail the bartender, and order drinks.

Bella holds onto my waist, resting her head on my shoulder.

The bartender drops off our drinks. I pay with a hundred and insist he keep the change.

A laugh breaks up the frustration in Bella's expression. "You're getting showy again."

"I can call a limo to take us home," I say.

"You can order bottle service in the VIP area." She takes a long sip of her drink. Her tongue slides over her lips, lapping every drop. "Is this the kind of place where you go to pick up women?"

"I pick up women everywhere."

She takes another long sip. "But the ones who know you're famous."

"Yeah." It's wrong downing my bourbon in one long

sip. I do it anyway. Fuck, that burns. I drop my glass on a nearby table. "Why? You want to have a threesome with another chick?"

"You're deflecting."

"You too."

"No. I think I'd kill any woman who tried to touch you." She downs the last bit of her gin and tonic and drops her glass next to mine. "You're really good at deflecting."

"You are too."

She wraps her arms around my waist. "I want to say something, but I don't think I'm brave enough yet."

I motion towards the bar.

Bella shakes her head. "I don't want that kind of courage."

I'm used to playing cool.

To walking away.

But I don't want to do that with her, not tonight, not right now.

My feelings for her are intense. It's fucking terrifying. And knowing that we might only have a few days…

Fuck, I'm not walking away from this. Even if that means I'll be devastated this time next week.

I lead her to the dance floor.

I press my hands against her hips to guide her. Bella has trouble finding the rhythm of a song, but when I'm leading, she catches it right away.

She presses her crotch against mine. Then she's looking up at me. "Joel, why did you ask me to marry you that night? Really? No bullshit."

"It's gonna sound stupid."

"Tell me anyway."

I look her in the eyes. "I've always operated on instinct. It felt right."

She stares back, not demanding an explanation, just listening.

I want to tell her everything. I need to do it now, because my cock is gonna take over soon. "That morning, when my parents told me they were splitting up, this light-bulb went off. Suddenly it was obvious that they'd never really been happy. My mom was looking at me like she'd break if I didn't play along and pretend I was happy about this. My dad was looking at me like I was the only person who could really understand why he wanted to go sow his oats after thirty-five years of marriage. They wanted me to be happy about the decision and, for the first time, I couldn't find a way to laugh it off. I couldn't find a way to deflect."

"You didn't want to put up with them bullshitting you?"

"Yeah, but it was more than that." I lean in close enough to whisper. "It wasn't a conscious decision. I went to Vegas to get out of my head. I thought I wanted to find a beautiful woman and fuck her until she was screaming my name. No, I did want that. But, deep down, I wanted a real connection more."

"But why me?" she asks.

"Why me?"

"You're deflecting."

"Answer anyway."

"You make me laugh."

"Is that all?" I tease.

"No… I like who I am around you. I don't like who I am around my dad. Or my friends at school. I didn't like who I was around Stan. I don't even like who I am when I'm alone. I don't even know who I am when I'm alone. I've been bending myself into the shape that best suits everyone else for so long…"

"I like who you are."

"Can you explain it to me?"

"You bite back. You're smart. Quick. You see through bullshit. You know what it's like to pretend like everything rolls off your back." I run my hand through her hair. "I like that you're wound up. I want to unwind you. I want to get you messy and dirty."

She digs her fingers into my back. Even through my t-shirt, I can feel the heat of her skin. The pressure of her touch.

I wish I had a better explanation. But I don't.

I brush her hair behind her ear and lean in close. My cheek brushes against hers. My free hand goes to her lower back.

I whisper. "There wasn't one reason. It just felt right."

She rubs her cheek against mine as she rises to her tiptoes to whisper in my ear. Her voice is shaky. Uncertain. "Does it still feel right?"

Yeah, but there's not enough blood in my brain for me to be sure which organ is making that decision.

I let my hands slide to her hips. Her ass. Fuck, she feels good. Soft. Warm. Mine.

She needs to be mine.

If not forever, then right now.

But then I'm losing my ability to think about anything but being inside her.

Now.

I pull her closer. She lets out a soft moan as my hard-on brushes her stomach. All these fucking clothes in the way.

I hold her body against mine. "I want to fuck you."

Her lips part with a sigh of pleasure. She sucks breath in through her teeth. "You're evading."

"Yeah."

"Joel..."

Her voice is shaky.

She wants to give in to her desire too.

She wants this as badly as I do.

"I *am* evading." I pull her dress up her thigh and run my fingertips over her soft skin. "I still want to fuck you."

She brushes her cheek against my neck. "Joel…"

"I'm too hard to think straight."

She groans.

"You're not going to convince me you want something else." I drag my fingers up her leg so I can press my palm against her. "You're so fucking wet."

She looks up at me. "At our appointment… No bullshit, no stupid demands, no lies. Okay?"

"Same goes for you."

"I know." Her eyes bore into mine. "You promise?"

I bring my hands to her ass to grind her crotch against mine. Fuck that feels good.

I can barely get my words out. I can barely remember I'm making a point about all my blood rushing to my cock. "You trust a promise from me right now?"

She places her hand over mine, pressing my palm into her panties. "You trust a promise from me right now?"

I laugh. "I promise."

"Me too."

I lean down to press my lips to hers. I don't want to talk anymore.

I'm not sure I *can* talk anymore.

She tastes so fucking good.

And she's aggressive. Needy.

Her tongue slides into my mouth.

Her moans vibrate down my neck.

Her fingers dig into my leather jacket.

Then she's sliding her hand under my t-shirt, pressing her palm against my stomach.

She's not holding anything back.

Neither one of us is.

I kiss her harder. I rub her over her panties until she's groaning loud enough to drown out the music.

Her fingers dig into my skin.

Right now, I need her desperate and panting.

I push her panties aside.

She breaks our kiss and sucks in a labored breath.

Her eyes fix on mine. She nods a *yes*.

I drag my lips over her cheek until my mouth is hovering over her ear. "I'm going to take you right to the edge angel. I'm going to get you so desperate you're begging me to fuck you right here in front of everyone."

She lets out a low, deep groan.

I don't have a fucking doubt that I can do it.

But I like Bella too much to get her arrested.

I know just where I'll fuck her.

But first things first.

I suck on her earlobe. Softly. Then harder. Then hard enough to get her moaning.

I keep my fingertips hovering over her clit.

She rocks her hips, brushing her clit against my fingers.

She does it again and again.

"Please," she breathes.

I suck harder. "Demand it."

"Touch me."

I do. I brush my fingers over her clit softly.

That's enough to get her shaking.

Fuck, I love the way she responds to me.

I brush my fingers against her again and again.

Until she's digging her nails into my skin, groaning that *you're an evil tease, Joel* groan of hers.

It's obvious what we're doing here.

But I don't fucking care.

I don't care about anything but getting Bella screaming my name.

I rub her harder. Harder.

She groans into my ear.

She drags her nails over my skin.

Her breathing gets heavy.

I stroke her until she's shaking. Until her nails are digging into my skin enough to draw blood.

I pull my hand away.

"Joel," she whines. She stares at me, her brown eyes wrecked with need.

Her entire body is wrecked with need.

She looks up at me with those dark eyes of hers. "Fuck me, Joel. I want to come on your cock."

My cock quivers. It doesn't care about my need to get Bella begging.

It's making quite a convincing argument.

Not yet.

I slide my arm around her waist. I keep her body pressed against mine as I lead her through the dance floor and past the bar, all the way through the side door.

Bella bites her lip as she looks around the alley. We're alone out here, but we are sandwiched between two busy streets. Someone might walk by.

But the music from the club is booming. It drowns out the sounds of the city.

That means we don't have to worry about being quiet.

That means I can get her screaming my name.

I bring my hands to her hips and I turn her around. She leans into the gesture, her back melting into my chest, her ass brushing against my crotch.

Bella grabs the bottom of her dress and pulls it over her hips. Her voice gets demanding. "Now."

"Put your hands on the wall."

She places her palms against the wall over her head.

"Spread your legs wider."

She spreads enough that I can get a good look at her.

Fuck, I need to be inside her.

But I need her begging me too.

I drag my fingertips over her ass, closer, and closer to where she needs them.

Her legs shake.

I brush her cunt with my fingers.

"Joel," she breathes.

I slide one finger inside her.

She gasps.

Two.

She's wet. And she's close. I can tell from the way she's pulsing. I push my fingers deeper to warm her up.

Deeper.

Harder.

She groans. "Fuck me, Joel." Her voice drops to something demanding. "Now."

Damn, I can't take any more teasing.

I slide my jeans and boxers to my knees.

I bring my hands to Bella's hips and I pull her closer.

My tip strains against her.

She groans with this perfect mix of agony and ecstasy.

Right now, she's mine.

Right now, I'm the only thing she wants.

Right now, I'm everything she needs.

I tease her again and again.

I tease her until her groans get needy and desperate.

She rocks backwards, pushing her body onto mine.

With one swift motion, I thrust into her.

"Fuck," she groans with pleasure.

God damn, she feels good.

I dig my fingers into her hips and I fill her with another hard thrust.

"Joel," she groans. "You feel so fucking good."

My body takes over.

I press my chest against her back, pinning her to the wall. With one hand, I tug at her hair to bring her neck to my lips.

With the other, I hold onto her hips.

I fill her with hard, deep thrusts. Each makes her shake and groan. Each fills me with pleasure. Each brings us closer.

She rocks her hips in time with my movements.

I get lost in the sounds of her groans. She feels so fucking good, sounds so fucking good. Then her breath hitches and her voice jumps two octaves.

"Joel. Fuck."

She's almost there.

I keep her hips pinned to mine and I fill her with those same deep strokes.

I fuck her through her orgasm.

"Joel," she breathes.

"Say it again, angel."

She screams my name again and again as she comes on my cock. Her cunt pulses around me, pulling me deeper. God, that feels good.

I lose track of everything except her groans.

Except her body against mine.

A few more thrusts and I'm there, groaning her name into her neck as I come.

Pleasure unfurls inside me.

I feel good everywhere.

But it's not just the ecstasy in her voice.

It's not just the aftershocks of my orgasm.

It's everything about being around her.

I kiss her hard then I clean up in the bathroom. When I'm done, she's standing outside the door waiting for me.

Neither one of us says anything about our impending appointment.

The entire drive home, the messy make out session in the shower, watching cheesy cop shows together on the couch—all night, neither one of us says anything about where we'll be this time next week.

Chapter Twenty-Six

JOEL

Bella and I wake up together. We shower together. We have breakfast together.

We spend the afternoon watching *Harry Potter* movies, only breaking to fix lunch together.

It goes too fast.

I blink and it's sunset.

And we're getting in the car, arguing over what we should play on the drive to Kit's place, parking, laughing as we race up the stairs to his apartment.

Then we're at the door.

I'm not ready for all the opinions of my bandmates. And I'm not ready to tell them how I feel about her.

Do I bullshit them the way I always do?

Or should I confess the truth?

There's no fucking way I'm going to let Mal or Ethan know the whole story.

But some of it…

Shit. I'm not good at contemplating shit.

Instinct…

I can do instinct. That's what I'll do here.

I knock.

A moment later, Piper pulls the door open. She looks as adorable as she always does in a red and white sweater dress, her blond hair falling over her shoulders.

Her blue eyes light up as she looks at Bella. She smiles. "It's so nice to meet you. I'm Piper."

"Bella." She shakes Piper's hand.

Piper motions *come in*. After we do, she closes the door behind us. "Okay, let me get this gushing out of the way." She holds out her left hand and wiggles her ring finger to show off her massive rock.

It's not as big as Bella's.

But then Kit's not the showy type.

Piper lets out a dreamy sigh. "Isn't it beautiful?"

Her expression is pure joy. There isn't a doubt in her mind that she and Kit should be together forever.

Bella smiles. "It is."

"It's only been a few hours. Right now, I feel like I'm never going to get tired of staring at this ring." She holds it up to the light, her eyes wide with wonder. "It's shiny. And…" She lets out another dreamy sigh.

"We can leave you alone with that thing. Come back after you two are *satisfied*," I tease.

"No, I… That's ridiculous," she says.

"So you're a right-hander?" I ask.

"What?" She clears her throat. "You don't mean—"

Bella laughs. "Of course you mean."

"Just curious. Some people go dominant hand. Some go non-dominate," I say.

"And you masturbate so often you have to switch hands because they get tired." Piper tries to make her voice teasing, but she's still blushing.

"You really think that would embarrass me?" I ask.

"Well... I guess not. Ahem." Piper looks to me. "Something tells me this proposal didn't surprise you."

I play coy.

She throws her arms around me and hugs tightly. "Thanks for helping him. Not just with this. But always... with everything."

Bella's gaze catches mine. She smiles knowingly. I'm not sure what it is she knows. Whatever it is, I like her knowing it.

If it was anyone else, I'd hate that look.

But I do want Bella knowing me.

All of me.

Piper pulls back with a smile. "Kit's parents went for a walk with your mom. She's so sweet and her sweater is adorable. It has this reindeer on it. She brought a matching one for you."

I have no doubt she's telling the truth.

"You're going to look amazing." Piper laughs. "It's just us, right now. Everyone else is on their way." She points out the bathroom, the tray of snacks, the drinks in the fridge. "Help yourself to anything. Or I can get you something."

"Thank you." Bella squeezes my hand. "I'll get some waters." She heads to the kitchen.

Piper waits until Bella is out of earshot then she leans in to whisper. "So..."

"So...?"

"What the fuck, Joel? I thought you and I were like this." She presses her pointer and middle finger together. "And I'm the last person to find out you were married."

"You'd have met Bella if you came to our show."

"It was twenty-one and over."

"That's never stopped you before."

"Excuse me for not going to my millionth Dangerous

Noise show." She puts her hands on our hips. "Why didn't you tell me?"

"I didn't want to steal your fiancé's thunder."

She shakes her head, not buying it. "I'm going to forgive you, but only because I know how much you've done for Kit."

"Generous, thanks," I tease.

"Seriously, Joel... I... I really do appreciate how much you've done for him." She wipes her eyes with the back of her hand. "Fuck, you're going to make me cry."

She has plenty of reason to be sentimental. Her fiancé is a recovering addict. He'd be in bad shape if I hadn't blackmailed him into rehab.

Maybe not dead...

But not good.

Piper clears her throat. She blinks hard. When she stares back at me, she's no longer wearing that sweet expression.

Her voice is demanding. "You should have told me."

"It's all over gossip."

"That makes it worse." She folds her arms. Her lips press together. "Well..."

"Well?"

"Come on, Joel. You can't show up with a wife and not explain." She looks at me with an earnest expression. "You and I have always been above bullshit."

"We have?"

"Yeah."

"What about when you were sneaking around with Kit?" I ask.

"What about when you were telling Kit not to be with me because Ethan and Mal would kick him out of the band?" she asks.

"They would have."

"No…"

I nod.

"They didn't."

True, but only because Violet was around to talk Ethan down. I love Piper like a sister, but Kit *is* family. Even if he's not blood.

He'll always come first.

But I'm not about to get all sentimental with her.

I keep my voice light. "Sorry, sweetheart, but Kit's always going to have my loyalty. And I'm always going to be straight with him."

She presses her palms together and shoots me a puppy-dog look. "You're not giving me any details?"

Damn. She really wants to know.

And Piper gets what she wants.

The woman is a force. She's used to holding her own with her over-protective older brothers.

Hell, she was strong enough to break down all the walls around Kit's heart.

It's hard to shake her.

But I know exactly how to do it. "I'll swap, detail for detail."

Her cheeks flush. "You don't mean…"

"I do."

"Why do you want…" She clears her throat. "What do you want to know?"

Piper's big, blue eyes, her long, blond hair, and her retro dress scream of sweetness.

I know better. Even if Kit refuses to share details.

She has a dirty side.

This needs to be something good.

Luckily for me, I know exactly the button to push.

"Do you ever steal any of Mal's bondage gear so Kit can tie you up and spank you?" I ask.

Piper makes that *eww* face. She hates being reminded of her brother's taste for domination.

I'm sure I'd feel the same if Mal was my brother. As it is, I enjoy hearing about his conquests second hand.

"You should see the riding crop I got him for his birthday," I say. "Would you rather use it on Kit or have Kit use it on you?"

Bella's laugh flows into my ears.

I turn back to her with a smile. "How long have you been standing there, angel?"

She hands me my water. "Long enough."

I'm obvious about checking Bella out. She's wearing the same snug black dress she was wearing the night we met.

Her hair isn't in a tight bun right now. It's falling all over her shoulders.

Her make up is dark. Her lips are fuck me red.

She looks undone.

She looks relaxed.

Happy.

And fuck does that make me warm all over.

I drop my voice to something seductive. "You look good enough to eat, angel. Have I told you that yet?"

"Not with words." She smiles.

Piper clears her throat.

"You want to try a riding crop?" I ask. "Or would you rather I tie you up first?"

Bella tries to fight her blush, but she doesn't make it. Her lips part with a sigh of desire.

She's too tongue tied to reply.

Again, Piper clears her throat. "Bella, have you said hi to Kit?" Piper's eyes go to the engagement ring on her left hand. Her voice gets as dreamy as her expression. "My fiancé."

She leads us over to the couch where Kit is sitting, reading off his Kindle. Well, reading is a strong word for what he's doing.

He's more pretending to read, shaking his head over my antics.

He rises to his feet to say hello to Bella. "Nice to see you again."

Bella smiles. "You too."

They actually shake hands.

I'd call him on how weird that is if Piper wasn't already wrapping her arms around Kit.

She rests her head on Kit's chest. "Did you hear what Joel said?"

"The building heard Joel." He leans in to whisper something in her ear.

"Joel likes to taunt me about my brother Mal," Piper says. "Everyone knows Mal is into bondage." She makes that *ick* face again.

"Not just bondage, sweetie. Mal is into every part of BDSM."

Piper's expression contorts into one of horror.

"He doesn't share enough to let anyone watch. Not anymore. But he did once," I say.

"I thought you didn't mix business and pleasure." She sticks her tongue out in disgust. "Why am I even asking?"

"I don't anymore," I say.

"You're married." Piper shoots Bella an apologetic glance. "I mean, it's cool if you guys are open that way. Or if you want to do threesomes… I mean, Ethan is taken now, and I don't think he and Vi are swingers. Oh God." Her cheeks turn red. "What if they are?"

This is hilarious.

Even Kit thinks so. He's smiling, running his hand through Piper's hair.

"Joel doesn't have threesomes with bandmates," Kit says.

"But maybe he swings." Piper shakes her head. "Whatever it is, I am happy for you. And I support you, as long as you're safe. But please do not fucking tell me about it."

Damn, I'm laughing so hard my abs are feeling it.

Piper looks to Kit. "They're not… they wouldn't."

He nods. "They wouldn't."

"You all think I'm naïve, huh?" she asks.

"It's sweet, baby." He presses his lips to her forehead. "But your brothers don't have honor. You don't have to protect it."

"Well… Mal… he only sleeps with his fuck buddies," she says.

"And he only has a few dozen," I say.

Bella laughs. She looks to me then to Piper. "We're not going to swing with anyone. I'm never letting another woman touch you."

"But you want another man to touch you?" I ask.

She tries to hold a poker face. It doesn't last long. She shakes her head.

"But you'd make an exception for Mal," I tease.

Piper clears her throat. "Ask him when he gets here. Or whatever you're doing." She turns red. "Um, Bella, so do you have any siblings?"

"A sister," she says.

"Would you want to know if your sister was into bondage?" Piper asks.

Bella presses her lips together, thinking. "I would. She's fiery. I can imagine her into anything, but her husband… he's about as interesting as white rice. It's hard to picture him in a leather mask." She looks to Piper. "But I wouldn't need the kind of details Joel is offering."

I slide my arm around Bella's waist and pull her body

into mine. "You saying you don't want me to tie you up and eat you out until you're begging me to fuck you?"

Bella blushes. "I'm not saying that at all."

Piper laughs. "You know, Kit's mom was worried about Joel and I being close friends. She really thinks Joel is charming."

"Only because she had no idea how perfectly we fit together." He leans down to plant a kiss on Piper's forehead. His voice is sweet. He's barely leaving room for a sexual implication.

She rises to her tiptoes to plant an equally sweet kiss on his lips.

They're adorable.

It's sickening… in a sweet way.

When she pulls back, Piper looks to Bella. "Can I borrow you for a while? I need dirt on Joel if I'm going to manage to torture him back. Mal's gotten really open about his… interests. Joel has too much material."

"Sure." Bella winks at me.

"You selling me out, angel?" I ask.

She smiles. "Only if Piper delivers some dirt on you."

"You're fucked." Kit laughs.

"I know." I watch them leave then I turn back to the bassist. "She as shy about threesomes as she says?"

He rolls his eyes. "You're so full of shit."

"I am?"

He nods. "Trying to make it about sex. That's bullshit."

"It is?"

Again, he nods. "You really fucking like her."

"I do."

He smiles. "Have you two decided to stay hitched?"

"Not yet."

"Good luck."

"Thanks." I need it.

Chapter Twenty-Seven

BELLA

Piper really is a fantastic hostess. As soon as Mal arrives, she brings him over to us.

Okay, she spends a while gushing over her engagement, jumping up and down, staring at her ring, insisting he stare at her ring…

Okay, maybe that takes twenty minutes. I don't mind. It's sweet. She's happy. She's sure she wants to be with him forever.

And the way he looks at her—he's sure he wants to be with her forever.

I've never seen two people that happy.

That in love.

Mom and Dad were happy, but they had that exhaustion of working parents. They had that comfortable *you're more a partner than a passion* relationship. They treated each other well. They loved each other.

But were entirely able to keep their hands off each other.

Mal holds up a bottle of sparkling cider. He motions

hello to me and Joel then turns to Piper. "You want to open this now or once Kit's parents are back?"

"Now. And, I think we have more, for when Kit's parents are back." She bites her lip. "Maybe."

"I'll ask Dad to pick more up," Kit says from the couch.

She beams. Her smile widens as she looks to her engagement ring. "Good idea." She looks to Mal. "Thanks." She reaches up and hugs him again.

He whispers something in her ear.

She whispers back.

They really are close. As close as any siblings I've seen. And it's clear they really love and support each other. Even if there was a lot of drama about Piper getting with Kit—Joel filled me in on the more gory details on the way here.

Piper pulls the wrapping off the bottle of sparkling cider and unscrews the cap. "It's too bad it doesn't burst the way champagne does."

"Not getting enough of phallic imagery lately?" Joel teases. "I'll have to tell your fiancé to step up his game."

"Please tell him nothing," she says.

"Tell him you want nothing? Shit, you're going to hurt his feelings, Pipes. Or is that your game? The brooding ones do fuck the best when they're hurting," he teases.

"What do you know about brooding women?" she asks. "You sleep with…" Her eyes catch mine. Her expression gets apologetic. "I'm going to get some glasses."

Mal chuckles. "You have her number."

"She's too much fun." Joel turns to me. His lips curl into a half-smile. He winks. "Pipes is only second to Bella."

"I'm too much fun?" I ask.

He nods. "Of course, if I start pushing your buttons, we're going to grab all the party's attention."

I know Joel's only teasing, but that does nothing to slow my racing heart. I want him pushing my buttons.

I want us tangled in bed, forgetting the rest of the world.

Forgetting that we still have an expiration date.

"Flirt when you can actually deliver on all those promises." Mal turns to me. "Nice to see you again, Bella."

"You too," I say.

"Don't worry. I already filled her in on your *tendencies*." Joel motions to Piper, bringing the glasses back towards us.

Mal shakes his head *you're ridiculous*. He turns to me. "Do me a favor, Bella, and don't let him get away with this shit."

"Joel does a lot of shit," I say. "You'll have to be specific.

"Hey." Joel mimes being stabbed in the gut.

Mal ignores him. "I'm going to tell you a secret." Mal raises his voice. "But I'm going to tell it Joel style."

Joel style must mean loud.

"Oh, whatever could you mean?" Joel shouts back. "I can't follow your subtle and hilarious comedy."

Mal blows him a kiss then turns to me. "Joel likes to watch. And listen. He plays up his wacky comedy routine to try to convince people he's teasing. But he's not. Don't fall for his shit."

"Joel likes to watch?" I press my fingertips into my sides to temper the heat racing through me. I like the idea of Joel watching me. I like it a lot.

"Should she tie me up?" Joel asks.

His voice is that teasing tone. Like he's trying to convince us he's joking.

But his eyes…

Fuck, his eyes are filled with this expression of pure need.

He does like to watch.

Mal chuckles, not buying it. "Yeah. She should tie you

up, strip, and make you watch her touch herself. She should fucking torture you making you watch."

"You inviting yourself to this party?" Joel asks.

Mal raises a brow. "You relaxing that *no threesomes with bandmates* rule?"

Uh…

Joel slides his arm around my waist. "You okay, angel?"

"I think so." No, I am. As attractive as Mal is—seriously, he's tall, broad, and covered in tattoos—I don't want him joining me and Joel in bed. However— "Well, I liked Mal's idea. I think we should try it later."

Mal chuckles.

Joel's pupils dilate. He really does like that idea.

Fuck, I'm hot.

I want to skip this party and go back home right away.

Damn, it's hard to think about anything but making desire spread over his face.

I want to tie him up.

I want to make him watch me strip.

Touch myself.

Fuck myself.

Fuck, I can't believe I'm actually considering this.

Not just considering it, but craving it.

"Joel didn't tell me how you met," Mal says.

"I didn't tell her how we met either," Joel says.

"How did you meet?" I bite my tongue so I won't add *there wasn't much about your band's origin on Wikipedia*.

Mal chuckles. "Your husband doesn't like being told what to do."

"Not by obnoxious vocalists." Joel winks at me. "I like certain people getting bossy."

My cheeks flush, but I manage to keep my breath steady.

Mal doesn't even blink. He's not at all moved by Joel's

banter. He turns to me, completely ignoring Joel's interruption. "You ever listen to Sinful Serenade?"

"Maybe. I mostly listen to pop from when I was in high school, Lady Gaga and Rhianna. But I think Anne, my sister, likes them. They have the singer who always sounds like he's coming?" I ask.

"As opposed to Mal, who sounds like he's in the middle of a fuck," Joel says.

"You've been listening?" Mal teases.

"You fucking know I've been listening." Joel shoots me a flirty glance. "I always listen."

Mal nods. "Yeah, their singer is always moaning. Seems to be working for them. Women eat it up."

"You don't seem to do too badly," I say.

Mal chuckles. "We do all right."

Joel moans through his words, copying the Sinful Serenade singer's style. "Is this kind, of, ooh, ooh, moaaaaaning siiiiinging really more disturbing than—" he switches to Mal's breathy style- "this, uh, uh heavy, breathing, like I'm fucking. So. Hard. I. Can't. Breathe?"

"I'm not sure what point you're making, but I would very much like you to continue making it," I say.

Seriously.

Joel moaning then panting…

Damn, my husband really knows how to torture me.

Joel winks. "You know how to get me moaning, angel."

I take a deep breath. It does nothing to cool me down. But it does bring clarity.

Joel is deflecting.

But why?

There must be something about this story that makes him uncomfortable.

"You don't think I can hold my own with the moans?" Mal's stare is a challenge.

"Don't you get enough attention on tour?" Joel asks.

"Define enough," Mal says.

"If you're still hurting for people to look at you and hear the pain in your voice, then go to some karaoke bar. Groan through a song and get women throwing their panties on stage. You'll get plenty of attention." Joel shakes his head with mock incredulity.

Mal chuckles. "What do you think, Bella? I think Joel should get up on stage and serenade you."

"Blue Oyster Cult didn't write any love songs," Kit calls.

"Nobody asked for your fucking opinion." Joel shakes his head. His hair falls over his eyes. "I know a lot of sweet fucking love songs."

"Everything by The Cure," Mal offers.

"It's not a fucking crime liking 80s music." Joel shoots me a panty-melting expression. "I was thinking *Like A Prayer.*"

I'm only somewhat aware of 80s music. I know that's a Madonna song, but I always thought it was about… well, I guess it's one big reference to oral sex.

Oh.

My blush spreads to my chest. "Um, I think Mal was telling me the story of how Dangerous Noise formed."

"Joel's good at derailing shit," Mal says.

He really is.

Mal continues. "Dangerous Noise used to be Joel and Kit. This guy named Gavin was their singer. And Drew, the guitarist who's in Sinful Serenade now, was—"

"Their guitarist," I offer.

Mal nods. "They all went to college together. Well, no, I think Drew and Miles were at a better school than Kit and Joel."

Joel flips him off.

Mal chuckles. "Kit and Joel dropped out pretty fast. Drew and Gavin too, actually. But now I'm getting off track." Mal shoots Joel a knowing look then his gaze goes back to me. "Gavin was good. Not as good as me, or as good as Miles, but he was good. Only he had an attitude. Even worse than mine."

"I still can't believe that happened," Joel says.

Mal nods. "It's hard to fathom."

"You're okay with everyone thinking you're bossy and annoying?" I ask.

"Who's calling me annoying?" Mal feigns hurt.

"Mal loves people knowing how bossy he is. He thinks it will make us all respect him," Joel says.

"You respect me, Young," Mal says.

Joel shrugs, but his expression is clear. He does respect Mal.

In fact, it's clear everyone respects Mal. Maybe he assumed the position of de facto leader, and maybe people get irritated about it, but they all respect him.

"We're all used to getting what we want, whenever we want it. Makes shit difficult. I'm sure you've noticed that about Joel," Mal says.

"She's too busy thinking about me naked," Joel says.

I am busy thinking about Joel naked. But not at all too busy.

Mal turns to Joel. "You want to stop interrupting or you want to tell the story?"

"I want to keep interrupting," Joel says. "Is that an option?"

I squeeze his hand. "I want to hear the story."

Joel nods to Mal *go ahead*.

He does. "Shit was okay with Dangerous Noise, until Drew started dating Gavin's ex. You know men with egos.

The last thing they can stand is a woman leaving them then coming with someone else."

I don't know that. My ex and I left on pretty amicable terms. But I do get his meaning. The thought of Joel with another woman is awful.

But the thought of Joel, naked, in bed, screaming some other woman's name…

Fuck, my stomach is already churning.

Mal continues. "Drew bailed to join Sinful Serenade. Their drummer and bassist used to be in a band with Ethan."

"He plays guitar, right?" I ask.

Mal nods.

"And you sing. Why weren't you in the band?" I ask.

"'Cause he was too busy getting laid." Joel clears his throat. "He didn't have time to waste with rock star bull-shit. He only remembers all this shit because it was how he got to be in charge."

He's covering.

Mal is nodding. He's on board with it.

Joel's eyes catch mine. Something passes between us, something I can't quite explain.

He knows I know he's full of it.

I nod *go ahead*.

He does. "Mal only puts up with us because it means he gets several thousand women screaming his name every night."

Mal chuckles. "Short story is, Tom, the Sinful Serenade drummer, is a force of nature. He wouldn't rest until Kit and Joel gave me and Ethan a shot. We'd been playing together for years. Joel thought I was bossy and annoying right away."

"I still do," Joel teases.

"But I'm more tolerable than Gavin or Drew," Mal says.

"Marginally."

"You're not so tolerable yourself, Young." Mal motions to me. "You're lucky you found a woman who wants to put up with you."

"Yeah. I'm really fucking lucky." He slides his arms around me and he kisses me hard and deep.

I melt.

Joel turns more and more "on" with every arrival. Then his mom and Kit's parents get back, and he's brighter than a 150 watt bulb.

He really is an entertainer. He teases all of his friends. He charms the pants off Kit's parents. He keeps the conversation going all throughout appetizers and dinner.

It's a nice party, a nice night. The home cooked food is fantastic. The conversation is flowing. And Joel is doing an expert job deflecting attention from me.

Every time someone asks about our engagement, our marriage, our wedding night, he finds a way to change the subject.

He's really good at pushing people's buttons.

But I can tell it's wearing on him. I can see the cracks in his smile. I can see the exhaustion in his eyes. I can see the tension knotting in his shoulders.

It's exactly how I feel at every family function, at every study group, at every one of my family's fancy catered affairs.

He's trying to keep the party going by entertaining.

I do it by keeping the peace.

It exhausts both of us.

I like Joel's friends. They're sweet and fun and they seem supportive.

But I still feel like I'm "on" too.

We say goodbye to our friends, drive Trish to the airport, say goodbye to her.

I'm very, very glad to be alone with Joel in his car.

To be heading back to our apartment.

To watch another *Harry Potter* movie on the couch.

To climb into bed with Joel.

He whispers in my ear as he runs his fingertips over my wrists. "Means the fucking world to me that you told me that."

My chest gets warm. "It means the world to me that you… that you didn't run away."

"No fucking way." He presses his lips to my forehead. "Tomorrow… I'll tell you about all that shit with my parents tomorrow."

"Yeah?"

He nods. "I've never shown anyone the ugly parts of me." He pulls me closer. "But I do really fucking trust you."

Chapter Twenty-Eight

JOEL

Two days until our divorce date.

I might only have two more days with her.

The thought nags at me through breakfast.

Through coffee.

I push it aside as we walk over to the hipster shops on Abbot Kinney. By the time I'm done with my second cup, I've got that dread in some tiny box at the bottom of my gut.

I'm here.

In this moment.

That's what I do. That's what I'm good at.

And it's what I want.

Bella buys two new outfits. Ones that would be ridiculously out of place in a New York winter.

Ones that show off her amazing tits and her fantastic ass.

That's got to be a good sign.

That, or I'm thinking with my cock.

But, I'd rather think about getting Bella off at lunch than about what happens if we call this off.

I manage to keep my hands to myself—mostly—as she finishes touring the shops. But when we're finally walking into a hipster sandwich shop, I can't help myself.

I slide my hand over her ass and pull her close.

Her body feels good against mine.

It's already afternoon. We're well past lunchtime. My stomach is growling and this place smells amazing. Like garlic and fresh bread.

But I still want her more than I want food.

More than I want anything.

The guy at the counter of this offbeat sandwich shop is giving me that *I know him from somewhere* look. Thankfully, he says nothing as he hands me my credit card.

I motion to the empty corner in the back. "Why don't you grab our seats?"

"Sure." Bella bites her bottom lip. She knows exactly what I have in mind for that secluded corner. She tries to play cool as she grabs our water cups, but her gait is unsteady.

She's in flat shoes. There's no reason for her to be stumbling.

No reason except her needing exactly the same thing I need.

I pull a hundred from my wallet, press it flat to the counter, and look the hipster guy in the eyes. "We want a little privacy."

The hipster guy nods with understanding. He takes the bill with a smile. "Sure thing." He motions to the mason jar filled with a bright red laminated 76. "Don't forget your number."

Okay, sure. We're the only people here. It's ridiculous that we need a number. But I know how this sort of thing goes. It's the way my dad thinks.

A policy is a policy. And since I don't give a fuck about the policy, I'm not about to argue.

I'm not about to do anything that could make it impossible to get what I want.

My cock rouses at the thought of spreading Bella's legs and stroking her to orgasm in that tiny booth.

Fuck, it's tempting.

Painfully tempting.

But my cock is going to have to wait.

I need Bella panting.

I need her dripping with desire.

I need to be sure that she's never wanted anything as badly as she wants my hands on her skin.

Shit. This isn't helping get blood back to my brain.

I grab another glass, fill it with ice and water, and down every drop. That does little to cool me off.

Bella is sitting in that tiny both, her pretty dress falling over her crossed legs.

When her eyes catch mine, she uncrosses her legs and spreads them apart. Her skirt hikes up her thighs. Then her legs are crossing again and she's wearing a coy smile.

Fuck, she looks cute in that dress. Its flower pattern is sweet and innocent. The purple cardigan over her shoulders only adds to the schoolgirl charm.

I take a seat next to her. My gaze goes straight to the creamy skin of her inner thigh.

It's hard to think about anything but getting my hand under that dress.

But I promised her I'd talk.

And I am a man of my word.

She hikes her skirt enough to show off her lace panties.

Her voice is bold, confident. "Your jaw is about to hit the floor."

"I asked the guy at the counter to give us privacy."

"Good." She smiles. "I want to talk to you."

"You're not encouraging conversation."

She presses her lips together. Then her knees. Her cheeks flush. Her voice gets needy. "Even so."

"If you pull that dress any higher, I'm going to make you come."

Her fingers curl into her thighs. That flush spreads to her chest. She wants me. Badly.

And I want that.

I want her.

She brings her mouth to my ear. "I want to make you wait."

My cock stirs. God damn, the confidence in her voice… "I like you bold."

"Me too." She presses her lips to my neck. "But you're not going to sweet talk your way out of this."

"This?"

"I'm making you wait." Her voice is shaky, but she presses on. "I'm going to make you desperate with desire before I give you what you want."

"Yeah?"

"Yeah." The shakiness is gone. Her voice is all confidence. She pulls back enough to look me in the eyes. "I *do* want to talk to you."

I cock a brow.

"Not dirty talk. Well, maybe a little." She wraps her fingers around her water glass. "I like who I am around you."

"I like who you are around me."

"I don't feel like that with anyone else." She brings her glass to her lips and takes a long sip.

Water dribbles over her lips and chin.

Her eyes fill with a fiery expression.

An *I'm enjoying torturing you* expression.

She's doing it on purpose.

There's only one place my mind can go.

Damn do I want to be filling her mouth.

Pushing her limits.

Coming on her pretty red lips.

Fuck, I've taught her too well. Blood is fleeing my brain at an alarming rate.

We're here for a reason.

But it's eluding me at the moment.

Bella laughs. "You're distracting."

"Speak for yourself."

She recrosses her legs and pulls her dress down her thigh. "Does that help?"

"Yeah, but I prefer it the other way."

Her voice gets serious. "I… I do want to talk."

I want to fuck her, hard.

But we need to have this conversation.

I nod and scoot far enough away to get my cock to settle down.

Bella smiles. "This sounds silly, but I really like when you look at me like that."

"Like I want you naked, under me, screaming my name?"

She blushes. "It makes me feel sexy. I've never felt like that before."

I cock a brow. Her voice is even. Her expression is earnest. Even so— "I have a hard time believing that."

"I've only been with two guys before you. One was a fling before law school. I didn't have enough time with him to really get into it. Stan, he wasn't verbal about that kind of thing. We had sex. And it was fine. He was attentive. But I kept thinking I needed to be what he wanted, to act how he wanted, to please him—"

"Did he get you off?"

"He tried, but I couldn't usually relax enough. I got anxious when he'd go down on me. Or when he touched me. I guess I shouldn't talk about sex with my ex-boyfriend."

"It's fine."

"It doesn't bother you."

A little, but— "I want to hear it."

"I guess I thought it should be all about him, about what he wanted. He wasn't selfish, but he didn't… well he didn't ever ask if I wanted to come on his face or his hands first in this way that made it clear that he needed me coming." She blushes as she stares into my eyes. "Joel, you're the only person I've ever known who makes me feel like what I want matters to you."

"It does."

"I know." She bites her lip. "And not just with sex, though I do appreciate it during sex. When I'm with you, I feel strong. Like I can stand up for myself. Like I might actually be able to figure out my life."

I offer her my hand.

She takes it. Her eyes go to her engagement ring. "I want to hear about your parents."

As much as I hate the subject, this *is* important.

Nobody really knows about my life.

Nobody except Kit and Daphne, and they only know because they were there for so much of it.

I bring my gaze to Bella's pretty brown eyes. "I should have realized a long time ago. They're different than each other in this way that… I thought it was good, but Mom wasn't happy."

"How's your dad different?"

"He's all logic. No intuition, no feelings, no emotion. It's easy to convince him of something, even if it doesn't quite add up."

"Like taking the letter of the law and ignoring its intent?"

"Exactly." Some of that tension in my chest softens. "I guess I could have been a lawyer."

"You could." She reaches over to run her fingers through my hair. "It's embarrassing how little I know about you, considering." She motions to my ring finger. "What were you studying in college?"

"I dropped out before I could decide. Mom was pissed about that for a while. No, not pissed. She was disappointed."

"That's worse."

A lot worse. I nod. "She thought I was running away because it was too hard."

"Were you?"

I say nothing.

"You were." Bella's voice gets bright. "I can't believe Joel Young has ever backed down from a challenge."

"It was one of the only times."

She shoots me an *I'm not sure about that* look.

I hold up my four fingers. "Scout's honor."

"Were you a scout?"

"I know how to tie a knot."

She laughs. "You're a flirt."

"You like it."

She nods. "But you don't fool me. I know you're evading because you don't want to talk about this."

She's right.

I want to share this with her, but the words are heavy. They lead to an ugly place. Everything about my parents leads to an ugly place.

They've been unhappy for a long time.

I've been lying to myself for a long time.

I call everyone else on their bullshit. I refuse to tolerate it. But I've been blind to my own shit for so long.

The hipster guy saves me from having to broach the subject. He winks as he drops off our sandwiches and takes our numbers. "Can I get you anything else?"

Bella shakes her head. "No, thank you." She takes a dainty bite of half her sandwich.

A laugh breaks up the tension in my jaw. "You're always so prim and proper."

"How's this." She lifts her pinky like she's having a formal tea. "Better?"

"Yeah."

She takes a bite, chews slowly, swallows. "You shouldn't watch me eat. I'll get self-conscious."

"What if you watch me eat in exchange?"

Her cheeks flush. "Oh. Well. I'm planning on making you watch first."

Fuck.

"Like Mal said." She smiles. "As long as you're game."

I barely manage to nod. I barely manage to think. Period.

She's going to tie me up and make me watch her touch herself.

I'm not exactly into bondage. I don't object to tying a woman up if that's her thing.

But I never let anyone tie me up.

I've never trusted anyone enough.

But then I'd never gone bareback before either.

I take a bite of my sandwich to buy my thoughts time to form. The tomatoes are firm. The avocado is ripe. The bacon is crisp. But this does nothing to satisfy me.

Food isn't what I want right now, no matter how much my stomach is growling.

I eat half the thing anyway.

"You're tongue tied." She laughs. "I like it."

I nod.

"We were talking about your parents."

"Who?"

Her laugh is louder this time. "About your dad and mom being different."

All right. She wants to have this talk. I need to divert my thoughts to something besides Bella stroking herself to orgasm if I want to get out of this restaurant without getting the two of us arrested.

I look her in the eyes. "Just after my mom went back to work, she tried to get me to sign up for soccer. I said no. I hate running. Still do."

She raises a brow. "Then how are you so…" Her eyes go to my shoulders, my chest, my hips. Then she's running her fingers over my skin. "You're very fit."

"It's mostly weights and the machines at hotel gyms. I have to keep up with shit if I want to keep my stamina up."

"For drumming."

I stare at her the way she's staring at me. Damn, that dress is tight on her tits. And it's cut low enough to show off the lace strap of her bra. "Amongst other things."

She blushes. "Now, you're distracting me."

I nod. "You really like that I'm built?"

"I'm sure you get that a lot."

"I'm sure a lot of guys like your tits. Doesn't mean you don't appreciate how much I love them."

That gets her blush spreading to her chest. Her nipples harden enough to make an impression in her dress.

Again, she presses her knees together.

She forces herself to look me in the eyes. "You're deflecting with sex again."

Shit, she's right. I nod.

"You don't want to talk about this?"

I nod.

Her eyes fill with affection. "Tell me anyway."

"I gave my dad a bunch of bullshit reasons why I shouldn't have to do soccer. They were technically true—soccer would mean less time for homework, and games would go late on school nights, and I did know kids who sprained their ankles doing it the year before—but they weren't things I cared about."

"Your dad bought it?"

"I don't think so, but he didn't care. He saw a logical reason, so he agreed. He told me I didn't have to do it. Even when I told him Mom insisted."

"Oh."

"She was furious. It was the first time I really saw them fight. It was the first time I realized shit wasn't perfect. He went right to what he knew would hurt her the most, saying she was a bad mother for going back to work. It was only part-time, while we were at school. And it wasn't like he could talk. He worked nonstop. Still does."

Bella rubs the space between my thumb and forefinger with her thumb. Her eyes are fixed on mine. She's really listening.

She really fucking cares.

I have to say this. Even if I don't want to. "I didn't hear much. They went to his office and locked the door. Then she came out, crying. And I made a joke and we laughed it off. And I convinced myself that it was fixed. Every time they fought, I cheered her up, and I convinced both of us that everything was perfect except for little hiccups."

"Until you couldn't?"

"Yeah. Every time Mom was upset… until she told me about the divorce. I couldn't make a joke. I couldn't laugh that off."

Bella rests her head on my shoulder. "She seemed happy."

"She did. But I'm still wrapping my head around the fact that I've been bullshitting myself for the last ten years."

"When you're usually the one calling people on bullshit?"

"Guess I'm a hypocrite."

"We all are." She intertwines her fingers with mine. "Do you still hate your dad?"

"Not his biggest fan at the moment. The shit he said when he told me about the divorce… he might as well have told me having kids was his biggest regret."

Her voice gets soft. "That must hurt."

"Yeah."

"Did you pretend to laugh it off?"

I chuckle. "How the fuck did you know?"

"It's easier to pretend like it doesn't hurt." She moves close enough that her body warms mine.

I slide my hand into her hair and pull her into a deep kiss. Then my hands are on her neck. I can't talk about this anymore. I don't even want to think about it.

Too much is changing.

I need to be someplace where things make sense.

And between Bella's legs—

That makes all the fucking sense in the world.

I bring my mouth to her ear. "I want to make you come."

"You're deflecting again."

"I know." I look her in the eyes. "I still want to make you come."

She smiles evilly. "I still want to make you wait."

It's easy talking to Bella, even about this ugly shit. We walk around the neighborhood, talking about everything and nothing for ever.

Besides her torturing me by deep throating her ice cream cone, I manage to keep my thoughts clean.

Cleanish.

They don't get dirty until we're back in my apartment. Bella is on her hands and knees, arranging her clothes in my closet.

Her skirt slides up and down her thigh. The damn thing keeps teasing me.

She gave me what I needed.

Now, it's my turn to give her what she needs.

She pushes herself to her feet before I can order her to hike her dress to her waist.

She turns to face me.

She's holding something in her hands.

A set of restraints.

She doesn't even blush. "Sit on the bed. I'm going to tie you up."

Chapter Twenty-Nine

BELLA

My hands are shaking so badly I can barely pull Joel's shirt over his head. My palms are so sweaty they slide right down his chest and stomach.

I fumble over his jeans. There's no reason why I should be fumbling. This is an ordinary button. An ordinary zipper.

He lifts his hips so I can pull the garment to his knees.

Now, Joel is wearing nothing but boxers.

His green eyes fill with desire as he offers me his hands. His expression is a dare. *Can you really tie me up? Can you really resist my hands on your skin? Wouldn't you rather come from my touch?*

I fumble with the rope handcuffs. They're simple and straightforward, no doubt designed with nervous fingers in mind.

Even so, I struggle.

Joel's pupils dilate as I cuff his wrist.

He keeps his voice bright. He's playing coy.

"You all right, angel?" he teases.

I swallow hard. Maybe. But that doesn't matter. "I want to do this."

I cuff his other wrist and tug at the restraint.

They have enough give they won't cut off his circulation, but they're on tight.

He's not getting out of them, unless it's what I want.

"Your shoulders okay?" I ask.

He nods.

My cheeks flush as I straddle him. "I've never done this before."

He tries to pull his hands apart. Nothing. His eyes go wide with a mix of desire and desperation.

What do I do here? I'm not exactly a master seductress.

But I know I want to drive Joel mad with desire.

That's all I need to know.

I hold his gaze as I grind my hips against his. Mmm, the friction of him against me…

I drag my hands over his shoulders and down his torso as I grind against him.

Joel lets out a low groan. "Take off your dress."

The tone of his voice commands me. God, the desire in his eyes…

I pull my dress up my thigh a little bit at a time. He watches with rapt attention.

His breath gets heavy.

His cock gets hard.

He's hard between my legs. Only his boxers and my panties are in the way. If I'm not careful, I'm going to strip him naked and mount him.

This first.

I need him desperate. I need him begging me.

His green eyes fix on mine. They scream *now*.

I take my time pulling my dress over my pelvis. Then up my stomach, over my breasts, off my head.

I drop it on the floor.

Joel rocks forward. His lips crash into my chest. Then he's dragging them over my skin. He doesn't have much control with his hands bound behind him, but he still manages to take my nipple into his mouth.

The pressure of his soft, wet mouth sends waves of pleasure to my core. I grind my hips against his, shifting so his cock is rubbing against my clit, pressing the fabric of my panties into my flesh.

Those boxers are still in the way.

God, I feel achy.

Empty.

I need him filling me. I want him claiming all of me. My sex. My mouth. My ass.

I dig my nails into his back. "Joel." My voice breaks into a whine. That's not right. He's the one who's supposed to be begging me.

He's the one who's supposed to be desperate.

I dig my hands into his hair and bring his mouth to my other nipple. He flicks his tongue against me again and again. Then he's swirling his tongue around the bud.

Sucking soft.

Sucking hard.

He scrapes his teeth against me. Harder. Harder. Hard enough I cry out.

I tug at his hair.

I rock my hips against him.

He feels so good like this, his mouth on my chest, his cock against my sex.

But I have to torture him.

I plant my hands on his shoulders and push myself up, off the bed. This is a cozy bedroom. The only other place to sit is the dresser. But it's just low enough that it will work.

I take three steps backwards. Then I push everything off the top of the dresser.

"Angel..." Joel's eyes fill with need as he looks up at me. "Sit."

I do.

"Take off your panties."

I push them to my knees then they fall off my ankles.

"Spread your legs."

I do.

"Wider."

I plant one foot on the dresser. Then the other. It's a difficult position. I have to lean my back against the wall to get the angle right.

But I know I've got it from the way all the breath leaves his body at once.

My eyes fix on his as I slide my hand down my torso, past my belly button, below my pelvis.

Waves of pleasure flow through me as I rub my clit with my middle finger. I'm already wound up, already needy, already close.

My need to come threatens to derail this.

I bring my gaze back to Joel. He's staring at me like I'm the best thing he's every seen.

His eyes are wide.

His teeth are sinking into his bottom lip.

He lets out a low groan. "Fuck yourself."

My sex clenches. "I don't usually—"

"Put your first two fingers together."

I press my index and middle fingers together.

"Wet them."

I slide my fingers into my mouth and suck on them. My fingertips are soft against my tongue. And my tongue is soft against my fingertips. Pleasure spreads through my torso. My head fills with thoughts of Joel's firm flesh in my mouth.

Of him groaning as he tugs at my hair.

I pull my fingers from my mouth then I drag them down my neck. Over my chest. I play with one nipple. Then the other. Then I have my fingers in my mouth again, my eyes fixed on Joel's.

His expression is pure desire.

He needs me.

Right now, he needs me more than he's ever needed anything.

This time, I bring my hand right to my clit. I stroke myself until my eyelids press together. Fuck. I'm close.

I force myself to open my eyes.

Joel meets my gaze. He nods *now* then his gaze shifts. He's watching intently.

I spread my legs a little wider as I tease myself with one finger. Then two. I've had guys touch me this way. I've had Joel touch me this way. But I've never penetrated myself.

My muscles threaten to clench up.

"Take a deep breath." Somehow, Joel's voice is steady, reassuring. He still has desire written all over his face, but he's looking out for me first.

I take a deep breath.

"Sit back so your legs can go slack."

I do. It doesn't give him as good a view, but it's a more comfortable position. My inner thighs are no longer straining.

I exhale slowly.

Then I bring my fingers back to my mouth. They taste like me. It spurs me on. It pushes the anxiety away.

Joel's voice drops back to that low, demanding tone. "Tease yourself, angel."

I do. First with one finger. Then two.

My eyes stay glued to his as I slip a finger inside my sex. It's different.

But not bad.

Not at all bad.

Slowly, I push my finger deeper. Deeper. It hurts, but in that good way.

In a really good way.

Pleasure fills my pelvis as I slip another finger in my sex.

I'm slow about stretching myself. Once I'm warmed up, I go a little faster, a little deeper, a little harder.

My hips shift to match the movements of my hand.

Joel's eyes stay glued to me. His jaw is slack. His cock is straining against his cotton boxers.

Right now, I'm the center of his universe.

Feminine power fills me.

Putting on a show is thrilling.

I watch him watch me. My movements get faster. Harder.

Then I'm going hard enough it hurts.

Harder than I ever thought I'd fuck myself.

His eyes meet mine. "I want to see you come."

"Soon." I steady my speed. It feels good. Too good. I'm close.

My eyelids flutter together.

My thumb finds my clit.

My body takes over. I rub myself as I fuck myself. I rock my hips so hard and fast I bang my head against the wall. It hurts, but I don't care.

I don't care about anything but falling off the edge.

Tension knots in my core.

Almost.

Almost.

There.

"Joel. Fuck." I scream his name again and again as I come. Pleasure spreads out to my fingers and toes.

Every part of me feels good.

But I'm not satisfied.

I'm not even close to satisfied.

Joel is still staring at me with rapt attention. Only now he's pulling at his restraints.

He's wrecked with desire.

I need him feeling as good as I do.

Now.

I push off the dresser and shift back onto his lap. He shudders as I press my crotch against his.

His eyes meet mine. "Now."

I reach around and unhook the cuffs.

Immediately, Joel pulls his arms free. His hands go to my hair and he pulls me into a deep, slow kiss.

His tongue claims my mouth.

God, I love kissing him.

It makes me feel complete.

He shifts his hips. The friction of his boxers against my clit has me ready to go again.

But him first.

He slides his hands to my hips and pulls me up with him. Together, we take a few steps away from the bed.

Joel palms my ass, pulling my body into his.

He's still wearing those stupid boxers.

He needs to be out of those boxers.

I push the things off his hips and wrap my hand around him. He shudders as I rub his tip with my thumb. His eyelids press together. A groan falls off his lips.

His voice is low, demanding. "You've been teasing me with that gorgeous mouth."

My sex clenches. I only barely manage to nod.

"This is going to be rough." He tugs at my hair. "I'm

going to fuck that pretty mouth of yours. Then I'm going to come all over those pretty red lips."

My nipples tighten.

"Tell me you want that, angel."

"Please."

He tugs at my hair. "On your knees."

Hell yes. I grab onto his hips and lower myself onto my knees.

He shudders as I take him into my mouth. I love the feel of him against my tongue, the taste of him, the way he shakes when I brush my lips against him.

I take a moment to taste every inch of him, to marvel in the way he groans and tugs at my hair, then I pull back.

I look up at Joel and nod *yes*.

He digs his hands into my hair, on the sides of my head. I lean forward to take him into my mouth. I suck on his tip. I flick my tongue against him.

I marvel in his pleasure.

His voice gets gruff. "Hands at your sides."

I press my hands into my outer thighs.

"If it's too much, grab my wrist. Otherwise, those hands better stay glued to those gorgeous thighs." He holds my head in place. "You ready, angel?"

I nod a *yes*.

My eyes lock with his.

Joel's fingers knot in my hair. He shifts his hips to thrust into my mouth. It's a short thrust. I only get a few inches of him.

Even so, it takes all my concentration to keep my balance on my knees. I press my palms into my thighs.

I look up at him.

He fills my mouth with another slow, short thrust. Another. Another.

His grip tightens around my head as he pushes deeper.

Deeper.

Deep enough I gag.

My hand goes to his hip reflexively. I pull it back to my thigh.

His eyes go wide as he fills my mouth with one long thrust. It pushes my limits.

I gag.

I swallow to relax my throat.

There.

He feels good in my mouth.

I want all of him.

I want to surrender to his pleasure.

He fills me with another long thrust. This time, I don't gag. I nod *keep going*.

He moves faster.

Deeper.

I suck harder as he thrusts into me. My thighs shake. My sex clenches. His groans fill the air. His stomach muscles clench.

He's close.

He thrusts harder. Faster. So hard and fast I can't do anything but take it. My thighs go slack. I give up on staying steady.

But he's got me. He keeps that firm grip on my head. He keeps his eyes fixed on mine, this look that screams *you're mine, angel.*

And he fucks my mouth.

Before, he was completely at my mercy.

Now, I'm completely at his.

The thought makes me hot all over. I groan against his skin, surrendering to the feeling of his cock in my mouth.

He goes deeper.

I gag. I try to pull back. But he's got me in place. He thrusts into me again and again.

Fuck.

It's intense.

But I like being at his mercy.

I suck hard as Joel fucks my face. His groans get heavier with every thrust. Then he's shaking.

His fingers knot into my hair.

"I'm going to come on those pretty lips," he groans.

Fuck.

I'm hot everywhere.

A few more thrusts and he's there. I can feel him pulsing. Then I can taste him, salty and sweet at once. I swallow hard as he pulls back.

He spills over my lips, chin, chest.

He groans my name again and again.

I lick my lips to get every drop of him.

Joel pulls me to my feet. He grunts as he throws me onto the bed.

I land with a soft thud.

He slides onto the bed. "Spread your legs."

I do.

"You're coming on my face now." He presses his palms into the inside of my knees to hold me against the bed.

This time, he doesn't tease me.

His mouth goes straight to my clit.

He licks me soft and slow. Every flick of his tongue fills me with this beautiful, diffuse pleasure. I shake. I groan. I writhe against his face, against his hands.

His nails dig into my skin, a gentle reminder that he's the one in control.

I really like him in control.

But I need to demand what I want too.

I slide my hand into his hair. "Harder."

He licks me harder. Harder.

Perfect.

"There," I breathe.

He licks me again and again. Until I'm so close to the edge I'm dizzy. It's not enough. I need more.

"Faster," I groan.

He goes faster. Harder.

There.

Almost.

The tension inside me winds tighter and tighter. So tight I can't take it.

With the next flick of his tongue, I come. All that tension unfurls. Threads of pleasure flutter through my pelvis, my torso, my thighs.

I tug at Joel's hair.

I scream his name.

I rock my hips to grind against him.

He keeps licking me. Again and again. It's intense enough I'm breathless. I try to shift away, to get a break, but he keeps me pinned.

I trust him. I *know* he'll release me if I ask.

But the way his nails dig into my skin—

The way he pins me into place—

Fuck.

My sex pulses as I come.

"Joel," I groan.

He licks me through my orgasm. Then he's pulling back, climbing up the bed, wrapping his arms around me.

I'm a sticky mess, but he doesn't care.

He holds me tightly.

I relax into his arms.

We lie like that, listening to each other's breath until the room is filled with the orange light of sunset.

"I have something planned for today. For after dinner." He slides his hand down my torso. "We have a while before we have to eat."

"Joel," I breathe.

"Yes?"

"Don't tease."

"No teasing." He slides his hand between my legs. "Just you coming on my hand again."

Chapter Thirty

BELLA

Joel won't tell me where we're going. He won't even tell me the proper dress code for our event.

I change into a pastel pink lingerie set and my clingiest dress. Heels are sexier, but it's dangerous wearing those things without knowing our location.

I stick with my black patent flats.

Then I follow him to his car. We tease each other about nothing on the drive to… well I'm not sure where we're going until we park and get out of the car.

The air is cool tonight. It will be cold soon. I pull my cardigan tighter, but that isn't enough to warm me up.

So I stick close to Joel.

I soak in the heat of his body.

We pass a Korean barbecue. A ramen place. A Japanese bookstore. A boba tea shop. A Japanese grocery store.

"This is Little Osaka." Joel points to the North/South street to our right. "It's mostly these three blocks." He motions to the storefront at the opposite side of the shopping center.

Only it's not a store.

It's a karaoke place.

He pulls out his phone to show off a text message.

Mal: A hundred bucks says I can out moan you.

"I was challenged." He slides his phone back into his pocket. "I figured you'd enjoy seeing my victory."

"What if you lose?"

"Angel, I'm going to pretend you didn't say that." He slides his arm around my waist and pulls me closer. "You get to hear me moaning either way."

"What are you singing for the moan-off?"

He smiles. "I can't divulge my secrets."

"Will you do a breathy singing off?"

"If you can name a band besides us that has a breathy karaoke track. Going up against Mal on a Dangerous Noise song is suicide."

"Where's your confidence?" I tease.

"There's confidence then there's a death wish. Two different things." He leads me into the karaoke joint.

The guy behind the counter looks too young to drive. He lights up when he spots Joel. It isn't the *he's famous* look. It's more *my favorite customer is back.*

"They're in room four." He points to the hallway on the right. "He's practicing."

Oh, that's what that sound is. It's hard to pick out the moaning vocals when they're competing with songs from three other rooms, but I'm pretty sure I can hear Mal moaning along to… something.

Joel smiles as he hands off his credit card. "You rooting for me?"

"Of course." The guy smiles back.

"You tell Mal the same thing?"

"Of course."

"You're going to make a great politician one day." Joel squeezes my hand and leads me down the hall.

This place already feels like it's out of a dream. The hall is bathed in blue light. The rooms are adorned with star-shaped windows.

On our right, a cuddled up couple is belting out love songs. On our left, a group of suits are joining forces to sing 80s songs.

I'm not sure a wiggle dress, flats, brown smoky eye, red lips, and hair that can only be described as *a just-fucked mess* are the right karaoke look. Right now, I don't care.

I feel like I belong here.

Even as we step into room four, an enormous suite with benches on three walls.

Mal is just finishing a song. He hands the mic to Piper.

She's still cute as a button. Her blond hair is in loose waves, her makeup is all sparkles, her fit-and-flare dress, Mary Jane heels outfit is stylish in an innocent college girl kind of way.

Not that I can talk.

She lights up when she sees us. "I thought you might back out." She winks at Joel. "You do hate to lose."

"Pipes, that cuts me. I thought you believed in me." He hugs her hello.

"What is it you always say?" She copies Joel's *I'm fucking with you* tone. "Sometimes you have to know when to fold?"

"Don't tell me you bet against me," he teases back.

Piper shakes her head. "If I bet, I can't be impartial." She turns to me. "You look really nice, Bella. How's married life treating you?"

"It's… exciting." I hug her hello.

She laughs. "Does that mean what I think it means?"

I nod. "Exactly what you think it means."

"I wouldn't expect anything less from Joel." She smiles.

"Kit's in the bathroom. Ethan and Violet are on their way. Well, they were on their way. Knowing them—"

"They're having sex someplace," Joel says. "You have to admire the man's stamina."

Piper makes that same *gross, that's my brother* look.

Joel laughs. He really enjoys teasing… all kinds of teasing.

Mal cuts in. He shakes Joel's hand then pulls me into a hug. "Nice to see you, Bella."

I nod. "You too."

"You force him to watch?" Mal asks.

I stammer. "Um… maybe."

Mal chuckles. "He went fucking crazy, didn't he?"

Piper clears her throat. "One more word and I'm leaving the room."

Joel laughs.

Even I laugh. It's cute how much she hates hearing about her brothers' slash surrogate brother's sex lives.

Mal turns to my husband. "Same terms as always?"

Joel nods. "Who's judging?"

"Bella can't be impartial," Mal insists.

Joel slides his arm around my waist and pulls my body onto his. "Of course. As soon as she hears me groan, she's going to hand me the title."

He looks to Piper. "You game for this?"

The door pulls open and Kit steps inside. He's wearing the same outfit as last time—a button up black shirt, black jeans, and motorcycle boots. His mass of curly dark hair hangs over his dark eyes.

He gives Piper a long once over then he shoots Mal a look. "Do I want to know?"

"Moan off," Mal says.

Kit chuckles. "And you're asking your sister to judge?"

"Sounds like you're volunteering, Lockhart," Joel says.

"Sure. I'll judge. You both annoy the shit out of me, so I'm plenty impartial." Kit winks at Joel.

"That cuts, Lockhart. I think we all know I'm more annoying than Mal," Joel says.

Kit chuckles. "True. But I think you can take it."

"I think we need three rounds," I say. "Each. At a minimum."

"How you doing Bella?" Kit asks.

"Good." I smile back. "I'm just concerned about fair play."

"Uh-huh," Kit says.

Everyone else shoots me the same *not buying that* look.

"We have a set of rules for this, angel." He motions for me to sit.

I do.

He sits next to me. "We each pick one song, any song. Then we both do the same song. Then the judges deliberate and crown a winner." He turns to Piper. "We need three judges, in case there's a tie."

"Vi and Ethan can do it," she says. "I think Violet is equally uninterested in the two of you."

"Baby, that's cold." Kit wraps his arms around her. "I like it."

"It's true." She turns to me. "I don't want to judge. I want to sit with Bella and throw shade."

"As long as you don't throw it at my husband." Warmth fills my stomach. I really like thinking of Joel as my husband.

I really want him to stay my husband.

I'M STILL LOST IN THOUGHTS OF FOREVER, MOSTLY oblivious to Mal and Joel's trash talk when Ethan and

Violet step inside. They have a just fucked look about them. His dark hair is in messy waves. Her short, blunt bob is in disarray. Her dark makeup is smudged. Her dress is sticking to her thigh-high tights.

"Told you." Joel motions to Piper.

She sticks out her tongue.

He laughs.

She flips him off.

Ethan shrugs. He turns to me with a smile. "Keeping Joel on his toes?"

"Of course." I smile back. "Have a fulfilling start to your evening?"

He chuckles.

Violet blushes. "Sorry we're late. We got—"

"We all know you were fucking at dinner," Joel says.

She turns to me. "I adore your husband, but he's a know it all."

"He is," I agree.

Piper brings us back to the contest. She looks to Violet and Ethan. "You two have been drafted as karaoke judges."

"Straight competition?" Ethan asks.

Piper shakes her head. "A moan off."

Ethan makes that same *ew that's my brother* look Piper made. He turns to Mal. "You singing only Sinful Serenade songs or you broadening your horizons?"

"Please. You really think he'd cede his home turf advantage?" Joel asks.

Mal chuckles. "I do what it takes to win."

Ethan and Violet take their seats on the bench. Kit comes over to plant a kiss on Piper's lips then he takes a seat next to his co-judges.

"Hey, why do you three look so serious all of a sudden," Joel says. "You want to go first for warm up songs, angel?"

"No. This time, I'd rather you go first." My cheeks flush. I don't mind saying vaguely dirty stuff around Joel.

But around his friends?

I'm going to die of embarrassment.

Only... no one seems to mind. If anything, they're charmed. I'm not sure what to make of the way they're looking at me. It's not like when everyone was staring like I'm from another planet.

It's more like they get why Joel married me.

Why I married him.

They see us together.

Joel nods. "As you wish." He punches in a song and turns towards me.

The lyrics to a familiar 80s song fill the screen. Joel keeps his eyes glued to me as he belts out the first verse.

He isn't a technically great singer. His pitch is a little off. But he sells every line. He thrusts his hips and strokes his mic and shoots me *fuck me* eyes.

During the breakdown, he slides into my lap and plays with my hair. He holds the mic away and leans in to whisper. "I'm going to fuck you in the bathroom in the hall."

He smiles as he shifts off my lap and goes back to seducing me from the makeshift stage.

When he's done, everyone claps. Mal and Ethan shoot Joel the same *that's more than I need to know about you* looks. It's funny. The two of them seem nothing alike, but they have the exact same mannerisms. They have the same blue eyes. Piper too.

The three of them are clearly siblings.

Me and Anne... the only things we have in common are the brown eyes and the inability to discuss our feelings.

I love my sister, but we're not all that alike. Or close.

Joel hands the mic to Mal then he takes the seat next to me. He holds me close through all the performances. Mal nails a sexy pop song. Ethan does his best impression of Tom deLong's nasally voice as he belts out Blink-182's *All The Small Things*.

Then it's Violet, channeling a rock goddess as she sings a Garbage song. This must be somewhere on Anne's playlists. It's familiar. And Violet is really into the song. The passion is written all over her face.

Kit gets up on stage and shoots Piper a panty melting look. "This is for you, baby."

The screen flashes with *I'm a Slave For You* by Britney Spears. It's not what I'd expect from a guy as stoic as Kit, but from the way Piper is turning every shade of red, I'd say it's working.

He isn't quite as obvious about his seduction as Joel, but he gets the job done.

He hands the mic to her but she shakes her head. "I need a minute."

He smiles victoriously, sits next to her, pulls her into his lap.

That makes it my turn. Okay. I can do that. I know what I want to sing too. I find my favorite sexy 80s song in the book and punch in the number.

The lyrics fill the screen. I try to sing from memory, but I don't quite manage. I'm stiff. Awkward. Unable to look at my audience.

Okay, maybe I'm not a performer.

But I do want to seduce Joel.

At least a little.

He's looking at me with his eyes wide. His expression is proud. He motions *keep going*.

I do. I look at him the entire song, but I do manage to get some feeling into my performance. When I'm done, I hand the mic to Piper.

"That was my first time," I admit.

Joel pulls me into a kiss. "Angel, that was an amazing first."

Everyone else offers similar sentiments. I can't absorb the exact words with Joel this close.

Piper takes the stage. She sings a familiar Gwen Stefani song and she does it well. When she's done, she pulls her boyfriend, erm fiancé, into a deep kiss then sends him to sit with the other judges.

"I have to confer with my opponent." Joel squeezes. "Give me a good luck kiss."

I plant a kiss on his cheek.

He shakes his head. "This is a good luck kiss." He slides his hands into my hair and pulls me into a long, deep kiss.

His tongue slides into my mouth. His movements are patient, like he's savoring this, like he has all the time in the world.

But we don't.

There's tomorrow.

Then there's our appointment.

I sigh as he pulls back. "Break a leg."

He blows me another kiss then he pulls Mal outside with him.

"I can't believe he did that." Piper bites her lip. "Kit hates to sing."

"It didn't seem like it," I tease.

She blushes. "I suppose you'll never be surprised by your husband doing something bold."

"I suppose not."

Joel is bold.

And he's confident.

And he makes me feel like it's worth being in the moment.

Maybe I can handle telling my dad about law school.

Maybe it's okay that I haven't figured out my entire life.

Joel and Mal confer in the hall for a minute. Then they're back.

He turns to Mal with a wink. "You can admit defeat right now if you want."

Mal chuckles. He punches a number into the machine and takes the mic.

Joel punches in a few more numbers then he takes a seat on the opposite bench. His eyes catch mine.

I mouth *good luck.*

He blows me a kiss.

I giggle as I catch it. It's a full-blown schoolgirl giggle. He has that affect on me. He makes me dizzy in the best possible way.

Someone flicks a switch. The lights go off. Then a polyphonic song is filling the room.

The lights flicker on. Then Mal is groaning through the first verse. Somehow, he manages to stretch every other word into a moan. It's incredibly sexy.

I'm not familiar with the original song. I can't say if Mal's version is in any way faithful to the original.

But it is amazing. And incredibly hot.

He groans through the last line of the chorus.

Then through the rest of the song.

When he's done, he shoots Joel a *top that* look and he hands off the mic.

Joel's eyes meet mine. He raises a brow *can I?*

I nod. This time, I blow him a kiss.

He mimes catching it and sliding it into his pocket.

God help me, I giggle again.

Joel wraps his hands around the microphone. "This is still for you, angel."

Lyrics to the Rhianna song *S&M* fill the screen. My cheeks flush.

He keeps his eyes on mine as he sings the first verse. He

doesn't stretch every word into a moan the way Mal did. Instead, he bleeds the last word of each line into a long moan.

He moans the melody between the verse and the chorus.

Then he's moaning all through the chorus.

He shifts his hips. He makes eye contact with everyone in the audience.

Joel gets breathy through the verse. He sounds like he's fucking hard and fast. He sounds like he's about to go over the edge.

Then he's moaning through the chorus and I'm on fire. If I didn't know better, I'd swear he was coming, not singing.

I lose track of where we are and what we're doing.

I lose track of everything but the sound of Joel's groans.

He bows as he finishes the song. People are clapping and teasing, saying something about how he does second and third, so it's his turn again.

The screen flashes. Sinful Serenade. *No Way in Hell.*

This is the song they're both singing.

It's one of Anne's favorites. She used to play it all the time. I know it well.

It's incredibly sexy.

He groans through the first verse.

Three a.m. and I can't slee-eee-eee-eep
A commooon refraaaiiiin I knoooowzw
As a sentiment, ah, uh, oh, oh it's cheap.
Someone to caaaalll
To hooold
To lo-e-e-e-e-ove
No way, uh, that word…
She smiles, mmmh, and I drift away.

God dammit. My entire body is buzzing. I let my eyes fall closed. I let the sounds of Joel's groans wash over me.

He's putting the original singer to shame.

Okay, maybe I'm a little biased.

Joel isn't nearly as on pitch as Miles is.

But the way he's moaning and groaning is every bit as good as the original song.

Better even.

He dials it up during the chorus, his eyes glued to mine. Then he's looking at his other fans, motions *give me more.*

"Sing this part with me," he groans into the mic.

And then everyone, even Mal, is singing the chorus with him.

Joel pulls his hand to his chest in a dramatic gesture. His eyes flutter closed. He belts out the last verse with all the heart he can muster.

He groans through the outro.

Then he hands the mic off to Mal, sits next to me, and whispers in my ear. "How was it?"

I try to play coy. "Not bad?"

"Not bad?" He turns his body, so he's blocking the rest of the room from view. Then he's sliding his hand under my skirt. "Should I check?"

"You were great."

He pulls his hand back to his sides and whispers in my ear. "I still want to fuck you in that bathroom."

God help me, I very much want him to fuck me in that bathroom. I nod.

"But not until we're done with this."

"Tease."

He smiles with pride.

We turn back to watch Mal's performance. It's every bit as good as Joel's, every bit as sexy as Joel's, but it doesn't affect me the same way.

It doesn't make me shudder with desire.

Joel teases me as the judges deliberate. It takes them forever.

Finally, Ethan stands up on the table. He's holding something up as the prize.

It's a Sinful Serenade CD.

He looks to Mal and Joel. "It was a close call, but the judges have decided that Joel wins this one." He bows to present the CD to Joel.

Joel nods as he takes the CD. "This is my tenth copy, but thank you."

Mal turns to him. "Real stakes this time?"

Joel raises a brow. "Terms?"

"Winner gets to cast the deciding vote on the album name."

Joel looks back to Kit and Ethan. All four of the guys share a look.

They all nod.

"Mal-style heavy breathing?" Joel asks.

"Unless you're afraid of a challenge," Mal teases.

They shake.

Joel's going to pant through another handful of songs.

God help me.

Chapter Thirty-One

JOEL

Technically, I lose the Mal-style sing off.

Really, I win by a landslide.

Bella's cheeks are flushed. Her tongue is sliding over her lips. She's pressing her knees together like she can't stand how wet she is.

She's been smiling all night.

Okay. I've paid more attention to the blushing and the groaning and the *fuck, I need you, Joel* looks.

But I've seen the way her eyes light up when she laughs. Happiness consumes her body the same way despair does. It's in her pretty brown eyes, in her relaxed shoulders, in her slight hip tilt.

I'm still not used to a woman liking me beyond *oooh, famous guy* or *I want to fuck him again*. Sure, I'm friends with Piper and Violet. I'm friends with lots of people.

But I'm not used to being in a relationship.

Probably should have thought about that before I got married, but I've never been one to do things in order.

Making her happy feels so fucking good. And right now, she's fucking ecstatic.

She's laughing with Piper and Violet over Ethan's impression of Mal.

Then over Ethan's impression of me.

Then over Piper's impression of Mal.

Shit, everybody takes a turn doing their best Mal impression.

Even Bella.

Hers isn't quite as bold as mine, or Ethan's, or Kit's, but it's good. It's funny, silly, hot as hell.

She's having such a good time.

I want this for her. I want her this happy all the time.

I'm almost tempted to hold off on dragging her to the bathroom and having my way with her.

Almost, but not quite.

After she hands off the mic, I wrap my arms around her.

She melts into my touch as she looks up at me. Her lips press together. Her eyes scream *please*.

She motions to the door.

I lean in to whisper. "Bathroom on the right. I'll meet you there in five minutes."

She doesn't say anything about how we could wait until we're at home where we can fuck on the bed. Or the couch.

She wants me so badly she's shaking.

Her breath warms my ear as she whispers. "Don't make me wait."

Fuck, I love when she gets bossy and demanding. I watch her hips sway as she walks away. That dress is tight on her lush ass. It fills me with all sorts of ideas.

Soon.

But, right now, I want to be deep in her cunt.

Damn, I'm getting hard just thinking about setting her on the counter, spreading her legs, and filling her.

I lean against the wall, attempting to pay attention to Violet and Ethan's Disney duet. It's cute, and I'm happy for them, but it's about as entertaining as one of my father's programming lectures at the moment.

Kit must know I'm in pain. He comes over and copies my pose. "I've never seen you this happy."

"I'm happy all the time."

"Not like this." He smiles. "It's good to see."

"Thanks." I guess. There's something about his look. It's the kind of look I usually give everybody. He's getting at something.

"Mal should pick the album title. He does write all the lyrics."

"Sure."

"You tell her to wait for you in the bathroom?"

I laugh. "Maybe."

"You might as well go now. We all know what you're doing."

"We're honeymooners."

"I'll give you some Joel-style advice." He chuckles. "Don't fuck it up."

I have to laugh. It is exactly what I would say.

"You really like her, huh?"

I nod.

"You love her?"

"I think I might."

His smile widens. "Shit, I'm out a hundred bucks."

"You bet against me?"

"With Piper."

"Hard to complain about Piper winning." I turn to Kit. "How did you deal with this?"

He raises a brow.

"I feel like I'm on a fucking roller coaster. When she

smiles, I'm warm all over. When she's upset, it's like the sun is never going to come out again."

His smile widens.

"What?"

"You're in love with her."

"This isn't going away?"

He shakes his head. His eyes are lit up with enthusiasm. "Damn. Joel Young is in love. Never thought I'd see the day." He chuckles. "It looks good on you."

"It feels good." Exhausting, but good.

"Go make love to your wife," he teases.

"Please never say *make love* to me again."

He chuckles. "You gonna tell her?"

"Eventually."

"You're scared."

Maybe.

"Shit. Never thought I'd see that day." He nudges me towards the door.

The man is mocking me, but he has good advice.

I nod goodbye and slip out of the room. The bathroom is at the end of the hall. I knock once. "Hey."

Bella pulls the door open. "It's small."

It is. But I'll make it work. I slip inside and lock the door.

There's little room to maneuver, but it's enough.

Bella holds out her clasped hands. Her eyes light up as she peels them back. She's holding her lacy pink panties.

Fuck, the mix of joy and need on her face—

The way she's teasing me—

I want to fill her with every kind of pleasure.

I am in love with her.

She runs her fingers through my hair. "You okay?"

I nod. This is a lot to take in. I pull her mouth against mine and I kiss her hard.

Words aren't happening.

My body needs to get the message across.

I bring my hands to her hips and lift her onto the countertop. She leans back, spreading her legs wide.

God damn, the sight of Bella on the sink, her legs spread, her cunt on display…

I drop to my knees and plant my lips along her thigh. I need to taste her, to feel her pleasure.

I lick her hard and fast.

"Joel." Her hands go to my hair. "I can't keep quiet."

"Don't. I want to hear you."

She groans.

I bury my face between her legs, tasting and teasing every inch of her. I lick her until she's dripping off my lips, until she's so wet I can barely keep a grip on her legs.

She's shaking so hard she's about to fall off the counter.

I press her thighs into the counter and I suck on her clit.

Bella groans, tugging at my hair as she comes on my face.

Her thighs press against my fingers.

Her cunt pulses against my lips. She gets wetter. Sweeter.

"Fuck me. Now." She grabs onto my shirt and pulls me up.

I slide my jeans off my hips. Then the boxers.

My hands go to her hips. I hold her in place as I tease her with my tip.

"Joel." She tugs at my t-shirt to pull me into a deep kiss.

Affection pours from her lips.

And mine.

I'm about to fuck her hard and fast in a dirty bathroom and all I can think is *I love her*.

My tongue slides into her mouth. I steady her hips. Slowly, I thrust inside her.

She groans against my mouth.

I'm inside her and I'm thinking *does she love me too?*

There must be something wrong with me.

No more thinking.

I need to feel every second of this.

I break our kiss. I watch pleasure fill her pretty brown eyes as I thrust into her.

She stares back at me.

All that affection passes between us.

She tugs at my t-shirt to pull me into a deep kiss. Her hips rock in time with mine. Her nails dig into my skin.

We stay glued like that until she's groaning with pleasure, coming on my cock.

She has to break free of our kiss to scream my name.

Then her lips are on mine again. And I'm filling her with deep thrusts. I'm fucking her so hard the mirror is shaking.

Fuck.

I go over the edge.

My cock pulses as I fill her. I groan into her neck.

She groans back against my neck.

We move together, groaning together, until I've spilled every drop.

When I'm finished, I help her clean up.

I help her back into her clothes.

And I kiss her.

I kiss her like her lips are oxygen.

At home, we collapse in bed.

Bella nestles into my chest. She intertwines her fingers

with mine and rubs her index and middle fingers over my wedding ring. "I… I think this is the first time I've really been happy in forever."

My chest warms. Fuck, my entire body is warm. "Yeah?"

She laughs. "You really are unlike everyone else I know." She turns so she's looking up into my eyes. "You're one of a kind, Joel Young."

I run my fingers through her dark hair. "Right back at you, Bella Chase."

"I'm not sure about that. But thank you." She presses her lips to mine.

Fuck, I really love kissing her. I run my fingers through her hair. "You're all mine tomorrow."

Her smile spreads over her cheeks.

"Don't look so happy. We're getting up at six a.m.," I tease.

Still, her smile gets wider. "I can't help it."

Chapter Thirty-Two

BELLA

It's still dark when we wake. But it's hard to complain about anything when Joel's body is pressed against mine.

God, it's comfortable in his arms. It takes me most of an hour to drag myself out of bed.

After a quick breakfast of scrambled eggs and black tea (black coffee for Joel), I dress in my most comfortable outfit and follow Joel to the car. Again, he refuses to tell me where we're going.

This time, he admits that my jeans, tank top, cardigan, canvas sneakers combination is ideal for our destination.

Even after two cups of tea, I'm tired. I rest my head against the window, watching the sun rise into the increasingly bright and blue sky. We must take four different highways. There's traffic on each. It's a lot for my *take the subway everywhere* mind to comprehend.

I'm about to get cranky over how long the drive is taking when we pull off the highway.

We pull into a massive parking lot.

Universal Studios Hollywood.

I rub my eyes. I pinch myself. I suck in a deep breath and let out a shallow exhale.

The sign still says *Universal Studios Hollywood*.

Suddenly, I'm flush with energy. I tap my feet together. I tug at my seatbelt. "You're taking me to the Harry Potter thing?"

"They have other attractions."

"Who cares about the other attractions?" I'm so excited I'm bouncing. It's right there on the sign: *Now open: The Wizarding World of Harry Potter*. "We're going to see Hogsmead. And Hogwarts. And we can have wands choose us. And get robes. And drink Butterbeer."

Joel's smile lights up his green eyes. "Damn, I thought you'd be more excited," he teases.

"Joel!" I squeeze his hand. Then I'm rambling about every single attraction I want to see.

I keep rambling about *Harry Potter* as we park in the VIP section. As Joel dons a baseball cap and sunglasses. As he takes my hand and leads me to the entrance—we already have VIP tickets that let us skip most of the lines in the park.

I'm still rambling about how much I wish I was more like fan favorite bossy, know-it-all Hermoine when leans in to kiss me.

His smile is so wide it's about to bust off his face.

His fingers skim my cheeks.

My skin buzzes from his touch. It's not just the heat of desire. There's a warmth of affection too.

He's taking me to the *Harry Potter* exhibit. And he's listening to my fan ramblings. He's really listening, not tuning it out the way Anne and Dad do.

He really cares what I think.

"You look so happy," I say.

"I'm happy you're happy."

He is.

The thought makes me warm all over.

He slides his arm around me as I unwrap my map. There *are* all sorts of other attractions, but none of them matter to me. I head straight towards *The Wizarding World of Harry Potter.*

Joel leans in to whisper, "You can be just as bossy as Hermoine."

"That's quite a high bar."

"Even so."

"You mean when we're… during sex?"

"Yes. But right now," he pulls me tighter, "you're taking charge, angel. If I don't follow you, I'm going to lose you."

That is true. I turn to Joel with a smile. I'm teasing him back. "Don't tell me you suddenly have a problem with me being bossy?"

He smiles back at me. "As long as you know I'm going to be the one in charge when we get home."

Desire pools in my core. Dammit, I want him already. I want him pressing me against the wall and issuing illicit orders.

But there's more than that. The way he's smiling, with all that affection—I want that just as much.

I want his heart as much as I want his body.

"Whatever do you mean?" I tease him back as we take the path on the left. The concrete is lined with bushes and trees. It's still very much a theme park.

This time, Joel doesn't whisper. He says this loud enough that anyone can hear. "I'm going to finally fuck that gorgeous ass of yours."

My cheeks flush.

My chest.

My entire body is red.

No one is gawking. No one is grabbing security to get us kicked out of the park.

"You okay, angel?" Joel runs his fingers through my hair. "You look a little flushed."

"I…" Um. I'm incredibly flushed. I bite my tongue. I squeeze my hands against my sides. Still, I'm hot all over. "Okay."

"Okay?"

"Don't talk about this kind of thing in front of Hogwarts."

Oh my God.

That's Hogwarts.

Okay, it's not really Hogwarts. Even from here, it's clearly too small. But it looks just like the wizard school, this grand grey castle on top of a rocky mountain.

We're standing at the start of the attraction. The street in front of us is modeled after Hogsmead, the small town by the wizard school. With the sun shining, and the sales kiosks, and the tourists in *Hollywood* t-shirts, I can tell I'm in a theme park.

But when I look up, at the castle, at the shop signs and the sloped roofs, and the fake snow atop the sloped roofs…

I throw my arms around Joel. "This is amazing."

He hugs me back. "It's just the beginning."

He's right. It's just the beginning.

For us, this really could be the beginning.

Thoughts of our relationship fade as I pull Joel into the attraction. No, I refuse to call it the attraction. It's as close to Hogsmead as I'm ever going to get.

I squeeze Joel's hand as I lead him around town. My conscious thoughts fade. My inner fan girl takes over. I squeal over sips of Butterbeer. It tastes just like cream soda.

All day, Joel holds me close.

All day, Joel smiles and laughs and gasps with me.

My happiness really is his happiness.

This is perfect.

He's perfect.

WE DON'T LEAVE THE PARK UNTIL TEN MINUTES BEFORE closing. My muscles are sore and achy. My stomach is stuffed with *Harry Potter* themed food (not the greatest, really. Theme park British food leaves something to be desired). My mind is full of sights and sounds.

And my heart—

My heart is so full it's ready to burst.

I squeeze Joel's hand as we pull out of the parking lot. He's still smiling wide. He's still looking at me like my happiness is the only thing he needs.

His voice is bright. "You look sharp in that Ravenclaw jersey."

"You think?"

"Blue and nerdy suits you."

"It's not too much?" I'm also sporting a matching scarf. And a track jacket. And a robe. Okay, and a keychain. A wand.

We did the whole, go to Olivander's, let a wand choose you thing.

And it was amazing.

He's been teasing me mercilessly all day, but he's done it in such a loving way. Like he's endeared by my love of *Harry Potter*. He wants to share it with me.

"I always thought I was a Hufflepuff," I say.

"The nice ones."

"They're also loyal and diligent. And humble." I tug at his scarf. "Not a good fit for you."

"Fuck no." He flips his scarf over his shoulder. "I'm

trusting you, that these gold and crimson guys brag the most."

I nod. "You must know Gryffindor. All the characters are in that house."

He smiles. "After today, I'm pretty sure I can ace any *Harry Potter* trivia quiz. They're the brave ones."

"Yeah. And they're loyal, and blunt, and maybe a little... impulsive."

He laughs. "If the scarf fits..." He turns back to the road.

I sink into my seat. "I don't want to be the nice, hard-working, humble girl anymore."

"You're not. You're nerdy, creative, and bookish. You're not allowed to have traits other than the ones described by your house," he teases. "So don't let me catch you being cunning or impulsive."

I play with my wedding ring. "It's a little late for that."

Joel laughs. "True."

"I know it's a little silly to put so much stock in which Hogwarts house I belong to."

He shakes his head. "It's not, and don't do that. Don't put yourself down like that."

"I'm twenty-two."

"So fucking what? These books mean something to you. They took you out of your life. They gave you a place to belong. A way to look at the world. That fucking matters. I don't make music for the money or the fame."

"Or the groupies."

He sticks his tongue out. "I never picked up women at shows. That's not the relationship I want to have with my fans."

"You don't want them to believe they only love you because they want to fuck you?"

He cocks his head to one side. "Maybe."

"Aww. You don't want to get by on your looks."

"Is that a crime?"

"No. It's cute."

"I don't mind playing that card."

"I saw your show. And that poster."

He laughs. "That poster is grade A spank bank material. And I get that the hot rock star fantasy is part of why I get to do this. I don't mind—"

"You love the attention."

"Maybe."

"And you're okay playing a role."

He nods. "It lets me spend my life making music. I get to brighten people's lives, three minutes at a time."

"You do."

"Yeah?"

"My sister… when she listens to Dangerous Noise, she has that look. Like she's where she belongs. Like someone understands her."

"Like you with these books."

Like me with Joel.

He's still smiling.

He's still looking at me like I light the stars.

I open my mouth, but words won't find the way to my tongue. I can't explain my feelings for him. Or his feelings for me.

I've never felt like I belonged anywhere.

But right now, I'm sure I'm where I belong.

"Thank you." It's all I can manage.

"Hey. You're the one who bought me this incredibly phallic source of power." He motions to his wand. "If I want to make magic, I have to grab my stick and recite the proper words."

"Joel…" I can't exactly protest. He's dead on about the wands being phallic. "You're ridiculous."

"You love it."

"I do." And I might even love him. But I'm not ready to face that possibility yet. Not with everything else hanging over my head. "Tomorrow is our appointment."

He nods. "It is."

"Are you thinking… what are you thinking?"

He says nothing.

Shit.

My need to fill the silence catches up with me. "I have to talk to my dad soon. Whatever happens tomorrow, I have to tell him about law school." And I have to hold strong. The telling him is the easy part compared to the *not crumbling under the weight of his disapproval* part.

"You're making leaving school official?"

"I think so. After I tell Dad." I swallow hard.

"You can do it." He rubs the space between my thumb and forefinger with his thumb.

I take a deep breath and exhale slowly. Already, the joy of the day is fading. Clouds are forming over my head. It's getting cold in here.

The scenery is getting ugly.

Joel's voice is calm, even. "Say it again."

"Which part?"

"That you don't want to be a lawyer."

My shoulders tense up. I have to force the words off my lips. "I don't want to be a lawyer."

"Again."

This time, it's a little easier. "I don't want to be a lawyer." My exhale breaks up the tension forming in my upper back. "I don't want to go back to law school."

"What do you want?" Joel squeezes my hand. "Besides my *wand*?"

"Ew."

"Baby, you want my wand so bad you're panting."

Maybe. I shake my head. "Wand is not a sexy euphemism."

"But this is the most powerful wand of all time."

I have to laugh. There's something about Joel. He's derailing me with sex, sure, but it's what I need right now.

I better tell him this now. Before he pushes my mind straight into the gutter.

"I'm not sure what I want to do. If I want to take that job offer from Alessandra... She's only offering it because you're my husband."

"That's how the world works."

"Even so." My voice is soft. What if Joel isn't my husband anymore tomorrow? She won't still want me as her assistant.

"You'd be good at it."

"Maybe."

"Absolutely." He looks to me. "You think you'd like it?"

"Yeah. Maybe I wouldn't love it, but it would be a good first job as a law school dropout."

"You get used to being a university drop out. Trust me."

I do.

That's the problem.

I trust Joel more than I've ever trusted anyone.

If we get to that appointment tomorrow and neither one of us calls it off...

I can't think about this right now. The anxiety is threatening to swallow me whole.

I take a deep breath and exhale slowly. "I, um, I'd like to get home as quickly as possible."

His voice drops to that low demanding tone. "Yeah?"

"Did you mean what you said before?"

He cocks a brow.

"About... wanting to..." I clear my throat. I've gained

a lot of sexual confidence, but I'm not even near Joel's level.

"You want my cock in your ass?"

"Yes."

"Not sure I can drive in this state, but yeah. Of course I meant that."

"Oh. Well—"

"Angel, I want to hear this. But if I want to get home alive—"

"It's that distracting?"

He clears his throat.

Feminine power fills me. I'm distracting Joel enough he's worried he's going to crash the car.

Ahem.

That is a concern.

I go back to babbling about *Harry Potter*.

Chapter Thirty-Three

BELLA

Joel is patient as we park the car, as we walk through the lobby, as we take the tiny elevator to the third floor.

He keeps a calm grip on my hand as he leads me down the hallway.

His posture changes as he unlocks the door.

It's like he's finally out of his cage.

In one swift motion, he pulls me inside.

He pins me to the door as he turns the lock.

His green eyes fix on me.

Then they're fluttering closed.

His lips crash into mine.

His hand slides between my legs. His fingers stroke my inner thigh. Even with my jeans in the way, the friction is divine.

I part my lips to make way for his tongue.

He tastes so good.

I need this so badly.

Need him so badly.

Bit by bit, all of my senses turn on. I'm not tired anymore. I'm wide awake.

Every inch of my body needs Joel. It doesn't matter that I had him yesterday.

I might not have him tomorrow.

I think I will.

I hope I will…

I should bring it up. We should talk about it. Like adults.

But I can't bring myself to do anything but kiss him back.

I need him right now.

I need to know he's mine.

That I'm his.

He pulls my scarf undone and tosses it aside. Then his hands are sliding under my t-shirt and he's grinding his hips against mine.

He's hard.

I want that.

I want everything with him.

But the thought of Joel filling my ass makes me clench up everywhere.

Can I do this?

What if it hurts?

His hips rock against mine.

With his size, it's going to hurt.

I try to push my thoughts aside as I kiss him back, but they won't go.

It's going to hurt. I'm not going to be exciting or dirty or bold enough for him.

I'm not going to be enough for him.

He's going to realize I'm a mess and run away.

What then?

His eyes flutter open as he pulls back. "You're nervous."

I nod. "I'm sorry."

He cocks a brow. "For what?"

"I'm not sure I can do this."

"Don't be sorry about that." His eyes bore into mine. His expression gets serious, caring. "Do you want to?"

"Well, you—"

"No, Bella. Do *you* want this?"

"Yes." I bite my lip. "I feel so dirty, wanting this."

"Say it."

"I…"

He cups my cheek with his palm, then he's rubbing my temple with his thumb. "Tell me where you want my cock."

My cheeks flush. "I…"

"You're not getting it unless you tell me."

I swallow hard and stare back into Joel's eyes. I *do* want this. And I can say it. "I want you to fuck… I want you to fuck my ass."

God, I'm red everywhere.

If Mom could hear me, she'd be turning over in her grave.

Chases are nice girls.

And nice girls don't demand anal sex.

Nice girls don't say *I want you to fuck my ass.*

Joel pins me to the door with his hips. "Say it again, angel."

This time, I don't hesitate. "I want you to fuck my ass." Still, my cheeks flush. I stare back into his eyes. "Will it hurt?"

"A little." He rubs my temple with his thumb. "If it's too much, tell me."

"You won't be mad?"

His brows screw in confusing. "Why would I be mad?"

"I don't know…"

"Don't bend yourself into some shape for me, Bella. Tell me what you want." His eyes bore into mine. "Promise you'll tell me if it hurts."

"Okay."

"Or if you're too nervous."

"I'm pretty nervous."

"That's all right. We don't have to do it today."

But we might have to do it today.

There might not be anything after tomorrow.

Neither one of us has suggested canceling the appointment.

Feelings are swirling around my stomach. I care about him. More. More than like. But I can't say it yet.

I have to be sure.

I can't… "Kiss me. Please."

"Promise."

"I promise I'll tell you if it's too much."

He nods. His eyes flutter closed. His lips brush against mine. Softly. Then harder. His tongue slides into my mouth.

He slides his first two fingers into the belt loop of my jeans and motions *come with me*.

I follow him to the bedroom.

Moonlight flows in through the curtains and bounces off the white sheets. Joel pulls me onto the bed.

He plants his body next to mine. "Close your eyes."

I do.

"I want you to feel good, Bella."

"Okay."

"I'm not going to hurt you."

I nod.

"You trust me?"

Again, I nod. There's no doubt in my mind. I do trust Joel. I trust him with my body.

And with my heart.

Maybe even forever.

He presses his palm into my lower back as he pulls me closer.

His lips brush against mine.

His hands slide under my shirt.

My body buzzes from the feeling of his fingertips on my stomach. My sides. My ribs.

He cups my breasts over my bra.

The soft fabric presses against my nipples as he rubs me.

I break free of his kiss to groan. "More."

He rubs harder. My bra is too thick. I can't feel enough.

"More," I groan again.

He slides his hands into my bra cups, one at a time. His thumbs toy with my nipples. He rubs me up and down, left and right, in zig zags, in slow circles.

Fuck, those circles.

I let out an incomprehensible groan.

My eyelids flutter closed.

My lips find his.

I kiss Joel deeply as he toys with my nipples. Each brush of his thumbs sends another wave of pleasure to my core. I forget what we're doing here. I forget everything but the desperate ache between my legs.

He presses his index finger to my nipple, holding it in place so his thumb can work its magic.

It's more pressure.

More pleasure.

I dig my hands into his hair to hold his mouth against mine.

I kiss him harder.

My body takes over. I sling my leg over his hip. I grind my crotch against his.

There's too much fabric in the way.

"Joel," I groan.

He presses his lips against my neck. "Yeah?" It's a tease. He's waiting for my demand.

"Make me come."

His voice gets heavy, breathless. "Fuck yes." He drags his lips down my neck. Then he's pulling my top over my head.

His eyes go wide as he peels off my bra. It's like he's never seen me naked before.

It's like he's never seen breasts before.

His stare makes me hot all over.

"Now," I groan.

He takes his time sliding his hand down my torso. Dragging his lips down my neck, over my collarbone.

His lips close around my nipple.

He sucks on me as he unbuttons my jeans. Undoes my zipper. His fingertips press my panties into my skin.

He rubs me over my panties.

The damn fabric is still in the way.

"Joel," I breathe. "Please."

Still, he rubs me over my panties. The pressure gets harder. Harder. Pleasure fills my pelvis, but it's not enough. I need his hands on my skin.

I push my jeans off my hips.

Then the panties.

I shimmy out of both garments. The damn things get stuck on my ankles. I kick them off so hard my foot smacks into Joel's shin.

He gives me a long, slow once over.

The desire in his eyes still excites me. It still makes me feel like the most beautiful woman in the universe.

I stare into his gorgeous green eyes as I take his hand and place it between my legs.

He doesn't tease. He rubs my clit with those slow circles. It's exactly what I need.

Pleasure knots in my core.

Almost.

Almost.

He leans down to suck on my nipple. Damn, the pressure of his soft wet tongue. It's almost too much to take.

Joel growls against my skin. "Say my name, angel."

My eyelids press together. "Joel."

He rubs me harder.

There.

I scream his name again and again as I come. Pleasure spills through my limbs. The world goes white. I can't see or feel anything but bliss.

Joel presses his fingertips to my lips. The gesture is so affectionate that I nearly forget what we're about to do. Then he presses his fingers into my mouth, and I taste myself on them, and I remember.

His eyes meet mine. "You ready?"

"No, but I trust you."

He nods and pulls off his t-shirt. I take my time exploring the lines of his chest. His stomach.

He groans as I cup him over his jeans.

I unbutton, unzip, slide the things off his hips.

He pushes them to his ankles.

Then the boxers.

Joel's naked in bed with me.

I stare the same way he did. He's still the best thing I've ever seen.

He kisses me hard and deep. When he pulls back, he shifts to grab something from the bedside drawer.

A bottle of lube.

And a sleek vibrator.

"Is that—" I'm not sure what I'm asking. Only that my muscles are threatening to clench up again.

"It's new." He runs his fingers through my hair. "Look at me, angel."

I do.

"I've got you. Just close your eyes and let me lead."

My eyelids flutter closed.

He plants a soft kiss on my lips. Then it's harder. Deeper. He lifts one leg and sets it over my hip.

His fingers brush against my clit. My sex. My perineum.

My anus.

It's the softest touch, but it's enough to wake up all my nerves.

It's different.

But not bad.

Not at all bad.

Joel squirts lube onto his fingers. This time, the brush of his fingers is slick.

He does it again. And again. He does it until I'm rocking my hips, pressing my body against his hand.

He slides a finger inside me.

Fuck. That's intense.

I stare into his eyes.

He stares back. *More?*

I nod. "Slowly."

Slowly, very slowly, he pushes his finger deeper. Deeper. His eyes go back to mine. He gives me that same look.

I nod. I want more. It's intense, but I want more.

He adds more lube and works me with his finger. I let

my eyes flutter closed. I forget everything but the sensations.

More lube. A second finger.

Damn. That's a lot of pressure. But it feels good.

Dirty.

Like I'm offering myself to him.

He works me with both fingers. Then it's more lube. And he's going deeper, faster.

He pulls his hand back. "Get on your hands and knees, angel."

Slowly, I shift into position on all fours, my legs spread as wide as they can go.

Joel positions his body behind mine. He spreads my cheeks, then he's working me with his fingers again. One. More lube. Two. More lube. Three.

I want more.

I want him inside me.

I can't believe how badly I want it.

"Please," I breathe.

He groans. Still, he works me. Every single one of my nerves is awake. I'm really ready for this.

He pulls his hand back. Then he's spreading lube over his cock. His hands go to my hips.

His tip strains against my anus.

Slowly, he enters me.

Fuck.

That's a lot more intense than his fingers.

But it feels fucking good.

Different, but good.

He starts with shallow thrusts. Then he goes deeper. Faster. Harder.

He reaches for the vibrator with his clean hand. Then he's turning it on, dragging it down my pelvis.

He presses it against my clit.

Against my sex.

He's going to—

Fuck.

"Yes," I groan.

He teases my sex with the toy again and again.

Then he slides it inside me.

Fuck, the pulsing of the toy—

Him thrusting into my ass—

I lose track of everything but pleasure. Of the overwhelming sense of being filled.

Of being his.

My fingers dig into the sheets.

He fills me with the toy.

He fills me with his cock.

"Fuck, Bella," he groans. "You feel so fucking good."

His movements get harder, faster. His voice drops to that low demanding tone. Only he isn't letting out any words.

It's all groans.

God, I love the sound of his groans.

I love how dirty I feel.

How full I feel.

With the next thrust of the toy, I go over the edge. I groan his name, my hips rocking as I come. Pleasure spreads out to my fingers and toes.

He's still rocking into me.

Still fucking me with that toy.

The sounds and sights of the room blur together. The sensations in my body blur together. Everything spins into this intense pressure. This intense pleasure.

Then Joel is groaning, shaking, digging his nails into my skin.

The pulsing of his cock pushes me over the edge.

Then he's there.

And we're coming together.

Groaning together.

Collapsing as a sticky, dirty mess together.

I'm really his.

And he's really mine.

Right now, I really believe this is a forever kind of thing.

Any other possibilities are too horrifying to consider.

Chapter Thirty-Four

JOEL

We shower together. We watch the last *Harry Potter* movie on the couch together. We go to bed together.

Neither of us says a fucking word about tomorrow.

Fuck, when did I become a coward?

Bella is sound asleep in my bed. In my arms.

It's a scene straight out of a movie. The moonlight is pouring over her closed eyes. Her chest rises and falls with steady inhales and exhales.

She looks comfortable.

Safe.

Certain.

Okay, she's asleep. She may be dreaming, but she's not thinking anything.

I don't want a divorce.

But I've been pushing her too fucking hard.

I can't do that here.

I need to listen to what she wants.

I should wake her up. Insist we deal with this now.

But I can't bring myself to do it.

Tomorrow.

We'll talk about this first thing tomorrow.

Before the ball is in motion.

Before this is over forever.

SLEEP ELUDES ME. SOMETIME AROUND FIVE A.M., I GET UP. I head to the gym down the street to sweat out all my thoughts. I head home. I shower.

I down several cups of coffee and a plate of eggs and bacon.

None of it tastes like anything.

None of it wakes me up.

Fuck, loving someone is difficult. I'm actually nervous. I can't remember the last time I was nervous about anything.

I watch the sun climb into the sky. It casts everything in an orange glow. Then it's that soft blue light of dawn.

In the bedroom, Bella stirs.

A few moments later, she opens the door and steps into the main room.

Her eyes meet mine. She stares at me like I have the power to crush her heart into a thousand tiny pieces.

Fuck.

I'm staring back with exactly the same expression.

"Joel. Um." She pulls her arms over her chest and rubs her triceps with her palms. "I… Um…"

"Yeah?"

"I should brush my teeth." She spins on her heels and locks herself in the bathroom.

I take a long sip of my coffee. It's still lacking taste, but the familiarity of it is almost comforting.

I can't let her dodge this.

I can't dodge it.

One of us needs to say something.

But when she steps out of the bathroom, my lips refuse to part. My tongue refuses to cooperate.

I stare back at her with that *don't break my heart expression.*

And say nothing.

Not one fucking thing.

Chapter Thirty-Five

BELLA

I hide out in the bedroom, poring over my wardrobe choices.

My clothing selection is limited. There are two dresses nice enough for a meeting at a law firm. One is dirty. That means I don't really have a decision.

It's emerald green pencil dress or nothing.

The dress is formal. Appropriate for a settlement conference. But it's not right for the end of my marriage to Joel.

How can it be ending?

He's not saying anything.

I'm not saying anything.

This, us getting a divorce, is the plan.

As long as we continue the silent staring contest, this is what's happening.

I change into my dress and I attempt to pep talk myself into calling this off.

Joel, let's stay married.

Joel, let's cancel this appointment.

Joel, please, fuck me now. Tell me you love me. Make me believe it. Make me believe I'm not out of my fucking mind wanting to stay married to someone I met a week ago.

By the time I have my hair in a bun and my makeup perfect, I almost believe I can say those words.

I touch up my pink lipstick. For luck, I guess.

I slip into a pink cardigan.

I step into my heels.

Fuck, even with all this makeup, I look as washed out and vacant as I feel.

My heels are more awkward than usual. My legs are jelly. It takes great concentration just to walk into the kitchen.

"Hey," I whisper.

"Hey," he whispers back. His eyes meet mine. For a split second, they fill with something luminous. Then they're dark, and he's staring at his coffee. He motions to the kettle. "It should still be warm."

"Thank you." I move into the kitchen and fix a cup of tea, but I'm going through the motions. The water is steaming.

It's hot enough to scald, but it feels like nothing on my tongue.

It tastes like nothing.

Joel, is this what you want?

Joel, tell me what you're thinking.

Joel…

Fuck, I don't know what to say here. My thoughts are going in circles. In my head, the divorce still makes sense.

But in my heart…

Joel fills his mug with coffee from the carafe. Still, he doesn't look at me.

I'm only barely managing to look at him. His eyes are filled with frustration, but he's not tense. Not exactly. His shoulders and jaw are soft.

He accepts this.

Is it what he wants or is he only barely tolerating it?

I won't know unless I ask.

But when I try, the words won't get out.

My mouth is dry. Finishing my cup of tea doesn't help.

I can't bring myself to ask. Hell, I can't manage to find any words much less get them off my lips.

I sit on the stool next to Joel's.

He turns towards me. Finally, he meets my gaze. "You want me to make eggs?"

My stomach is spinning. Food might help, but I'm not willing to risk it. "No thanks."

"We'll leave in twenty." He slides off his stool. "I should get dressed."

"Sure." I press my palms into my thighs. As much as I appreciate Joel in a pair of boxers, I have to agree that he *should* put on slacks and a collared shirt.

The thought of him in a suit does something to me. It makes it hard to remember we're heading to our divorce.

It fills my head with images of stripping Joel out of his suit, of binding his wrists with his tie and forcing him to watch me touch myself, of need filling his green eyes.

THE REALITY OF JOEL IN A SUIT IS A HUNDRED TIMES better than my mental image. The slate fabric brings out the grey in his eyes. His one shade darker tie does too. It would look so perfect around his wrists. Or mine. Honestly, I don't care. I just want his body pressed against mine again.

I just want his eyes filling with desire.

With his hair neatly combed, and his suit covering most

of his tattoos, Joel really does look like a nice guy I could bring home to Dad.

No matter what, Dad won't like Joel. I'm not sure it's possible for my dad to like a guy I married in Vegas. But Dad will come around once he realizes how successful Joel is. How well Joel treats me. How much Joel...

Well, I guess I don't know if Joel loves me.

I can't blame him for his silence. It's not as if I'm getting any words off my tongue.

I contemplate my inability to open my mouth during our incredibly silent drive. There isn't much traffic and we aren't going far. The drive only takes ten minutes, maybe twenty, but it feels like hours pass.

My entire body is cold, numb.

Then we pull into the parking garage, hand the keys to the valet, and step into the elevator and my head starts spinning.

This is really happening.

In the next hour.

Neither of us is stopping it.

Fuck.

The elevator is a tiny space. And Joel is sticking closer than necessary. His palm is still pressed against mine, his grip firm and steady.

There are no signs of nervousness in his posture or his expression.

He's a rock.

Or maybe this is what he wants.

Maybe he's looking forward to being done with this.

My eyes go to the sign on the wall.

Lux and Lawrence. Third floor. The green light flashes Lobby. Then Two. Three.

The mirrored doors slide open.

Joel nods to the lobby. "You ready?"

No, but this is as ready as I'm going to be. "Thank you."

My legs wobble as I step into the lobby. It's a beautiful office. The walls are cream with oak accents. The furniture is all brown and grey hues, much of it the same oak hue.

I would be lucky to work somewhere this beautiful. With these big windows. With all this light. With a view of the crystal blue waters of the marina and the ocean behind it.

Joel squeezes my hand. He leans in to whisper. "You okay?"

No. Definitely not. But I can't exactly be cuddling up and taking his comfort right now. I force myself to smile. "I will be." In theory.

His expression gets incredulous. Still, he moves towards the front desk.

His hand stays glued to mine.

"Chase and Young," he says.

"The divorce. Of course." The woman at the front desk tries to paste a smile on her face, but she keeps staring slack-jawed. Her gaze stays on our pressed together hands, even as she presses the intercom. "Chase and Young are here."

Our names sound good together. Like a law firm. Or a married couple. It rolls off the tongue, Mrs. Bella Chase and Mr. Joel Young. It looks great on a Christmas card. Mom and Dad always sent Christmas cards, with pictures. Dad stopped after she died.

We could pick up the tradition.

Only we can't.

We can't do anything.

We're ending our relationship. By the end of the day, we will no longer be married.

This will end, and I'll fly back to New York, and Joel

will become that interesting story I tell my friends. *Did you hear the one about how I accidentally married a rock star?* And we'll all laugh about how improbable it is that I did anything bad. Because I'll have some new clean cut doctor-slash-lawyer-slash-MBA husband.

No.

I can't do this. "Joel, I don't know—"

A voice interrupts. "Sweetheart, how are you?"

That's my dad.

I look up, and sure enough, he's there, in a sleek black suit, standing next to the man who must be my lawyer.

The other man extends his hand. "Nice to meet you, Ms. Chase. I'm Leonard Shaw. I'll be your counsel."

"Nice to meet you." I pull my hand from Joel's to shake his. I can feel Joel's posture stiffening from the change in the air. It gets colder, harsher. Or maybe I'm imagining things. "Daddy, what are you doing here?"

"You think I'm going to let you do this with a stranger?" he asks.

"Oh." That's fair. As far as Dad knows, Joel is my one-week mistake.

Neither one of us is calling this off.

Which means…

I guess Dad is right.

My stomach churns. I look into Joel's eyes. I can still see all that affection in them, but I guess that's not enough.

He's silent.

I'm silent.

There's another lawyer coming towards us. He's not as neat as Mr. Shaw. His hair is shaggy. He almost looks like Joel's brother, but Joel only has a sister.

He nods hello to Joel. "Nice to see you again, Mr. Young."

Joel nods back. His mood must be as shitty as mine,

because he doesn't make a joke or ask the guy to call him Joel or your highness. He doesn't even smile.

The lawyer turns to me. "You too, Ms. Chase. I'm Adrian Lux." He offers his hand.

I barely manage to shake.

That's Joel's lawyer.

And this is my lawyer.

And that's my dad.

I motion from my dad to Joel. "Oh, I'm sorry. Daddy, this is Joel. Joel this is my father."

Dad offers his hand. "Vincent Chase."

Joel shakes. "Joel Young."

"Divorce is never fun, especially with such young clients, but we'll get you two out of here and back to your lives as quickly as possible," Mr. Shaw says.

My father nods back to him.

My lawyer nods to everyone in the fucking room.

Then to the other lawyer. "I need a moment to confer with my client."

Mr. Lux nods back. "Of course." He leads Joel into an office down the hall.

My dad and Mr. Shaw, my lawyer, lead me into a sleek conference room. The sturdy oak table is surrounded by sleek black chairs, the mesh ergonomic ones. He hits a button and shades slide down the glass walls.

We have privacy.

To discuss the settlement.

Only my mind isn't going to paperwork. It's thinking up all sorts of positions for me and Joel. God, that table is the perfect place for him to bend me over and fuck me.

What the hell is wrong with me?

I can't think dirty thoughts with my father ten feet away.

My dad offers me a reassuring pat on the shoulder. "This will be okay, sweetheart."

Mr. Shaw opens a folder and places a contract on the table. He motions for me to sit.

I don't want to sit, but standing is taking all my strength. This is the only way I'll be able to read the paperwork.

I sit and pick up the contract. The first page is standard stuff. The next is details on our finances. A lot of detail.

There isn't much to know. The only money in my account is what I earned at my summer job. And there's only enough to get me through June. Not that I ever hurt for money. My dad pays my tuition. He sends money anytime I ask for it.

As long as I go along with the plan, as long as I keep up appearances, I have it made.

"Mr. Young has quite a bit of money." The lawyer takes a seat and points to the section detailing Joel's finances.

He underestimated the other day. He's worth about five million.

Five.

Million.

Dollars.

"You're entitled to a lot more than this." The lawyer turns the page.

There it is on the contract, the settlement terms.

Half a million dollars for me.

I keep the rings.

I sign a non-disclosure.

Those are the only terms.

"He agreed to this?" I ask.

"Mr. Lux will convince Mr. Young that signing this agreement is in his best interests."

That's a no.

But he will.

I swallow hard. "I don't want any of his money."

"According to the state of California, all of that money belongs to the two of you. You're entitled to more than this, Ms. Chase."

"She said she doesn't want his money." Dad's voice is irritated. "My daughter doesn't want to live off a technicality that allows someone to ply money from something that barely qualifies as a marriage."

That's not right.

Well, I don't want Joel's money.

And maybe this wasn't the kind of marriage my parents had.

But it is a marriage.

And it hurts that it's ending.

That Joel won't be mine anymore.

One day, he'll be someone else's.

He'll love someone else.

He'll come with someone else.

Fuck.

Everything hurts.

I can't let this happen.

I have to do something.

The lawyer is calm. Even. "As your counsel, I'm advising you to take this offer or to ask for more."

His voice is effortless.

No doubt, he's used to dealing with emotional clients. He's a family law attorney. He deals with child custody. Half a million dollars is nothing compared to winning primary custody.

He looks at me. "This is the law, Ms. Chase. You're a law student, aren't you?"

"Yes."

"This money can help you graduate debt free. It can allow you the freedom to work as a public defender. Or to work for a non-profit. Wouldn't you like to do pro-bono work?"

Of course, but I'm not going back to law school.

"She said no." My father stares down the lawyer. "Are you going to honor your client's wishes or not?"

The lawyer clears his throat. "You're a lawyer, sir. And you're a first year law student, Ms. Chase. Both of you understand the power of the law. It's not what's right or what's fair. The law is simply the terms of the game we play by. It's foolish to do anything but manipulate it for your gain."

Daddy is glaring at Mr. Shaw like he's about to deck him. "If I have to repeat that my daughter doesn't want this man's money one more time, we're going to find new counsel."

The lawyer shakes his head. "If that's your decision."

"Sweetheart?" Dad looks to me. "He needs a yes from you."

"Oh. I… Yes, but, actually…" I look up at Dad. "I got Cs my first semester."

He raises a brow. "We can talk about that later."

"No. I have to say this now." I take a deep breath and exhale slowly. "I want to drop out."

"Because of this Joel?" Dad says Joel's name with distaste.

"No. Well, a little, but only because Joel helped me realize it. I don't know what I want to do, but I know it's not this." I blink back a tear. "I'm sorry I wasted your money."

"Sweetheart, I have plenty of money." Dad sets his hands on my shoulders. "Are you sure this is what you want?"

I nod.

"Infatuation can cloud your judgment," he says. "If you're still hung up on Joel, thinking you can't be with him if you're a lawyer—"

"No, it's not that. Joel wouldn't care. He just… he just wants me to be happy," I say.

"Will leaving school make you happy?" Dad asks.

"Once I get over the shock." My heart is thudding against my chest. I can't believe I'm having this conversation in front of my divorce attorney. Or at my settlement conference.

But I'm glad it's happening now and not later.

I'm glad Dad is here.

I look back to Dad. "You trust me?"

He nods.

"Let me talk to Mr. Shaw alone," I say. I whisper my next set of instructions in Dad's ear.

"Are you sure, sweetheart?"

I nod. "I'll see you at lunch."

My father looks to Mr. Shaw. Despite the clear disgust in Daddy's eyes, he nods, shakes Mr. Shaw's hand goodbye, and takes his leave.

The lawyer perks up. He's sure I'm about to ask for money. "Not everyone feels comfortable making demands in front of family."

"No, that's not it."

I swallow hard.

I want…

Fuck. My mouth goes sticky. I can't say what I want. Not yet. Not to him.

I have to say it to Joel first.

I turn to my lawyer. "Can I speak to my husband?"

His face screws. "Ms. Chase, I don't recommend

speaking to your husband before divorce proceedings. It's best to keep emotions out of these things."

My skin burns. I'm hot, but it's not desire or embarrassment. How can this guy stare at me, telling me to keep emotions out of a divorce?

This is my life.

My marriage.

Sure, it's a week old, but it's still my marriage.

It still means something.

I push myself out of my chair. For some reason, my legs are steady. It's not like before. "Now, please."

"I'll confer with Mr. Young's counsel." The lawyer frowns, but he still leaves to fetch Joel.

Or to try to convince Joel's lawyer to convince Joel not to do this.

Sounds of office work fill the room. Maybe Mr. Shaw is right. Maybe it's wrong asking to see your husband before you're supposed to divorce him.

But I need to talk to Joel right now.

I need to get this off my chest.

A few moments later, there are steps in the hallway. Joel, plus both our lawyers, step into the room.

My lawyer looks at me. "Mr. Lux and I agree that it's best if the two of us supervise."

I shake my head. "I don't want that."

Joel nods to his lawyer. "It's fine."

"Mr. Young—"

Joel's voice drops to that demanding tone. "Now."

Slowly, our lawyers leave.

The door closes.

We're alone in here.

Tension flees my shoulders and back at an alarming rate. I move closer to Joel. Closer than I should, given the circumstances, but I need the comfort of his body.

He pulls me into a deep hug.

"I'm not taking your money," I whisper.

"You should."

"I won't."

He nods *fine* then he pulls me closer. "You're going to be okay, Bella. You'll bounce back."

"No." I pull back enough to look him in the eyes. His green eyes are bright. Not like before. This is a respite both of us need. But we need more than that too. "I don't want this."

"Don't want what?"

"I don't want a divorce. I want to stay married to you."

Chapter Thirty-Six

BELLA

Joel's green eyes fill with surprise.

He stares back at me.

He says nothing.

I stammer. "You should respond."

He moves closer. "You don't want a divorce?"

"I don't."

"I don't either."

"Yeah?"

He nods.

My fingertips graze the back of his hand. Then I'm intertwining my fingers with his. In my heels, I'm only a little shorter than Joel. I barely have to look up at him. "This is crazy. We've known each other for a week."

"And?"

"People don't do that."

His lips curl into a smile. Tension falls off his brows, his jaw, his shoulders. "I'm not people."

"You're really not." I move close enough to rest my head on his chest. Then his arms are around me, and I melt. This is what safety feels like, what home feels like. "If this is about proving something about love being real and marriage being important—"

"It's not."

"Would you tell me if it was?"

"Yeah." Slowly, he removes the elastic band holding my bun in place. "We promised. No lies, no bullshit today."

With my hair falling over my shoulders, I feel wild. Like I'm ready to shed off the prim and proper clothes and get dirty. But I have to get this out first. I look up at Joel. I stare into those earnest green eyes of his. "If you're being stubborn, you probably won't realize it."

"True."

"I'll ask anyway. Are you sure you're not being stubborn?"

"Yes." He runs his fingers through my hair. "I never wanted this." He motions to the contract on the table. "I love you, Bella."

My chest warms. I believe him. My entire body believes him.

I stare back at Joel. "I love you too."

He beams. "Fuck, angel." He slides his hands to my hips and pulls me closer.

I let out a soft sigh. "Is that enough, loving each other?"

"You want to stay married."

"I do."

"That's the reason that matters." He takes a step back, breaking our connection, and he locks the door.

He can't mean...

Joel turns back to me, his eyes fierce. "Take off your panties."

My sex clenches. I want him right now, and not just his body, his mind and his heart too. But— "Someone will hear."

He shakes his head. "You'll stay quiet."

"I can't."

His voice drops to that demanding tone. "You can."

I can… I'm not sure about that, but, at the moment, I'm more than willing to try. I press my back against the conference table. "We're really married."

"Fuck, say that again."

"You're my husband."

His pupils dilate.

"And I'm your wife."

His teeth sink into his bottom lip.

It fills me with just as much desire. This, staying married, is crazy. It's not the crazy of marrying him in Vegas—that was a spur of the moment, gin-soaked decision.

This isn't.

I'm sober. I'm lucid. I'm in my right mind.

This is what I want, Joel as my husband.

Me as his wife.

Fuck.

I don't care about the consequences anymore.

I need our bodies joining.

His voice is a growl. "Panties. Off. Now."

I'm tempted to test him, to see what he'll do if I disobey. But last time I called his bluff, I ended up desperate and wanting.

I can't take that now. My emotions are a cresting wave. They're going to knock me down if I don't get the reassurance that he really is mine.

I pull my dress to my waist, plant my ass on the conference table, and spread my legs. "Why don't you help me with that?"

Desire spreads over his expression. "You teasing me, angel?"

My tongue slides over my lips. "Maybe."

Two steps and his body is planted between my legs. He looks down at me as he drags his fingertips from the inside of my knee, up my thigh, over my panties, back down the other leg.

He does it again and again.

He does it until I'm panting.

"Joel," I breathe.

"Don't tease if you don't want me teasing you back." He presses my knees together and drags my panties down my thighs.

They fall off my knees landing on the ground.

I tug at his jacket. I'm not sure what I'm asking for. Only that I need more of Joel and now.

He reads my mind. He slides his suit jacket off his shoulders and tosses it aside. The garment is nice. It deserves more tender care. But I don't give a fuck about that at the moment.

I need his body pressed against mine.

I need all of him.

His fingers dig into my thighs. Slowly, he presses my legs apart.

He lowers himself to the floor.

I tug at his hair. "I can't stay quiet."

"You can." He blows cold on my inner thigh. Then hot.

Then his breath is on my sex, sending desire out to my fingers and toes.

My hips rock of their own accord. I barely manage to catch my balance.

Joel reaches up to me. He places my right hand on the table. He takes my left hand and sucks on my fingers, one at a time.

The pressure of his mouth on my sensitive skin… I can barely stand it.

When he's done, he slides his hand up my torso. His thumb catches on my lip. It's an instruction.

I take his thumb into my mouth and suck hard.

He lets out a low groan. Then his other hand is on my thigh, pinning my leg to the table.

He nips at the skin of my inner thigh.

He does it again and again.

He does it until I'm so desperate with desire that I bite his thumb.

"Please." My words are muffled by his digit.

But he understands.

He licks me from bottom to top. It's mercilessly slow and soft. I can't take the tease right now.

I need Joel.

I need to come on his face.

I need him inside me.

"Now," I groan.

He slips his index finger into my mouth as he licks me a little harder, a little faster.

It's sweet, painful agony. I suck on his finger. Then I'm nipping at it. Then I'm biting hard enough to draw blood. He's a musician. I shouldn't.

But he groans against me.

He slides another finger into my mouth.

I suck on it like I'm sucking his cock. His pressure stays unbearably soft. His speed stays unbearably slow.

It feels so fucking good.

But I need more.

I throw my head back. "Make me come, baby. Now."

He drags his hand down my torso. Then it's curling into my other thigh.

He presses his lips to my inner thigh and groans against my skin. "You've got to stay quiet, angel."

"I will. Please."

His eyes are on fire. He nods *now* then he leans closer.

He licks me harder this time. Faster. Pleasure spreads out through my torso. Down my legs. Up my chest. The bliss is diffuse. I need more.

I need to come.

"Harder," I groan.

He licks me harder.

Harder.

Perfect.

"There." I tug at his hair. "Don't stop."

He doesn't. He licks me with that same pressure. A little faster. A little closer to just where I need him.

Tension knots in my core.

Almost.

Almost.

There.

I tug at his hair as I come. I bite my tongue to mumble all the groans that fall off my lips. My thighs press into his cheeks tightly enough to suffocate him.

All that tension in my core unwinds, sending waves of pleasure through me.

"Fuck me." I tug at his hair to pull him up.

He looks up at me, a dare in his green eyes. Or maybe that's the pride of accomplishment.

Either way. I need him right now.

"Joel, now. Please." I tug hard enough to hurt him, but it only makes him groan with ecstasy. "I need you inside me."

"Fuck." He pushes himself up. "On your back."

I lower myself onto my back.

He pushes my dress farther up my waist. Then he's grabbing my hips and pulling my body towards his.

He undoes the knot of his tie and tosses it aside.

Then he's undoing the first few buttons of his shirt, undoing his belt, unzipping his slacks.

He pushes his pants and his boxers to his knees.

There he is, hard and ready for me.

We're both pantless in this conference room.

We shouldn't be fucking here.

But I don't fucking care.

"Now." My fingers curl around the side of the table as he plants his hands under my knees.

He brings my legs to his torso, so I'm bent at ninety degrees, my ankles at his shoulders.

He rocks his hips and his cock strains against me.

Fuck, that feels good.

I look up at him.

He looks down at me.

Satisfaction fills his green eyes as he thrusts inside me. His fingers dig into my hips, holding me in place. He pushes farther. Farther.

There.

I have all of him.

It's intense.

Intimate.

So much more intimate than it's ever been.

We're staying married.

This really is forever.

He really is my husband.

He holds my gaze as he fills me with long, deep thrusts.

He fucks me so hard the table shakes.

I hold on tightly to the side, but I'm still bouncing with every thrust.

This is loud.

Someone is going to hear.

Everyone is going to realize what we're doing.

But I still don't fucking care.

"Harder," I groan. I need more of him. All of him.

He holds onto my hips, pulling my body towards his. His fingers dig into my flesh as he thrusts into me harder and faster. I still shake, the table still shakes, but his grip is tight.

My body stays pressed against his.

It's intense.

Good intense.

I let go of my last conscious thought. My hips rock in time with his. It pushes him deeper.

Judging by the way he breathes harder, it drives him out of his fucking mind.

I match his movements.

I stare into his gorgeous green eyes until I can't take it anymore. My lids press together.

Words fall off my lips. "You feel so good, baby."

He lets out a low, deep groan. "Fuck, Bella."

He moves harder.

Deeper.

My fingers dig into the table.

"Touch yourself," he groans. When I hesitate, he adds. "I've got you."

I bring one hand to my clit and I stroke myself. Tension knots in my core.

Fuck.

"Joel," I groan.

I force myself to look up into his eyes.

God, the pleasure in his expression…

I rub myself harder. I groan louder. I feel too good to care.

With the next brush of my fingers, I'm there. My sex pulses as I come. It pulls him closer, takes him deeper.

It sends bliss to every bit of my body.

I feel good, relaxed, at peace.

But I still need him there too.

"Come inside me," I breathe.

He thrusts a little harder. His fingers dig into my skin. Then it's the nails.

Then he's shaking.

His teeth sink into his lip.

"Fuck," he groans.

And he's there.

His cock pulses as he comes inside me. I watch pleasure spread out through his body. His thighs shake. His brow knits then softens. He gets this dreamy look in his eyes.

He leans down to plant a kiss on my lips.

I kiss back hard and deep.

He untangles our bodies, grabs tissues, helps me clean up, helps me into my clothes.

His tie isn't knotted. My underwear is on inside out. His buttons are off. None of that matters right now.

He motions to the door. "You ready for this?"

It's not like before. His voice is bright. Happy.

This time, I am. I nod. "Yeah."

Joel slides his arm around me and he leads me out of the conference room.

Mr. Lux and Mr. Shaw look at us knowingly. They don't seem upset or shocked. They don't move either. They stand there with that *are you ready to go on* look. Either they wear good poker faces or this isn't the first time a randy couple has decided on a pre-divorce fuck.

"We're not going to get a divorce," Joel says.

Mr. Shaw turns to me. "Ms. Chase, I can't recommend being swayed by—"

"This is what I want."

It really is.

Epilogue

JOEL

It's not until I step into the elevator that I actually consider the possibility of Alessandra's text being true.

I have no time for your lovely dovey bullshit. We have real rock stars to deal with. Headliners. Not just opening acts with egos too big for their tour dates. If you steal my assistant, you'll feel it.

She's always been a hard ass, but the *don't fuck with my assistant* thing is harder to gauge. Alessandra was never protective of her other assistants.

With Bella…

I absolutely believe she'll make me feel this.

But I don't care.

It's been three weeks since I've seen my wife.

Two days since I've heard her voice.

Fuck, I need her right now. My head is already filling with ideas. Ideas that are threatening to make this elevator ride incredibly fucking awkward for the suits riding with me.

The door opens on five. An intern shoots me a nervous

glance. He presses his lips together, no doubt reminding himself he's not supposed to gush over the talent.

I've always loved showing up at our label. The crowd is a fun mix of starstuck interns and blasé execs. But now that Bella is on the ninth floor…

I appreciate that the guy's a fan, but I don't have time for him to hold up the elevator.

I nod to him.

His jaw drops. He forces himself to step out of the elevator. Then he turns and watches the doors close. Well, he watches me. Not that I'm doing anything other than standing here.

Down to two. They're both suits. They're both apathetic to me. They're both getting off on seven.

They snicker to each other, no doubt mocking the intern, then they turn to me with apologetic glances.

"Some people." The woman shakes her head. "It's been a while, Mr. Young. How are you?"

She seems familiar, but I don't have any interest in small talk today.

I offer her a hello nod. "I'm about to find my wife and fuck her in the conference room. I'm fantastic."

She smiles and turns to her fellow suit. "What did I tell you about Alessandra?"

"She speaks very highly of Ms. Chase," the guy suit says.

"Ms. Chase is fucking amazing," I say.

"Yes, there's a lot of talk of offering her a position in—"

The lady suit clears her throat. "We shouldn't tell her husband that."

The guy nods. "Always nice to see you, Mr. Young."

I nod back.

Finally, the elevator stops on their floor. They get off.

And from the way they're looking at each other, they're probably about to get off again.

None of my concern.

But hearing them gush over Bella…

Fuck. Everyone else knows she's amazing.

It makes me warm all over.

It's been six months now. Bella started working as Alessandra's assistant just after we got back from our honeymoon. I knew Bella would be amazing, but I wasn't sure if she'd love the job. After all, music industry assistant is a far cry from lawyer to be.

It's not the status she expected for herself.

Or the money.

Or the crowd.

It's a different kind of work.

But she's great at it.

And she loves it.

The elevator stops on the ninth floor. I check my phone again. There's that same teasing text from Alessandra.

And that same picture message from Bella: a pair of crotchless panties and a quarter cup bra in black lace. Tragically, the lingerie is laid out on our bed instead of on her body.

But that only gives my imagination more room to grow.

Fuck, I'm going to *grow* right here and now if I don't put this thing away.

I step onto the ninth floor. It's quiet today. It's always quiet in the afternoons when everyone heads to the coffee shop down the street for their caffeine and sugar fix.

There's Alessandra's office, the curtains down, the door closed, the lights off.

And there's Bella, sitting at her desk, talking into her headset. Her eyes catch mine. Her lips curl into a smile.

Slowly, she stands.

Fuck, I never get tired of seeing her in her work clothes. Her pink button-up shirt is tight around her tits. Her black pencil skirt hugs her hips in a way that calls for my hands. With the bun and the glasses and the hint of makeup, she has the *professional good girl* thing down, pat.

But she's wearing her lingerie under that outfit.

She's my angel.

And my devil.

I move closer.

Her eyes stay on mine, but she continues talking into the phone. She holds up her finger *one minute*. Her smile spreads wider.

She's enjoying teasing me.

"I'm sorry, sir, but Alessandra has demands. I wish I could talk her down, but I can't. It's eighty percent of the door or nothing." She presses her headset to her ear. Her eyes go to her computer. Then they're back on mine.

"What's he saying?" I whisper.

She shoots me a thumbs up.

She's fucking good at her job.

I almost want to watch her do her thing.

Okay, that's bullshit.

I want to make her come several times.

"Fax it over and we'll sign right away. Thank you." She ends the call and tosses her headphone on her desk.

She practically leaps into my arms.

"It's been too long," she murmurs.

I look up at her. Fuck, those brown eyes of hers are beautiful. And they're filled with that mix of affection and desire.

This was our first tour together.

Our first time dealing with the long separations.

I finally understand why Ethan and Kit are so

annoying all the time. It's hell being away from her. But the reunions are almost sweet enough to make up for it.

"Alessandra threatened to make my life hell if I stole her assistant." I set Bella on the ground. My hand goes to the back of her head. I undo her bun and watch her hair fall over her cheeks.

"She's at a meeting for the rest of the day."

"Good." I lean in to press my lips to hers. God, the taste of her lips. Honey, tea, and Bella.

She pulls back with a needy sigh. "You don't care about Alessandra's threats."

"I don't." I run my fingers through her hair. "But you do."

She presses her lips together. "Maybe."

"Maybe?" I laugh. "That's the worst lie I've ever heard."

"Maybe." She tries to hold a poker face, but it only lasts a hot second. "Okay. A lot. I like this job."

"You love this job."

She nods. "I love you." She rises to her tiptoes and presses her lips to mine.

Her kiss is hungry.

Fuck, I'm hungry for her.

I can't believe how good it feels, knowing I'm back. Knowing we have another few months before we have to deal with the off/on of touring again.

For three months, I'm all hers.

And she's all mine.

Fuck. I need her. Now.

I slide my hands to her lush ass and pull her body into mine. We're in plain view of a dozen offices and desks. At least half a dozen people are here. I'm sure they're all watching.

But I don't care.

Nothing is going to stop me from reuniting with my wife properly.

"Joel..." It's a plea as much as it's a warning. "Not here."

I motion to the empty conference room down the hall.

She doesn't hesitate. Her eyes light up as her teeth sink into her lip.

She takes my hand and leads me down the hall.

It must be two dozen steps. That feels like a thousand miles.

She pulls me into the room, locks the door, lowers the curtains.

"Sit on the table," I say.

She slides onto the table and spreads her legs. Her eyes fix on mine. Her hands go to the hem of her skirt. "I missed you so much, Joel."

"I missed you more."

"Not possible." She tugs her skirt up her thigh. Her eyes go to the ground. Her cheeks flush.

"It kills me to say this, but we *can* wait until we get home."

"I can't."

Thank fuck.

"That's not it. I... um..." She pulls her skirt up another few inches. "I have to show you something."

"Fuck yes."

"Not that. Well... that. But this first." She slides off the table, turns around, and motions to the zipper of her pencil skirt. "Undo that for me."

I place my body behind hers. She groans as my hard-on brushes against her ass.

All these clothes in the way.

They need to be gone.

But I need to torture her too.

I slide my hands over her hips and hold her body against mine. She purrs as I bring my lips to her neck.

I plant soft kisses along her skin.

Then hard ones.

Then I'm sucking on her earlobe.

She grinds her ass against my crotch. "Joel… I… I'm going to lose my nerve."

And I'm going to lose my ability to form coherent sentences.

I don't mind. But this is clearly important to her.

I drag my hands over the edge of her skirt then I pull down her zipper.

She looks back to me. "Tell me you like it." She pushes her skirt and panties off her hip in one smooth motion.

There's the soft skin of her lower back. Her side.

Her hip.

And there's my name, curving over her hip. *Joel* in some fancy black script. There are hearts around it, red ones.

It's girly as fuck.

It's perfect.

She turns so we're face to face. "Joel…"

Her tattoo is on the opposite hip as mine. Right now, with us face to face, our ink is aligned.

Fuck, it's romantic.

"You haven't said anything." She tugs at my t-shirt. Her expression is uncertain. Right now, I have the power to crush her heart into a million little pieces.

I won't.

I couldn't.

I'd die first.

Besides— "I fucking love it."

"Yeah?"

I nod. "When did you get it?"

"Last week." She presses her palm against my chest. Her voice is still soft. Vulnerable. "You swear you love it?"

"Cross my heart and hope to die." I push her skirt to her knees, so it's out of the way.

That's my name on her skin.

Forever.

This is as permanent as it gets.

My fingers trace the lines of her ink again and again. "It's fucking perfect, angel."

Her expression fills with relief. "Really?"

"Fuck yes." I drag my hands to her blouse then get to work on the buttons. "Did that hurt?"

She nods. "Terribly." She slides her hand under my t-shirt. Her fingers curl into my skin. "But it was worth it."

"I love you."

"I love you too." She brings one hand to the back of my head and pulls me into a deep kiss.

Fuck, I need her.

My tongue claims her mouth. My fingers do away with her buttons. I push her blouse off her shoulders.

Bella shrugs it all the way to her hands then it flutters to the ground.

There's my wife, in that quarter-cup bra and those crotchless panties and her work pumps.

"Fuck, Bella…"

"I missed you so badly." She pulls my t-shirt over my head. Her eyes fix on mine as she rakes her hand over my chest.

My stomach.

She undoes the button of my jeans.

Then she's pushing them off my hips.

Bella lowers herself onto her knees. She looks up at me as she pulls my boxers to my feet. As she wraps her hand around my cock.

As she takes me into her mouth.

It's been too long. The sensation of her soft, wet mouth has my nerves in overdrive.

One hand digs into her hair, guiding her.

The other reaches down to play with her nipple. She groans as my fingers find the tender bud. I rub her harder.

She works me harder.

I tug at her hair.

She groans against my cock, working me harder, taking me deeper.

Fuck, the way she's looking at me like she needs me coming in her mouth…

Any other day, I'd scream *fuck yes* from the mountaintops.

Today, I need to be inside her.

I tug at her hair to hold her head in place. She grunts with an equal mix of pleasure and pain.

Fuck, that sound is tempting.

But nothing is stopping this.

"On the table," I groan.

"You too." She climbs onto the conference table and scoots to the middle. Her eyes are on fire, this mix of confidence and pure need. "I need to feel your body against mine as I come." She slides her index and middle fingers into her mouth, wets them, and drags them down her torso. "I need to look you in the eyes as I scream your name."

Fuck. "Bella…"

She holds my gaze as she spreads her legs and brings her fingers to her clit.

Her eyelids flutter closed.

Her lips part with a sigh of pleasure.

She looks fucking beautiful wrecked with pleasure.

I watch her touch herself until she's at the edge. She's shaking and panting and groaning my name.

"You're coming on my cock," I growl.

She nods.

I press myself onto the table and place my body next to hers.

She looks up at me, her eyes filled with every ounce of trust in the world.

Every ounce of love in the world.

I plant my hands outside her shoulders and bring my body onto hers.

She shifts her hips. Her cunt strains against my cock.

One inch at a time, I enter her.

Fuck.

She sighs with relief. "Joel..." She wraps her arms around my chest. Her nails rake over my back. "I missed you."

"I missed you, angel." I kiss her hard as I fill her with deep, steady thrusts.

She feels like home.

I let go of my conscious thoughts as I drive into Bella. Her hips rock to meet mine. Her groans vibrate down my mouth.

Need flows from her to me.

From me to her.

We're fucking in the conference room of her office. She's still in her lingerie. Still in her heels.

But it's still so fucking romantic.

I groan into her mouth as I drive into her.

She's too good with her mouth. I'm almost there.

But then she is too.

I break our kiss so I can stare into her pretty, brown eyes. "Come for me, angel."

She nods. Her eyelids fall together. Her back arches.

She throws her head back as she rocks her hips.

Her clit presses against my pelvis.

Her lips part with a sigh.

A few more thrusts and she's there, groaning and shaking and clutching at the table as she comes.

"Joel… fuck… Joel…" Her eyes blink open. She stares back at me, her expression pure bliss.

She tugs at my hair and pulls me into a deep kiss.

All that love and affection pours from her to me.

From me to her.

I'm about to come inside her and all I can think is *I love her.*

I missed her.

I need her.

I dig my hands into Bella's hair, holding her head against mine. A few more thrusts and I'm there.

Pleasure spills through my pelvis. My cock pulses as I fill her. She shifts her hips, rocking me through my orgasm.

She kisses me.

I kiss back just as hard.

We stay a sticky, tangled mess for minutes.

Eventually, I untangle our bodies. We help each other into our clothes.

When Bella finally has her buttons straight, she takes my hand. "Come on, baby. Let's go home."

I nod and pull her into a deep kiss.

But the truth is, I'm already home.

Wherever I am, when I'm with her, I'm home.

It's that fucking simple.

Want More Dangerous Noise?

Sign up for the Crystal Kaswell mailing list to get the extended epilogue to *Dangerous Rock*. You'll also get bonus scenes, teasers, and updates on new releases.

Join my Facebook fan group, Crystal's Groupies, if you want more regular (and silly) updates.

Dangerous Fling, Lacey and Mal's story, is available now.

Turn the page for a teaser.

Already read *Dangerous Fling*? Check out *Sing Your Heart Out*, the first book in the Sinful Serenade Series.

Dangerous Noise

Dangerous Kiss - Ethan

Dangerous Crush – Kit

Dangerous Rock – Joel

Dangerous Fling – Mal

Dangerous Encore - series sequel

Dangerous Fling Teaser

LACEY

Get *Dangerous Fling* Now

For the millionth time, I smooth the sheets on the bed. Now, they aren't mussed enough.

They need to look lived in without looking messy.

No.

They need to looked fucked in.

This bed is the place where Malcolm Strong is fucking a glamour model turned actress. Only, in the music video, she won't be a model turned actress. She'll be…

Well, I'm not exactly sure what she'll be besides the woman Mal is fucking.

I scrunch the sheets. That's closer to where they need to be. Not that it *really* matters.

Most days, I don't mind sitting here, waiting for our celebrity client to show.

Today…

Fuck. That's a car pulling up outside.

Parking.

Turning off.

Its door opens and slams shut.

Footsteps move closer.

Those are steady footsteps. The footsteps of a beautiful six-foot-three, musclebound, inked-up rock star sex god.

The butterflies in my stomach rise up in my throat.

This is my job.

I can't freak out.

The butterflies ignore my logic. They spread out to my fingers and toes. My chest gets light. My head too.

The door pulls open.

And there's Mal, surrounded by the soft glow of the morning light.

He steps inside.

It's not like with other famous guys. They're always lacking something, plain, ordinary, dull when they should sparkle.

Mal is as brilliant as he is on stage, in photographs, in the band's six earlier music videos.

He's shining like the star he is.

His deep blue eyes fix on mine. His soft lips curl up at one side. It's a half smile. It's a tiny expression but it still lights up those piercing blue eyes.

God, he's beautiful.

His brown hair is hanging in messy waves. His grey t-shirt is snug around his strong shoulders. And his skinny jeans—god damn, this man is the poster child for form-fitting denim.

Get a grip, Lacey. Your number one job description is not fangirling over hot rock stars. So what if Mal is the only guy with a permanent place in your spank bank? So what if you respect him as a writer as much as you lust after him as a tattooed, tortured celebrity bad boy?

Future music video directors don't gush, no matter how

many times they've touched themselves thinking of their actor. Musician. Whatever.

Danielle Kubbie's assistant certainly doesn't gush.

Mal takes another step into the studio. Suddenly, it feels smaller than its 800 square feet.

His deep voice flows from his perfect lips. "I thought the actress was a redhead."

He half-smiles at me. Then at Danielle.

He's teasing.

Or... does he really think I'm the video actress? I am standing next to the bed in a tiny, incredibly unprofessional tank top–and-shorts combo. But Danielle doesn't care. The studio air conditioning is crap and she'd rather I "look like a whore than smell like sweat."

Mal gives me a long, slow once-over. There's something about the shift of his hips. About the ways his pupils dilate.

He wants me in that bed.

As the actress in the video.

Or as...

No. I'm getting ahead of myself. I'm letting my sex dreams bleed into reality. There's no way that Malcolm Strong, celebrity millionaire, rock star sex god wants me.

Danielle laughs. "Mal, sweetheart. It's nice to see you." Her eyes go to the clock on the wall then to him. "Traffic?"

He nods. "It's a long drive from Orange County."

She purses her lips. He's late and Danielle doesn't allow anyone else to out diva her.

She forces a smile. "You don't have to explain. You're the rock star." She motions to the bed. "You ready to start?"

Mal cocks a brow. "No foreplay?"

His deep voice is as hard to read as his beautiful face, but I'm pretty sure he's joking.

His eyes light up.

Yes, definitely joking.

"I'm afraid I'm out of time for romance." Again, Danielle motions to the bed.

Her voice is easy to read. She's irritated he's late.

I offer Danielle a smile. I try to direct it towards Mal, but the moment my eyes connect with his, my cheeks flush.

My chest too.

Fuck, I'm hot.

It's too early in the morning for me to feel this hot.

He's moving closer.

Closer.

Three feet now.

He extends his hand. "Malcolm Strong."

Somehow, I shake. "Lacey Waltz." I bite my lip to keep from adding details. *I love Dangerous Noise* is the only acceptable compliment. *I've been picking apart your lyrics for years and I regularly fuck myself thinking of you* is far, far beyond an acceptable level of gushing.

Somehow, I pull my hand back to my side. It seems impossible that my brain is doing anything with the way it's filling with familiar fantasies: Mal throwing me on that bed, pulling off his t-shirt, ripping off my jeans, planting his face between my legs, and groaning against my skin the way he groans through my stereo.

Ahem. "I hate to disappoint, but I'm Danielle's assistant."

He nods, an *I understand* kind of nod. But he's still looking at me like he wants me in that bed.

God, I want to be in that bed with him, his hard, sweaty body on top of mine.

Snap out of it, Lacey. You are not currently masturbating. You are at work. You are not losing this job because you're in love with Mal's persona. You know better than to buy into image. You're here to help craft his image.

Danielle's voice pulls me back to reality. "Where is your leading lady?"

She's not hiding the irritation in her voice anymore. Rock stars can pull diva shit—Mal is the lead singer and frontman of Dangerous Noise. He's the face of the band. He's irreplaceable.

The music video doesn't happen without him.

The video vixen is just another pretty model. She's one of thousands. Tens of thousands even.

"She's in makeup." I pull my cell from my pocket. My hands are slick with sweat. I can barely keep my phone in my palms. "I'll get an ETA."

Danielle taps her pen against her clipboard. "We need to move into a studio with space for a makeup room. This happens too often." She turns to Mal with a barely apologetic smile. "We're usually on location." Again, she motions to the bed. She does it in a *this is the third time I've suggested you hop onto that bed. Are you dense or just difficult?* kind of way. "We can get the solo stuff first."

A hint of regret flares in Mal's eyes. He looks back to Danielle. "Sure."

He moves onto the bed in an impossibly sensual manner. How can one person be this sexy? It defies logic.

Danielle goes to the camera, and I take my place behind her, waiting for instruction.

This is as it should be. The hot musician is posing. The brilliant director is taking in the light in the room. And I'm here, learning everything I can from her as I tend to her beck and call.

Only, Mal is still looking at me like he wants me in that bed.

He's not exactly wrong, creatively.

His image is pure tortured bad boy. He's someone who fucks because he hurts, not because he loves pussy and fake tits. The actress on her way is a former *Playboy* model. She's undeniably beautiful, but she's firmly in the *cheap groupie* type—as directors, it's our job to sort actors into types.

I'm in the *normal girl* type. In Hollywood, that means pretty and thin but not drop-dead beautiful.

That's what this video needs. Not me. But a woman who looks a little less glamorous and a little more everyday.

Suggestions rise up in my chest. I have to bite my tongue to keep from spilling my ideas to Danielle. She has a vision. And she doesn't want my feedback. She doesn't want anyone's feedback.

This is a great job. I'm learning a lot. If things were different, if I was still with Adam, maybe I could risk it. But I need the cash more than I need to honor my inner Dangerous Noise fan or my inner filmmaker.

My inner filmmaker whines, but I'm going to keep my mouth shut.

For half an hour, I move lights and hold reflectors as Mal moves around the tiny studio.

He stares out the window longingly.

He tears off his t-shirt.

He climbs into bed, tugging at the sheets, raking his hand down his torso, staring at the empty spot next to him.

The man is somehow expressive and stoic at once. He has a quietness to him. But he still manages to convey this deep pain that goes all the way to his soul.

His blue eyes are filled with anguish.

His posture is heavy. Tired.

Then it's strong. In control. Demanding. *I want you. I'll have you. I know you want that too.*

He tugs at the waistband of his jeans.

He unbuttons them.

He goes to push them off his hips.

My heartbeat picks up.

My breath hitches.

Malcolm Strong naked.

In front of me.

Yes.

Now.

Please.

This is a fucking dream.

Only it's not.

Because there's this buzzing in my pants. My cell.

A text.

Karen: Twenty minutes. Sorry. She was late and wearing last night's makeup. And hungover. And cranky.

Lacey: Your new favorite model?

Karen: You're my favorite, babe. Let me do you after this. Please <3

A boring sit in the makeup chair is the perfect way to get my mind off Mal nearly naked.

Off Mal nearly naked with some groupie-type.

Lacey: If Danielle doesn't mind.

Karen: Thank you. I'll rush. I promise.

I slide my phone back into my shorts. "Karen will be here with the model in twenty minutes."

Danielle breaks from her cinematography trance. She studies the window on our left. Then the one on our right. "We're losing the light."

We are. It's still early enough that the light in the room is soft and pretty. But this is August in Los Angeles. We're quickly approaching the harsh light.

"Should I hang the blackout curtains?" I offer.

"No." She taps her fingers against her camera.

Her eyes go to the window. To Mal, kneeling in that bed with his jeans undone, all sexy and perfect and yummy.

She looks to me.

Oh no.

I don't like the expression on her face.

"Lacey." She points to me, then to the bed. "Stand in for me." She doesn't wait for an answer. She goes right back to her viewfinder. "I want to race the light."

Standing in is a normal part of my job description. It's usually for the hot celebrity, not the model, but it is a regular occurrence.

This is a normal work duty.

It doesn't matter that I'm standing in as the girl in the Dangerous Noise video.

It doesn't matter that I'm climbing into bed with Mal.

I can do this.

My inhale is sharp. My exhale is shallow. Slowly, I move my left foot. Then my right.

Danielle makes one of those *hurry up* noises.

I take another step. Another. My knee brushes against the bed.

I plant my palm on the sheet and slide onto the mattress.

This is normal.

Only it's not.

There's nothing normal about being in bed with Mal.

With the one musician who has a place in my heart.

That's Mal, three feet from me.

His jeans unzipped.

His blue eyes on mine.

His hands…

Fuck, his hands are skimming my hips.

My heart pounds.

Breathing—what the fuck is breathing?

"Sweetie, you're fucking him. You can't do it from that far away." Danielle taps her camera in that *you're irritating me gesture* of hers.

"Right." I'm fucking Mal. As the stand-in. The actress. Whatever.

I took several semesters of acting classes at USC.

I know acting.

I move closer.

There's only a foot between us. This is kissing distance. Fucking distance. The closest I've been to any guy who isn't Adam since high school.

My thoughts evaporate as Mal slides his hands around my waist.

He presses his palm into my lower back to pull me closer.

He stares down at me. "You okay?"

So much for my epic composure. But then he doesn't know I'm nervous because he's my celebrity crush. For all he knows, it's normal stage fright.

I force myself to look up at him.

God, he has beautiful eyes.

I force a smile. "I'm used to being behind the camera."

"Took me a while." His palm presses against the bare skin of my lower back. "It's fun once you get used to it."

It's fun, being in front of the camera with Mal.

I nod.

He raises a brow. *You sure you're okay?*

Again, I nod.

He doesn't waste time. His hand slides up my back, over my tank top, across my exposed skin.

He undoes my ponytail and drags his fingers through my hair.

I press my lips together. I exhale though my nose. I try,

hard, to keep from moaning. Or groaning. Or falling back onto the bed and pleading with him to literally make my dreams come true.

Danielle's voice barely registers. "Keep going. You two look perfect." She's happy. She's never happy. "Really, Lacey. You should act."

I'm perfect as the girl in Mal's bed.

I...

He digs his hand into my hair. It's rough. It's tender. It's raw power and it's fucking intoxicating.

That's Mal.

The one in my head.

The one on the album.

The one in that poster that used to hang in my dorm room.

My eyelids flutter closed as he leans in.

Slowly, his lips brush mine.

It's for the cameras.

A fake kiss.

Pretend.

But God, it feels so fucking real.

My entire body is buzzing.

Those are Mal's lips on my lips.

Mal's hands on my skin.

Mal's hard body against mine.

I slide my fingers through his short hair. I tug at his jeans. And I sink into his touch.

Slowly, he lowers me onto the bed.

Then he's pinning me with his hips.

Lifting my arms above my head.

Holding my wrists down with his palm.

He stares at me, his eyes full of desire.

But then he looks to the camera. He *is* acting.

As we change angles.

As he pins me from behind.
As I climb into his lap and wrap my legs around him.
It's all pretend.
But his body is in this as much as mine is.
He's hard.

Get *Dangerous Fling* Now

Sing Your Heart Out Teaser

Between the throbbing house music and the dance floor full of beautiful people grinding, it's difficult to move. It's harder to think.

I need to pee. Now. Waiting in the line snaking around the corner is not an option.

How can there only be one bathroom downstairs? One hundred people plus one bathroom equals far too many tortured bladders.

Kara must know where the bathroom is. Wherever she is.

I push through the crowd, but there's no sign of my best friend.

Someone bumps into me, her hip pressing firmly against my pelvis. Dammit, my bladder is going to explode at this rate.

Screw upstairs being off-limits. This isn't a church. It's some up-and-coming band's Hollywood mansion. I'm not about to pee my pants respecting the sanctity of rock stars' bedrooms.

There's a couple making out on the curving staircase. I step past them and make my way to the second floor. The sounds of music and conversation fade to a murmur. I'm tempted to hang out here until Kara is ready to go home.

Parties are not my scene. Even my bladder hates them.

I scan the wall, trying to figure out which of the five doors is attached to the smallest room. There. Second on the left. That must be it.

I turn the knob and push the door open.

Not a bathroom.

Definitely not a bathroom.

There are two people on a bed. The woman is on all fours. The man is kneeling behind her.

They're naked.

They're having sex.

Then they're not. The grunting stops. Flesh ceases to smack together.

The man looks at me. There's no sign of embarrassment or awkwardness on his face. He's totally unmoved.

The woman shrieks. She scrambles off the bed, pulling a sheet over her chest. "Miles, you fucker. I told you I don't do threesomes!"

Miles. There's something familiar about him. I try to place him but my thinking abilities are back to zero.

He's tall, broad shoulders and chest, sculpted abs, and below his bellybutton...

He's hard.

He's hard and he's huge.

Save for the condom, he's completely and utterly naked.

A blush spreads across my cheeks. I stammer, attempting and failing to speak. I've never seen that before. Not in person. In movies, sure. Textbooks, of course.

But never in person.

I can't look away.

The guy, Miles, makes eye contact. His voice is even. Calm. "You mind?"

I take a step backwards. My foot sinks into the plush carpet. I only barely manage to hold my balance. "Excuse me. I thought this was the bathroom."

"Next door on the left."

I know I'm red. Beet red. "Thanks."

I pull the door closed so I'm alone in the hallway. Next door on the left.

I step into the bathroom, lock the door, and die of embarrassment.

It takes twenty minutes for my cheeks to return to a normal color. I slink back to the sprawling main room and do my best to blend in amongst the partygoers.

Every inch of the hardwood floor is packed with beautiful people talking, flirting, or making out.

It's like the up-and-coming models, actors, and musicians are attracted to each other. They have a certain glow that mere mortals lack. And here I thought this was a normal college-students-with-a-keg-and-cheap-vodka kind of shindig.

Kara's friend invited us. He's in a band. Are they really this popular? I can't remember their name, but then it's hard to think of anything but Miles naked on the bed, hard and ready for action.

The lines of his hips and torso are burned into my brain.

And his…

Dammit, I'm not going there.

I find the closest thing to an empty corner and try to clear my head. I fail. My mind keeps going back to that vivid mental image.

Miles. He was unfazed, like the sex meant nothing to him. Like the girl on his bed meant nothing to him.

The man is a player. He's not the kind of guy I need in my life. He doesn't deserve my thoughts.

This stops. Now.

I scan the room for some better way to stay occupied.

It's no use. He's here. Miles is still effortless and aloof. He's still unaffected.

The guy has already moved on from the blonde in the bedroom. He's flirting with a redhead in a designer dress and stilettos.

She's model gorgeous with perfect hair and makeup. I'm standing here in an H&M skirt and blouse, my brown hair its usual frizzy mess, my black eyeliner doing little to enhance my plain-Jane brown eyes. Liner, mascara, and under-eye concealer are the extent of my makeup knowledge. I think I'm the only woman here who isn't contoured. Hell, I know I'm the only one wearing canvas sneakers.

I don't belong here.

It doesn't make sense that Miles is looking at me instead of the pretty redhead.

But he is. His clear blue eyes are fixed on mine. They're gorgeous. I couldn't see them in the dark but out here, they're practically shining.

Heat spreads across my chest. I'm gawking.

He smiles, reveling in my attention.

I press my eyelids together to temper my out-of-control blushing. It's no help. My head fills with that beautiful image of him in nothing but a condom.

Why did I let Kara talk me into coming to this party?

I push my way through the crowd, trying to get as far from Miles's gaze as possible. A dozen steps and I'm standing in the clean, modern kitchen. It's dark and mostly empty.

"You're not big on respecting people's privacy, huh?"

It's the same voice I heard upstairs. Miles.

I could swear I've heard it before. A lot, even.

I turn so we're face to face. Why does Miles seem so familiar? I don't go to parties. Hell, I've been MIA the last few months.

I wouldn't forget his strong jaw, his messy brown hair, or his gorgeous blue eyes.

Those eyes are fixed on me. He's staring at me, picking me apart.

I don't like the scrutiny. Sure, I'm hiding. But I'm not admitting that to him.

I clear my throat. "No, I'm not big on alcohol. Can't find anything else to drink."

He reaches past me. His hand brushes against my shoulder as he pulls open the fridge. He nods to a row of water bottles on the middle shelf. "Help yourself."

"Thanks."

Miles looks so familiar. And his voice is familiar too. Almost like he...

No. That's not possible.

There's no way this guy is the singer of alternative rock band Sinful Serenade, the guy who sings *In Pieces*, the guy who's been haunting my thoughts for the last three months with his breathy, tortured voice. With all the pain in his soulful eyes.

I try to recall the song's music video but my damn brain goes right back to the image of Miles naked on the bed.

Damn. I watched that video a thousand times. It was a

massive hit. The song hit the top 40 for a week or two, a rarity for alternative rock in this day and age.

More importantly, the video and the song went right to my soul. The singer was whispering in my ear. He promised that I wasn't alone. He promised that I wasn't the only person who had ever felt this way.

I understood him and he understood me. We were the only two people in the world who knew how badly it hurt, losing everything that mattered.

The man who sings *In Pieces* is a tortured soul. He doesn't screw one woman, wash up, then move on to flirting with lay number two.

Kara keeps playing down how famous her friend is.

He lives here. I know that much.

This Miles guy seems to live here.

Fuck.

Why didn't Kara warn me her friend was in *that* band?

Miles clears his throat. "You okay?"

I nod a yes and attempt to hold his gaze. "Don't walk in on casual sex very often."

"Mhmm."

"I was looking for the bathroom."

He laughs. "Is that the best you can do?"

"I was." I take a half-step backwards. "Excuse me. I should go."

His voice drops an octave. "You're not going to let me formally introduce myself?"

"Okay." My stomach flutters. "I'm Meg Smart."

"Miles Webb." He takes my hand with a strong grip. His eyes pass over me like he's trying to place me. "How is it we haven't met before?"

"I don't go to parties."

"Guess that makes this my lucky day." His hand

brushes against my wrist. Then it's back at his side. He leans in a little closer, his eyes on mine. "Why'd you decide to come tonight?"

I should be the one asking him that. "My friend convinced me I wouldn't hate it."

"What's the verdict?"

"I still don't like parties." I take a deep breath. "Why'd you come tonight?"

"That was my bedroom you burst into."

Somehow, my cheeks burn hotter.

His eyes rake over me. "Can't blame you for looking. I'd do the same."

My knees go weak at the seductive tone to his voice. That's him, the guy who sings *In Pieces*, the man who has been haunting my dreams.

That song is the centerpiece of my *listen on repeat and fall apart* playlist.

I try to formulate some excuse for why I need to leave immediately, but nothing comes. "You're um… you're in the band? The one that is throwing this party?"

"Yeah. Sinful Serenade. I'm the vocalist." His eyes pass over me again. He takes his time, like he's sure I'll be in his bed in thirty minutes flat.

A pang of desire shoots straight to my core. My damn body isn't obeying my commands. It can't help wanting Miles Webb. There's something appealing about the tattoos poking out from under his t-shirt. About the confidence in his eyes.

It's not like me to fall for the bad boy.

Even when he's so tall. Two inches taller than me at least. I'm 5'11', a giant for a women. I tower over most of the men I know.

But not Miles.

I take a deep breath, trying to convince my body it doesn't want him.

He's bad news.

A player.

A rock star even.

But I can't stop staring.

I clear my throat. "I was looking for my friend, Kara. She's tight with some guy in your band. They go way back."

"Oh, yeah, Drew's friend. Heard a lot about her last tour."

"So, I should really find her." I step aside. "And go home. I have to study. You know how it is. Or maybe not, being a rock star and all. But I have a test tomorrow."

I turn and make my way out of the kitchen.

There are footsteps behind me. "Meg?"

I spin, eye to eye with Miles again. Once again, my mind flashes with the image of him kneeling on that bed, his cock hard, the muscles of his thighs and torso taut.

How is it possible that Miles is the guy who has been singing me to sleep? He's not a poet.

He's a manwhore.

"Yes?" I ask.

"Your friend isn't in a state to drive."

He points to Kara, curled up on the couch. Her dark eyes are filled with an expression of drunken excitement. She looks especially short and curvy next to her tall, muscular friend. That must be Drew. His black hair and intense brown eyes are appealing. No wonder she's staring at him like she wants to devour him.

She bounces to her feet and throws her arms around me. "Are you having fun? Please, tell me you aren't completely miserable."

I hug back. "Only partially."

She laughs. "That's a start!"

Good. She still happy. Kara is an endlessly patient friend. She's been dragging me out of mourning for months now. I'm not going to ruin her night.

"I'm about ready to go home," I say. "I'll take a cab."

"No. I can drive. It's getting late," she says.

The dark-haired guy, Drew, butts in. "Kendrick, you are way too drunk to drive. If you even think about getting in your car, I'll throw you over my shoulder, carry you to my room, and strap you to my bed."

Her eyes light up the second he calls her by her last name. "I didn't know you were into that. Do you have rope or handcuffs or what?"

"I'll call you a fucking cab." His voice is equal parts playful and protective.

She nudges him and points to me. "This is my friend Meg, who you are so rudely ignoring in favor of lecturing me."

He pushes off the couch and offers his hand. "Drew Denton. Nice to meet you."

I shake. "Meg Smart."

"Miles giving you a hard time?" Drew asks.

"I can handle myself," I say.

"If you won't listen to reason—" Drew turns back to Kara "—then I will drive you home."

Kara looks Drew in the eyes. "You were drinking too."

"I can." I bite my tongue. Dammit, Kara's car is a stick. I can't drive us home. "Never mind."

Miles butts in. "I'll drive you guys home."

Drew's eyes narrow. He shoots Miles an incredulous look.

"Not letting you drive tonight." Miles throws back a stern look. "You'd do the same."

Slowly, Drew's protective expression melts. He and Miles share a look of understanding.

The cocky singer turns to Kara. "Your keys."

"It's a manual." She digs through her purse.

"That's fine." He smirks. "I know how to handle my stick."

Want more cocky rock stars?

Check out the Sinful Serenade series. Miles, Drew, Tom, and Pete each have their own standalone novel. But be warned: the *Sinful Serenade* series is known to cause sleepless nights and melted Kindles.

Sinful Serenade

Sing Your Heart Out - Miles
Strum Your Heart Out - Drew
Rock Your Heart Out - Tom
Play Your Heart Out - Pete
Sinful Ever After – series sequel

Author's Note

Thank you for reading *Dangerous Rock*. I started this book with every intention of keeping it a light, fun, dirty romp. Let's face it. Kit and Piper's book was a little heavier (as it deserved, with Kit's past). A little more slow burn. And that slow burn is really fucking delicious. But it's as frustrating for me as it is for you. Sometimes, the hero and heroine just need to let their bodies do the talking.

If you've read my other books, you know they usually end up with a vibe a lot like this one—fun and sexy with a nice helping of emotional weight and character development. And maybe a little angst. (If you haven't read my other books, you should— start the Dangerous Noise series with *Dangerous Kiss*). Joel and Bella had their own ideas about what they needed from me and from each other. They would not allow this book to stay as firmly in romp-land as I had hoped.

Bella is different than my other heroines in that she doesn't know what she wants to do with her life. And she ends her story still uncertain of what she wants to do with her life but open to possibilities besides the one that was predetermined for her.

It was difficult for me to write this type of character—I'm incredibly type A and hyperfocused on exactly what I want to do—but I'm glad I did. It's not easy being 22, having everyone's expectations thrust upon you, not knowing if what you want is your voice or someone else's. Even though I've always wanted to write, I felt that same pull after I graduated college. My dad, my boyfriend, my mom, my friends—they all had different ideas about how I should go about accomplishing my goals. Half the people I knew told me to forget everything else and follow my dreams. The other half told me to table my dreams as a hobby and go after something practical. But the idea of writing full time as a dream never clicked with me. A dream is a wish. A dream is out of your reach. A dream is not something you can accomplish with actionable goals.

What did I say—very type A, right? It took me a long time and a lot of mistakes and life experience to figure out how to hone in on my ideas and my intuitions (even if that meant blocking out advice of people with good intentions). This is always difficult, even for the most headstrong among us (that would be me). Especially for women—we are used to putting other people's needs ahead of ours. We are used to hearing so many other people's ideas of what we are supposed to prioritize.

If you've read my other books, you know that my heroines' arcs are important to me. I want my heroine to come into her own as much as I want her to fall head over heels for the hero. I hope I've accomplished that with Bella.

And I hope you fell for Joel as hard as she did.

As always, thanks for joining me on this journey.

I hope to see you soon for Mal's book, *Dangerous Fling*.

Acknowledgments

My first thanks goes to my favorite Hufflepuff (and a proud Hufflepuff too), my husband, for his support when I'm lost in bookland and for generally being the sun in my sky. The second goes to my father, for always encouraging my love of reading and for taking me to the bookstore when I was supposed to be grounded.

To my favorite Slytherin, Athena Wright, you are the best author BFF a girl could ask for. Thank you for your feedback, for being my chat buddy, and for always being there to give me the perspective I need. You gave me the kick in the ass I needed with this book AND you talked me down from the *oh God, it's not right yet, everyone will hate it* ledge more times than I can count. If anyone else had told me that my ending sucked and needed to go, I'd have ignored them. But, girl, you and I are just on the same wavelength in a way that continues to blow my mind.

A special thanks to my fellow Ravenclaw, Molle, for fangirling over pop-punk albums with me, and for reminding me that loving my work matters as much as all the marketing money in the world. To my cover designer

Sara Hansen, thank you for your work in making my rock star series perfect. To my editors, Tonya and Nicole, thank you for whipping the story and the prose into shape. And thanks to Giselle at Xpresso and to all the book bloggers who helped get the word out.

And thanks so much to all my beta readers!

As always, my biggest thanks goes to my readers. Thank you for picking up *Dangerous Rock.* I hope you'll be back for the rest of the *Dangerous Noise* series.

Also by Crystal Kaswell

Sinful Serenade

Sing Your Heart Out - Miles

Strum Your Heart Out - Drew

Rock Your Heart Out - Tom

Play Your Heart Out - Pete

Sinful Ever After – series sequel

Just a Taste - *Miles's POV*

Dangerous Noise

Dangerous Kiss - Ethan

Dangerous Crush – Kit

Dangerous Rock – Joel

Dangerous Fling – Mal

Dangerous Encore - series sequel

Inked Hearts

Tempting - Brendon

Hooking Up - Walker

Pretend You're Mine - Ryan

Hating You, Loving You - Dean

Breaking the Rules - Hunter

Losing It - Wes

Accidental Husband - Griffin

The Baby Bargain - Chase

Inked Love

The Best Friend Bargain - Forest

The First Taste - Holden

The Roomie Rulebook - Oliver

Dirty Rich

Dirty Deal - Blake

Dirty Boss - Nick

Dirty Husband - Shep

Dirty Desires - Ian

Dirty Wedding - Ty

Dirty Secret - Cam

Pierce Family

Broken Beast - Adam

Playboy Prince - Liam

Ruthless Rival - Simon - coming soon

Standalones

Broken - Trent & Delilah

Come Undone Trilogy

Come Undone

Come Apart

Come To Me

Sign up for the Crystal Kaswell mailing list

Printed in Great Britain
by Amazon

27093708R00229